THE
DELI COUNTER
OF JUSTICE

Edited by
Arlo J. Wiley

D1707433

For Erin
who is more super
than anyone in a cape.

- Eric Sipple

∞

For my wife, Pam, whose love and patience makes
her the true hero of the family. And for my collaborators,
Arlo and Eric, who infuriate as often as inspire me, but in
any case are the ones that finally made me write something.

- Paul Smith

∞

To my dad, who still takes me to the comics shop.

- Arlo J. Wiley

Table of Contents

Introduction

by Mere Smith

"…with a superhero here, and a superhero there,
here a superhero,
there a superhero,
everywhere a superhero…"

- with apologies to Old MacDonald

☯

Let's talk about superheroes.

But first, a little chat about the late 19th century revival of Gothic novels and their expression of the *fin de siècle* mindset.

(Wow, I nearly fell asleep typing that – but stick with me, maybe this'll go somewhere interesting.)

Now I'll grant you, as far as conversational topics go, superheroes and Gothic novels may appear on the disparate side. Yet I would make the argument that all our modern superheroes' *true* "origin stories" lie within these *fin de siècle* (that's fancy Franchese for "turn of the century") Gothic novels. After all, who are the characters that populate these books? Dr. Jekyll, Mr. Hyde (1886), Dorian Gray (1891), and of course – the Superman of his day – good old Count Dracula (1897). And what do all these characters have in common?

Simple. They're monsters.

But more than that, they're supernatural – *superhuman* – monsters.

Much has been said about the global zeitgeist at the end of the 19th century, and considering World War I erupted only 14 years after the *"fin"* – something to ponder in 2014, the year this book is being published – you can safely assume that back then most people thought the world was going to hell in a big old handbasket. A handbasket already woven of fire and spiders.

And as art is wont to do – especially the art of writing, where the communication of ideas is at its most precise – Gothic novels reflected prevailing attitudes: dread, pessimism, cynicism, and lamentations over the degradation of society. People at the end of the 19th century knew the world simply could not go on as it had done for centuries – notions of empire were disintegrating, social constructs regarding religion, class, gender, and race were eroding, creating dangerously chaotic identities (hello, Dr. Jekyll). And yet these people also knew they were on the verge of The Future, for the dreariness of the *fin de siècle* had its flip side: an excitement – dare I say optimism? – to be found in the light bulb, the telephone, in street trolleys, even airplanes! Humanity's common dream for millennia had become reality: we could *fly!* There seemed no end to invention – that anything, *everything*, eventually would be possible. Even cowering in the caves of their existential crises, people stoked embers of hope in the recent technological revolution.

Any of this sound familiar?

What if I said "9/11" and "the internet"?

But wait! I hear you protest. *A-ha and attend!*

If **our** *turn of the century was so much like* **their** *turn of the century, how come* **they** *popularized monsters, and* **we** *popularized superheroes? They made bad guys, we made good guys! Doesn't that make us morally better? It totally does, doesn't it?*

Uh… I'd dismount your high horse before it bucks you.

Whereas our predecessors looked to the future with at least some hope to warm them, our generation looks forward and sees only cold dystopia.

Dystopias have dominated our vision of the future for decades – from *Blade Runner* to *The Road* by Cormac McCarthy to the zombies of *The Walking Dead* – the bottom line is: *none of us sees this whole human thing working out.* Whether it's a plague that wipes out humankind, global warming that trashes the planet, or a nuclear war that destroys both humankind *and* the planet – it is generally accepted that we, denizens of the 21st century, are looking at some pretty grim prospects.

And this time, rather than being a hearth for hope, our great technological revolution has only emphasized our "inevitable" damnation. Thanks to the internet, the globe has shrunk, our awareness has grown, and we are now capable of not only knowing of, but *seeing*, tsunamis drown hundreds of thousands of people; the injured, bloody children of war; the murders of hostages – each act a villain in its own right. Today's world may not be worse than it was at the end of the 19th century – by certain rubrics like life expectancy, it's objectively better – but nowadays we sure as hell know a lot more about all the awful things that happen outside our private caves.

Is it any wonder that during the 20th century *fin de siècle*, instead of creating monsters – nope, already got a shitload of those, thanks – we should instead turn to superheroes to defeat them?

So this is right off the top of my head, without the – already-ingrained – use of Google. Thor, Captain America, Wonder Woman, Black Widow, The Hulk, Hawkeye, Superman, Catwoman, Batman, The X-Men, The Watchmen, Spider-Man, Iron Man, Hellboy, The Fantastic Four, and Blade. Off the top of my head.

We both know I've left far more names off my Super List than I included, and with a single exception, every one of these superheroes has appeared in a major American film.[1] Breaking down the various collectives, that's well over *thirty* superheroes, the large majority of whom would be classified as "good guys."

We love good guys.

We *need* good guys right now. We need good guys to save us in a world that is suddenly superhumanly big, in which we often feel too small to save ourselves, much less our fellow man, like those superheroes we admire.

We need hope.

But then again, how much frickin' hope do we really need to generate such *prolific* media about superheroes? *Los Angeles Times* and NPR film critic Kenneth Turan wrote recently, "The one big thing (Hollywood) knows how to do is make sequels and superhero movies, and sequels to superhero movies." And it's not just movies. It seems every individual superhero has their own comic books, TV shows, toys, cartoons, video games... the list goes on.

Maybe a simpler question would be, *why do we need so* **many** *superheroes?*

---

[1] At this point in time, the sole exception is that epitome of female strength, the original Überfrau: Wonder Woman. Between her and Black Widow, it appears dismantling the patriarchy is going to be a *tad* more annoying than planned.

At least, that was my knee-jerk response when I was first approached about writing the introduction to *The Deli Counter of Justice*.

More superheroes? I thought. <u>*Really?*</u>

But then I read the stories.

Have no fear, they are indeed about superheroes — but they're also about so much more — like the complex and sometimes fucked-up human beings under the masks. Ask me, that's *way* more interesting than watching Superman flounce around in his tights being unquestionably virtuous. Because sure, I may want Superman out there protecting me — but he's not somebody I'd wanna have a slice of pizza with. I can't imagine he'd be anything but stultifying and self-righteous. (Soul-searching reboots notwithstanding.)

However, the characters in *The Deli Counter of Justice* — well, most of them, anyway — I'd like to sit down with and split a BLT.

You see, Cook's Deli is not your run-of-the-mill diner. In a universe where superpowers almost seem the norm (a nice reversal that calls into question what, exactly, a "superhero" actually *is*), it's also a hangout for off-duty "capes" and "masks." Cook's was founded by Carl Cook: superhero emeritus, who once went by the *nom de guerre,* Piecemaker. Not only has Carl retired from the superhero scene, Carl has retired from this entire book — though he owns the namesake, he's never featured in his own story — a choice I find pretty well sums up *Deli*'s intent.

For while some superheroes (not naming names, Mr. Stark) eagerly play the "Look at me! Look at me!" card while performing grand acts of valor – the heroes of *The Deli Counter of Justice* mostly go about their business saving people – and themselves – with more self-awareness than self-aggrandizement. And in our current *fin de siècle* moment, much as we might need good guys to defend us, to save us, to remind us of the heroes we ourselves can become – we also need superheroes for another, perhaps even more important reason: to remind us of the humans *they* become after the mask is removed. To show us that their frailties are our frailties, that weakness need not break us – that in fact, confronting (and not *fighting*, but *making peace with*) our own imperfections may be what saves us all in the end.

That by embracing our humanity, we learn to be superheroes again.

And those kinds of heroes?
There's no such thing as too many.

Prologue

Carl Cook turned 52 last month.

He considers that number with some amusement; hard to believe he's made it this far. There was a time, not too terribly long ago, when he didn't think he'd make it past 40. Didn't even want to make it past 40.

Carl unlocks the door to the deli, the one with his name on it—Cook's Deli, the sign says—and walks in to an empty restaurant. Whenever he can, he likes to be the one to open; more often, he's the one who closes up at the end of the night. Blame all those years of catching sleep wherever he could, crashing until the late afternoon.

Seeing those spotless tables and empty chairs reminds Carl of what he has, what he's responsible for. He likes this responsibility. It grounds him. Until a couple years ago, until right around the time he hit the "half-century mark," as his daughter teased, his life revolved around a very different sort of responsibility.

Once upon a time, Carl Cook wore a black-and-gold costume and called himself Piecemaker. If you live beyond New Caliburn city limits, you might not recognize the name. But if you're a resident of the country's—maybe even the world's—hub of superheroic activity, there's a good chance he saved your life, even if you didn't realize it. Carl never asked for that responsibility. He wasn't born with any powers, unless you count the time he ranked first in the state's High School Wrestling Championship, Non-Superhuman Division.

That changed one day when he found himself in the middle of a genuine hero/villain battle and took a stray blast to the gut. He didn't know why, maybe it was his chemical make-up or his genes, or maybe Commander Lazer was using his raygun to create an army of mutant freaks to control the world, but Carl woke up with superpowers. Stranger things have happened.

Whatever the case, Carl discovered he could now... well, he could take things apart. With a flick of his wrist, he could break any complex object in sight into its component parts. Guns, knives, getaway cars, basically every tool at a criminal's disposal. And this, this was the neatest part: he could control those parts with his mind. In his early 20s, he didn't even know what the word "telekinetic" meant. Soon enough, he found out. Add in those award-winning wrestling moves, and what choice did he have but to become a superhero?

Over the years, Carl as Piecemaker worked his way up through the ranks, even landing a spot as a reserve member of the Heralds. Big-time stuff. Big-time stuff comes with big-time responsibilities, though.

The costume meant he wasn't always around when his

family needed him. Eventually, it cost him his marriage. Lost custody of Tabitha, too, except for every other weekend. Carl was very good at taking things apart. Less so at putting them back together.

He felt very much like he was at an end.

Then he met Tommy, that brave, unflappable kid, and whatever parental instincts he ignored when Tabitha was born suddenly kicked in. That's how he went from Piecemaker, tired and alone, to Piecemaker and Crashtest, rejuvenated and alive. For the first time in years, his head was really and truly back in the game.

But 50...50's a big number. A nice, big, round number. A man turns 50, he starts taking stock of things. It was time to hang up the cape. 30-some-odd years fighting crime on the streets of New Caliburn was nothing to sneeze at. Piecemaker had his turn in the limelight. Now it was Carl's. He took the money he'd socked away after some ill-advised endorsement deals in the '90s, back when every down-on-his luck hero was pushing some dot-com disaster, and found a little place on the Row.

His dad had coached his wrestling team, but his mom taught him how to cook. So he did the furthest thing possible from slipping on spandex and beating up crooks: he opened a deli.

That was nearly two years ago. Now, as he surveys those tables and chairs, Carl thinks about this little experiment. Has it worked? Has it made a difference? As he preps the deli for another exciting day of sandwich-making, he allows himself a moment's indulgence.

He asks himself this question:

Was it worth it?

Pixelated

by Eric Sipple

The tip of Tabitha's finger came off cleanly and without pain. The streak of red on the blade's spinning, stainless steel surface caught her eye immediately, but it took her a moment to realize it was *her* blood. Tabitha lurched away from the meat slicer and pulled her finger defensively toward her body, releasing the safety button as she did. The slicer's brake brought the circular blade to a stop so fast it was still before the ten-pound chunk of smoked turkey breast hit the floor with a moist thud.

She swore. Not because of the pain (there still wasn't any), but out of anger. She'd drifted off. And cut herself. *Again.*

A fat drop of blood fell out of the red disc of her former fingertip and landed on her dirt-gray sneakers. She swore again. Then the pain and more swearing.

Then the phone rang.

Tabitha glared at the phone, finger raised to eye level, other hand squeezing the wounded digit. She didn't actually need to do anything to stop the bleeding, but there were customers watching who didn't know that. All she needed was a few minutes out of sight to give her finger a chance to heal. Except the phone was ringing, and Pike was out on a delivery. The only time she dared ignore the phone it turned out it was Dad calling. When she finally answered (he didn't give up, not for dozens and dozens of rings) Tabitha had to listen to a fifteen-minute lecture on the importance of prompt customer service.

She grabbed a washcloth and made a fist around it, said *Keep bleeding until I'm in the back* to herself (well, not exactly to herself), and crushed her finger against the fabric while she answered the phone with her free hand. It was Dad, just as she'd feared.

"You watching ENN?"

"Why would I be watching ENN? I hate the news." *Especially ENN.* The last thing Tabitha wanted to watch was ENN and its 24-hour feed of superheroic news.

"What the heck's on the TV, then? I told you, it's either news or—"

"—or sports, I know."

"There's no sports on right now."

"Soccer's on." Tabitha glanced up at the too-small TV in the corner of the deli to double-check. Getting caught in a lie would drag this call out even more. Satisfied, she said, "I'm watching soccer."

"Soccer's not sports, Tabs."

"Dad, I've got to go, okay?"

"Turn on ENN."

"Dad!"

Self-conscious, Tabitha looked around the deli. Luckily, it was mostly empty. An older couple watched her from one of the booths, concerned. Probably parents. It didn't matter that Tabitha was twenty-two; to them, she was a kid making her poor dad's life hell. The only others were the five teenagers at a table near the door. They were managing not to laugh.

"Your brother's the Mask of the Day. Turn it on or you'll miss it!"

That explained everything. Anything Tommy-related was a reason to celebrate. It meant maybe, finally, Tommy — her step-brother, technically, and even then only by a very technical adoption to cover his role as Dad's boy sidekick — would finally do his own thing and stop trying to drag Dad out of retirement.

"I'm hanging up now. My finger's bleeding all over the place."

Shit, that was a mistake.

"Your finger's what?"

"It's nothing. I cut it on the slicer."

"You cut yourself on the slicer *again?*"

"I'm fine." A little too fine. The bleeding had nearly stopped. *Slow down, you little shits. Slow down.*

"Tabitha."

"I said I'm fine! I just need a bandage."

"You gotta stop spacing out." He crushed so much worry, admonishment, and exasperation into the five words, it was hard not to be impressed.

"I'm not doing this right now," Tabitha said. Dad was looking for an opening. She had to get off the call before he found a way to make this about giving college another try.

"C'mon, I *know* how bored you are. I love having you at the store, but you know you're too smart to be making sandwiches all night for drunks."

Tabitha clenched the washcloth. "Yeah, never heard this shit before. Thanks. I like the drunks. Gives me people to feel superior to."

"Tabs, don't swear in front of customers."

"I'm hanging up for real. And yes, I'll turn on ENN."

Tabitha dropped the phone on the ground next to the smoked turkey breast, and grabbed the television remote. She kicked the metal door open as she flipped the channel to ENN, then slipped into the back room. Out of sight, she closed her eyes again. *All right, guys. Do your work. Scab this bitch up before Dad calls back.* No one told their family everything. A girl was allowed some secrets. Tabitha's were in her bloodstream. Billions of them, racing through her arteries and veins. Her friends. Her creations. Her Pixels.

☡

Growing up with a superhero for a father never seemed that weird to Tabitha. Mostly her life was like other kids'. Divorced parents, a dad absorbed by his job, the sudden intrusion of a step-sibling. She couldn't talk about his job, sure, but even that wasn't so bad. It was like having a spy for a parent. Tabitha told kids Dad was a salesman or a computer installer or (when she wanted to screw with someone) in waste management which *probably* meant he was a capo in the mob but *shh don't tell anyone*. Still, Tabitha couldn't deny that having a Superdad had inspired some strange hobbies.

Did she ever wish it was her and not Tommy - who she loved like the whole brother thing wasn't just a sidekick cover - out there with Dad, doing awesome things while Tabitha went to school? Sure. Yeah. Whatever. But it wasn't all about the once-somewhat-notable Piecemaker. This was about her. This was about what *she* could do. What she needed to prove. That she could do something everyone said was impossible.

As Tabitha struggled to convince her overzealous nanoscopic helpers what a bad idea it would have been to repair her finger with people watching, she still wasn't sure she'd succeeded.

⚖

Finger wrapped in two layers of gauze, Tabitha stared across the now-empty deli at the television. She'd caught most of the fifteen-minute Mask of the Day segment, enough to feel the simultaneous pride and envy she always did when she heard about her stepbrother's exploits as Crashtest. Now that they'd moved on to recapping the day's newsworthy superheroism, all Tabitha felt was envy. She looked for where she'd left the remote, but before she could find it, the front door's electronic chime sounded.

She had customers. Two of them, both women, both her age, and both members of the super-duo Tragicom.

Yeah, fucking great. Just what I need.

They weren't in costume, obviously. Supers didn't get dinner wearing their colors. No one wanted to be saved by someone with mustard stains on their spandex. Lyta Lim (aka Thalia, aka Comedy) stopped by the entrance, eyes sort-of-but-not-quite on the wall-mounted menu. She ignored her friend, Bridget Borders (aka Melpomene, aka Tragedy), who paced, cell phone up to her ear, demanding that sound check be done before she showed up. *Gig night,* Tabitha thought. Tragicom always stopped by when Bridget's band was playing somewhere in the Row.

Lyta slipped a hand under her shoulder-length black hair and scratched her neck. She stared up at the menu with a look of feigned concentration, her pink-lipsticked mouth scrunched to one side as she shifted her weight from leg to leg. Her tight green skirt crept up her muscular thighs with each movement. Lyta Lim, soloist with the New Caliburn Ballet, even fidgeted gracefully.

"Hey, Lyta. How's it going?" Tabitha asked.

"You know," Lyta replied with a shrug. She glanced

over her shoulder "Hey, B., what should I get?"

Bridget shook her head at Lyta, pressed the phone hard into her ear, and turned her back to both of them.

Tabitha sighed. Lyta got the same thing every time. Every. Single. Time. There was only one reason she'd pretend to care about the menu: she was stalling until Bridget got off the phone. Tragicom was here to have words. Tabitha was used to it at this point. They'd been having words with Tabitha since they shared a dorm room. Even dropping out of school hadn't been an escape.

"What's up, Tabitha?" Bridget slid her phone into the pocket of her leather jacket. Tabitha was with Bridget the day she found that jacket. There'd been rips in the leather across the back and up the arms, tears that Bridget had carefully stitched up that night in their dorm. The stitches were so perfect they looked purposeful, part of the design. The jacket probably looked better now than it had when it was new.

"Just working. Where you playing tonight?"

"McDonogh's?" Bridget asked Lyta.

"Uh, no. It's…" Lyta turned to Tabitha. "You know that Irish place where the coffee shop used to be?"

"McDermott's. Haven't been there yet." Tabitha felt a thin, petty thrill at getting to correct them, a thrill that died with Bridget's dismissive shrug. Bridget, lead singer of Miss Andry (whose self-released, crowdfunded album was *the* hot thing on college campuses), got so many gigs she didn't *need* to know the names of the places she played.

"So," Bridget began, but trailed off and took a sudden interest in her glittering violet nails.

Lyta picked up where Bridget left off, "We heard about a thing and we thought of you."

"A thing?" Tabitha asked.

"Yeah, a thing," Bridget said.

"Hashtag," added Lyta.

"Hashtag?"

Lyta nodded, glanced from side to side to ensure they were still alone, then leaned in to say, "The new Hashtag. There's a casting call."

"A secret casting call." Bridget looked up from her nails for a second, but returned her attention to them when Tabitha tried to make eye contact.

"Secret, but we know where. And when."

Fucking Hashtag? Hashtag was a techie sidekick, known for sitting in a black conversion van and hacking computers while his partner Howl cut a bloody, vengeful swath through the underbelly of New Caliburn. They wanted her to be a fucking sidekick? Not even a sidekick. A sidekick *auditionee*. Tabitha stared at them, her dorm mates through the worst year of her life, the closest thing to friends she had, and wondered how hard it would be to accidentally slam their faces into the counter.

"I mean, since Hashtag's always been a boy, it's pretty much time to get a lady in there, right?" Lyta kept her voice low and quiet, but made up for it with aggressive, emphatic gesturing. "That could be your thing, you know? Prove that the chicks can hack it, too. Hah! Hack it!"

Bridget cracked a smile, but not much of one. "Hack it? Really?"

Tabitha's instincts took over, the defenses she'd built up over years of the disappointment and oh-so-helpfulness of family and friends. "Seriously?"

"What's wrong?" Lyta asked. "We thought you'd be excited."

"You thought I'd be *excited*?"

"Forget it, Tabitha," Bridget said.

"Yeah, whatever. You're on a real career path here. Sorry to get in your way."

The Pixels were sparks of flame in her veins, feeding on adrenaline, begging to be used, demanding to prove just how little Tabitha needed their goddamn sidekick auditions. They flooded her muscles with oxygen, wrapped the bones of her hands in a dense, protective shell, readied themselves for the punch Tabitha wanted to throw into Lyta's smug little ballerina face. *We're ready*, they said, and with her last shred of restraint, Tabitha replied, *No, we're not*.

The Pixels were her proof, but only if they worked. Only if they didn't fail like they had before. Failed to listen, failed to work when she needed, in the way she needed. They'd burned her into unconsciousness when they wouldn't stand down, and gone comatose themselves when she pushed them too hard. If she revealed them now, if she showed them off to *prove* what she could do, and they failed…if they failed in front of everyone…

Pike crashed through the door and hopped the counter. Without another look at Bridget and Lyta, Tabitha walked towards the back room and said, "Where the hell have you been? Take their order for me. I need to get ready for tonight."

ॐ

The first wave of drunks crashed through the doors at 1 a.m. Most were the impatient, get-a-jump-on-traffic kind of drunks who hated waiting in line for anything, even a post-drink snack. Others were so far gone that the bars had cut them off and they had nothing to do but stuff down a corned beef sandwich on their way home. The rest were designated drivers, so shell-shocked by their hammered friends that they couldn't help but share their misery with any sober person in shouting distance.

This was usually Tabitha's favorite part of the night, when it was finally busy enough to keep her brain quiet. The crowds didn't bother her. The drunks just wanted to talk, and didn't notice (or didn't care) if Tabitha was listening. The designated drivers were less fun but at least had a good excuse to be jerks. Tonight, though, Tabitha wished she could trade places with them. A couple shots of tequila sounded like a better escape than hiding here, working the drunk shift while Bridget and Lyta danced and sang and fought crime like they were born to succeed.

Tabitha's current drunk leaned over the counter, chest draped across its surface. Since he'd come in, he'd been rambling about some street performer he'd seen. She glanced up from the Italian sub she'd hastily wrapped as he continued. "Oh, man, you should *see* it! He's incredible! You like magic?"

She shrugged. "You ever seen a particle accelerator? Kind of hard to be impressed by card tricks after that."

"Card tricks. You hear her? Fuckin' *card tricks*!" The drunk slapped his friend on the arm. The friend, clearly sober and even more clearly sick of being slapped on the arm, shook his head. The two of them looked about 50. The drunk one was balding and wore a Caliburn Merlins jacket that might have fit him 20 pounds ago. Sober friend was a foot taller, gaunt, and needed to shave. Drunk friend returned his attention to Tabitha. "Lady, I'm tryin' to make sure you don't miss the best magic act you've ever seen, and you're on about card tricks."

"Yeah, don't call me lady," Tabitha said. She slammed his sub on the counter and turned to his sober friend. "You want something?"

The skinny one shook his head. Tabitha sidled over to the register and punched in the order with an eye on the rest of the store. Eight or so other people, including the

three with Pike at the other end of the counter. Not too
bad. The first wave would be over soon, and if Tabitha was
lucky she'd have enough time to straighten up before the
bars closed and the tsunami hit. The only ones that had
Tabitha worried were at the end of the line. Four drunk
girls, probably in college and possibly underage, with
designer-torn stockings and factory-stressed denim jackets.
One of them was bound to cry when Tabitha told them
they didn't serve gluten-free vegan tofu wraps.

"It wasn't nothing special," sober friend said when
Tabitha took his money. "The show, I mean. Just some guy
on the street with a smoke machine and a bunch of old-ass
tricks. Smoke stunk like a swamp, though. That was
something."

"If he's running a smoke machine on the street, the
cops'll want to have a talk with him. That might be worth
seeing."

One of the faux-punk girls pushed her friend right
onto her ass. It was hard to tell if the girl was laughing or
screaming when she hit. Tabitha wished it was worth the
hassle of kicking them out. Instead, she smiled at the
thought of their oncoming hangovers and went back to
ignoring them.

Drunk Italian sub guy was less understanding. "Why
don't you keep it down, you fuckin' drunks? I'm havin' a
conversation here!"

One of the girls (the one who'd pushed her friend)

lifted a hand, made a fist, then slowly raised her middle finger.

"You see what I'm talkin' about, Gary? What I was sayin' before? Goddamn drunks are ruining this neighborhood. This used to be a nice place."

Gary — the sober one — rolled his eyes and smirked at Tabitha. "The whole walk over here he was like this."

Tabitha smiled back. "Self-loathing is an ugly thing."

All four of the girls were laughing. Gary's drunk friend pointed a stubby finger at the girl who was flipping him off, his face bright red. Tabitha tensed. Loud drunk was one thing. Angry drunk was another. He said, "Look at what that shit does to you! Just a bunch of dumb, drunk whores is what you are."

"You might want to get your friend out of here before I have to," Tabitha said.

Gary nodded, but his friend had already abandoned his sub on the counter. The girls backed up as he approached. The bird-flipping one dropped her hand to her side.

"You think it's just a good time, don't you? You think it's all a fuckin' party!"

Tabitha went for the gap in the counter, but Pike was closer. He got between the drunk and the girls. "Okay, dude, calm down. Ain't no reason to fight, okay? Ain't no reason."

The man ignored Pike and kept coming. When Pike

didn't move, he took a clumsy swing, one Pike was too off-balance to dodge. The blow knocked Pike backwards and into the arms of the girl whose laugh had started everything. Gary charged toward his friend, begging him to stop. With his friend on one side, and a steadied, angry-looking Pike on the other, the drunk realized he was in over his head and stumbled toward the door.

Gary chased his friend out, shouting, "Hey! What the hell, Ken? Wait up!"

Tabitha sighed, turned to the four girls and held her hands apologetically in the air. "Don't know what that was about. You okay, Pike?"

"Think so," Pike said. "Nothing broken."

"Good. You cool to help these girls out?" Tabitha asked. Pike nodded as she passed him on her way to the door. She pushed it open and took a cautious look. The street at night was a river of flickering neon, the aura of multicolored light shining off of sequined dresses and overly gelled hair. The drunks were out in force, some in the middle of the street itself, crossing in groups too large to worry about oncoming traffic. She caught sight of Gary waving his arms at a crowd of people, yelling something she couldn't make out over the noise. Ken — sloshed, ragey Ken — was still making trouble.

It wasn't her problem. Irrational, angry drunks were nothing new in the Row. Why worry about this one? So what if it was weird that someone that wasted was ranting like a prohibitionist?

The crowd parted and she saw Ken being pulled off a very large bald man with very large, tattooed muscles by an even larger (bald and tattooed and muscled) man. She thought she could still hear his teetotaling rant, except…it wasn't Ken's voice. It was a woman's, and it was coming from Tabitha's left. Tabitha watched as she dashed across the street towards Ken, like she was headed to help him.

Tabitha knew — *knew* — this was no coincidence. A Drunk Prohibitionists' League hadn't opened up shop in the Row. There was something or some*one* behind this. Someone who had to be found. And stopped.

Good thing Tragicom is here, Tabitha thought. Except…

…except the Row wasn't Tragicom's home. It was her father's. It was hers.

"Pike!" Tabitha pointed to the bag on the counter. It was plastic, tied at the top, and held three Italian hoagies ready to go out after the first rush cleared. It was all the excuse she needed. "I'm taking the delivery. Keep things together while I'm gone."

⚖

It wasn't the first time she'd worn it. Of course it wasn't. Not only had she gone out in *the* costume (she was pretty sure this version was *the* costume, but she'd been fickle before), she'd gone out in the five previous ones to see how they felt in the field. She hadn't done anything in them but crouch on rooftops and study the streets and alleyways of the Row, but she *had* put them on.

She'd trained, too. Taken kickboxing and jujitsu and Eskrima, fought in competitions, took beatings from better fighters so she wouldn't be afraid of pain. Tabitha knew she needed be ready for *the day*, because screwing up on the day could be the end of her.

Tabitha exited the deli out the back and stopped beside the dumpster. *This is it, boys. Dress me.* The Pixels snapped into action and flooded out of her pores. Piece by piece, they began to break her clothes into a sort of molecular soup. Too late she added, *I want the purple one.* The arms of her shirt had already dissolved into an off-white goo that clung to her skin. It felt like warm snot. She was going to get whatever costume the Pixels wanted to give her. Tabitha backed further into the shadows but was careful not to touch the wall. The last time she did that, it left a Tabitha-shaped indent in the bricks. The Pixels weren't always sure where she ended and the world began. *Shit, my shoes.* She hopped from foot to foot, her soles never in contact with the cement for more than a second.

The sturdy black mesh of her outfit formed rapidly out of the goo. It was material she'd designed, a tight webwork of carbon nanotubes that (in theory) armored her against blades and bullets. She'd considered patenting it, but then she'd have to explain how it was made, which meant revealing the Pixels.

Tabitha glanced at her legs. The color spreading through the mesh was red, not purple. *Figures.* She felt a cowl form over her head, though, which meant the Pixels had at least picked the right design. Better than nothing.

She flipped her hand palm-side up, where a mass of the goo had pooled. It stretched and formed into a dark red mask. She pressed the mask to her face, where it stuck as if she'd glued it there. *Good boys. Very good.*

The sound of metal smashing against metal echoed down the alley, followed by screams. Tabitha pushed aside the fear that she wasn't ready, that the Pixels were too new, too untested. It was now or never, and there was no word Tabitha hated more than *never.*

☼☼

White smoke rose from the smashed hood of a grey sedan, its fender pressed into the driver's side door of a red minivan. The doors to the sedan were open, its seats empty. The driver of the minivan was still inside her vehicle. Her head was slumped over the steering wheel, red hair over her face and arms limp at her side. The sedan had crumpled the door in towards her and shattered the glass of the window. Whatever caused the sedan to swerve into the van's lane, Tabitha doubted it was an accident.

There was a small crowd gathered around the accident.

A half-dozen people had a woman surrounded in the middle of the street, the one who'd run to Ken's aid shouting the same prohibitionist crap he had. Tabitha's best guess was that the sedan swerved into the minivan to keep from hitting her. Whatever had happened, the crowd had her contained.

Ken, though, had slipped free of the large, tattooed man's grip. He burst out of the crowd, shouting, headed for the minivan. "You could have killed her!" he said over and over. He stumbled onto the hood of the sedan and gabbed the minivan's crushed door. "You could have killed her. Goddamn drunk drivers! You could have killed her!"

The crowd did nothing to stop him. They just watched him pull himself in through the window towards the unconscious woman. Ken kept one hand on the car door and reached through the broken window with the other. His hands were bloody from grasping the glass shard-covered bottom of the window frame. If he felt any pain, it didn't show.

Tabitha could see the deli, which meant anyone who looked out could see her. She needed information, but even Pike was never high enough to miss a Tabitha-sized girl in a costume fighting the guy they'd just chased out. She'd have to take this somewhere a *little* more private. Tabitha picked a path through the traffic and broke into a sprint.

The crowd noticed Tabitha and quieted enough for her to hear a man in the crowd ask, "Who the hell is that?"

Stuff of legends. That's what you are, Tabitha. She angled her run to take her along the side of the minivan and right into Ken, who had a hold of the woman's hair and was trying to pull her out through the window. The Pixels flooded her legs with a warm surge of strength. She took two steps along the ground, then a third onto the hood of the car. Focused on the unconscious woman, Ken never saw her coming. Tabitha hooked the crease of her elbow under his shoulder and shoved him up and away. Ken rolled over the hood and landed on the pavement back-first. Tabitha spun, pointed at a man in the crowd (the man who'd made sure *everyone* knew Tabitha was a nobody) and said, "Make sure she's okay."

Now would be a good time to be strong. Tabitha grabbed the front of Ken's shirt and lifted him as high as her chest as if he was no heavier than a small dog. *Love you, boys. Keep it up.* Strength like this took a lot out of the Pixels. She needed to work fast. Tabitha sprinted towards a pink and blue neon sign halfway down the block. Prix Luxe, the clothing store of choice for over-rich teenagers desperate to pay $300 for a pair of handmade jeans. Not Tabitha's kind of place, but the huge glass window cases that flanked the shop's door were the best refuge she was going to find. She could already feel herself weakening, and Ken, no longer stunned, had begun to struggle. He took a clumsy swing that just missed her face. Before he could take another, Tabitha tossed Ken ahead of her and onto the sidewalk of the entryway.

Tabitha came down on his chest before he could move, pinning his arms under her knees. Ken started to shout, so she clamped a hand over his mouth. "Jesus, shut up. I have to work." She pushed her fingers into his still-open mouth and really, really hoped the mesh of her gloves would hold up if he bit her.

Let's see what's going on in there, shall we?

The Pixels were designed for Tabitha. Specifically. Carefully. Outside of her bloodstream, their lifespan was limited. So long as the Pixels dissolved after leaving her, they couldn't be studied or used by anyone else. Tabitha remembered hiding in a coffee shop as a child while someone in a stolen suit of Technocrat's powered armor leveled half the financial district. She couldn't let anyone do the same with her creations.

The Pixels didn't die immediately, though. They could survive for a little while. Not long, but long enough.

Streams of carbon nanobots poured out of Tabitha's hand, down her fingers, and into Ken's mouth, where they passed without resistance through his soft palate and into his bloodstream. The rapidly decaying Pixels formed a daisy chain back to Tabitha's nervous system, conducting tiny electrical impulses from Ken's arteries and into Tabitha's brain. What the pixels saw, Tabitha saw.

Tabitha's mind began picking apart the situation as soon as she heard the woman echoing Ken's rant. She'd run through the possibilities — what could cause two unrelated people to say the same *exact* thing, and settled on the most likely culprit: mind control. If it was magic (and there was nothing Tabitha hated more than the verifiable existence of unscientific garbage), there'd be nothing for her to find. If it was something else, *anything* else, it would leave a trace that the Pixels could find. Tabitha *really* hoped it wasn't magic.

Images of molecules spun across her field of vision (the visual thing was *still* twitchy, no matter how much she practiced) as the Pixels inventoried what they found. Red blood cells, white blood cells, proteins, hormones, and... *wait, where's the alcohol?* She ran back through the list until she came across a large organic compound that didn't belong. A molecule bonded with some of the ethanol saturating Ken's body. Something she recognized. *Remote impulse receivers.* People had tried and failed for years to accomplish what Tabitha had with the Pixels — the creation of autonomous nanomachines — but the research produced lots of byproducts. One had been so dangerous it was outlawed as soon as it was invented. A molecule that, when present at a sufficient density in the body, could receive a remote signal and override a person's neural impulses. Provided, of course, it had a set of keys to someone's neurotransmitters. Alcohol, for instance. Crude but effective mind control. *Bingo.*

She ordered the Pixels to fan out through Ken's body, break the bonds between alcohol and receiver, and metabolize the ethanol. On their own own, the receiver molecules had no way to transmit commands. All she had to do was process enough of it out and…and…

Tabitha lurched to the side and vomited everything she'd eaten and drank for the last day onto the concrete. She felt Ken pull himself out from under her, but there was nothing she could do to stop him while her body purged itself. She'd pushed the Pixels too hard. Now she was paying the price. A thick hand touched her shoulder. Tabitha rolled onto her back and brought her hands and feet up defensively, like a frightened cat. She didn't need to see the look on Ken's face to know how ridiculous she looked. *Wait, the look on his face.* He wasn't shouting or attacking. He was worried.

Ken sat beside her, his body as wobbly and weak as Tabitha's. He asked, "You okay, lady?"

"Dunno." Tabitha pushed herself onto her knees. Her muscles spasmed with every move. "Maybe. You okay?"

"Yeah. I wasn't right in the head, was I?"

"Nope."

"But you fixed it," he said.

Tabitha considered that, smiled, and said, "I think so."

Afterimages of the molecules the Pixels had seen still floated across her vision. One of them, something she'd barely noticed as the Pixels had done their work, was the atom that served as the bond between the ethanol and the organic receiver. One simple atom. Sulphur. *Sulphur. Why does that…oh, shit. Swamp gas.*

"Thought so. Thanks, lady. Thanks a bunch."

Still distracted, Tabitha replied, "Thank the Pixels."

Tabitha stood. Ken's friend, Gary, said he'd smelled swamp gas earlier that night, coming out of a smoke machine used by the very magician Ken had praised before he lost it. The smoke could have delivered both the organic receiver and the sulphur that bound it to the alcohol. Anyone, *everyone*, who watched the show after having a drink would be affected, and the bars were about to turn an army of drunks out onto the street. She stepped out of the darkness of Prix Luxe's entryway to see the chaos had already begun.

Her first thought was that she needed to have a talk with The Row's newest street performer.

Her second: *Thank the Pixels? What the fuck kind of line was that?*

☿☿

The crowd seemed to part before Tabitha as she ran. She felt her weakness give way to elation. *I'm doing it*, she thought, and spared a glance at the deli as she passed. Pike had followed her father's disaster plan and locked the front door. The deli was safe and Pike wasn't watching. Perfect. All around her, people were losing their minds, shouting nearly identical rants and attacking whoever or whatever was closest. Maybe a quarter of the crowd was affected, but it was enough. The Row wasn't ready for a riot and Tabitha didn't have the power to stop one. She had to find the source. She had to stop the puppet-master.

Tabitha jumped from sidewalk to car to street, avoiding crowds too large to push through. At the end of the next block was another wreck; a pickup truck had rear-ended a cop car. The driver of the pickup held the cop by his collar and was slamming him repeatedly into his own car. Tabitha kicked her left foot into the side of the driver's knee as she passed. He cried out in pain, released the cop, and fell to the ground. *Serves you right for watching a fucking magic show.*

Just ahead, the main drag of the Row split, the lanes arcing in opposite directions. Between them was a barely functional fountain surrounded by an oval of grass that the city had the nerve to call a park. If someone wanted as many people as possible to see their show, the park was the best choice.

She shoved through a clot of people and skidded to a stop. A greenish aura surrounded the streetlights, and the sickening smell of rotten eggs was everywhere. Dozens stood shoulder to shoulder, their attention on the man before them. He wore a crisp white shirt with gold buttons, black leather pants, and shiny black boots that stopped midway up his calves. His blonde hair was long and pulled into a ponytail. Over his shoulders was a black and purple velvet cloak. He stood on the edge of the fountain, a dove cupped in his hands. He was speaking, but Tabitha couldn't hear over the cheers of his audience. An entire crowd of people under his control, forced to applaud his show as anarchy broke out around them.

So he's a narcissist. Perfect. Let's get this started.

Tabitha felt something in her throat, the tickle of the Pixels strengthening her vocal cords. She'd played this out so many times in her head — the chase, the discovery, the announcement of her arrival — that the Pixels already knew her next move. Tabitha leapt onto the sloped cover of a trashcan and stuck there, bound to it the same way her mask stuck to her face. She took a breath. A very deep breath.

"This show sucks! Get off the stage, you hack!"

Tabitha's amplified voice cut through the cheering of the crowd and the shouts of rioters. It echoed off of brick walls and down alleys. The magician turned towards her, and the eyes of his audience did the same. She had his attention. Which meant…*shit, now I have* everyone's *attention.*

The magician smiled and flipped his cape over his shoulder. "It's about time! I was afraid you wouldn't come! To be honest, I hoped there'd be more of you, but it's a start."

"Yeah, whatever. It's time to shut it down. Pack up the smoke machine and tell me how to stop this before anyone else gets hurt." Every word pushed itself out faster than the last, like her whole body knew what to say, what to do.

Whatever doubt she'd felt when she put the mask on was buried under the thrill of the moment. *Hope he doesn't ask my name, though. Really should have figured that out before now.*

The crowd's head moved back and forth between Tabitha and the magician as they spoke.

"You think stopping me will keep that poison from hurting people?"

"I was talking about hurting you, Teetotaler."

"Teetotaler? That's catchy. You mind if I use that?"

"You won't be for long."

"Oh, I know. Once your allies are here, they'll stop my little demonstration, but by then I'll have made my point." He raised his arms as he spoke, white-gloved hands spread wide. "The city will see alcohol for the menace it is, and this row of filth, this temple to debauchery, will be in ruins!"

Tabitha blinked. This guy was leaning hard into the ranting villain curve. "Sorry, but this temple to debauchery is my home, and I like it the way it is. Last chance to give up quietly."

"Not until the Heralds arrive. Not until this city's greatest heroes are forced to confront the poison they defend."

He thinks he ranks the Heralds? *He'll be lucky if they bother to read about him in the paper.*

Dammit, Tabitha, you're supposed say this shit out loud!

"You think you rank the *H—ahh!*"

A hand closed on Tabitha's ankle and yanked her foot

free. The bond the Pixels created to stick her to things was made to release under strain. Better to fall than to hang by a broken ankle. Tabitha bounced off the top of the trashcan on her way down, then hit the cement tailbone-first. The magician's audience was already closing in around her. Tabitha kip-upped to her feet and kicked the closest person in the chest to clear some space. *My ass is numb, boys. Anything you can do about that?*

Someone grabbed Tabitha by the shoulder and spun her around. A woman; tall, broad-shouldered and strong. She pulled Tabitha close and said, "You don't even know the Heralds, do you?"

Tabitha shrugged free of the woman, but two more hands closed on her from behind. She jumped, supported by the person's grasp, and kicked both feet into the tall woman's chest. The force pushed Tabitha backwards and knocked both her and her attacker to the ground. *Need a strategy. How do you fight a crowd?* She rolled into an empty space and leapt back to her feet. This time, before the crowd could close on her, Tabitha charged, elbows out like a linebacker's. Strength poured into her legs, and her skin hardened in the second before the impact. *Ass is still numb, though.* Her elbows hit someone's jaw with an unexpected crunch. She reminded herself that these people were under someone's control and dropped her arms to chest-level. At least they wouldn't lose any teeth.

"You're just some small-time nobody," Tabitha heard

as she plowed through the crowd.

Another voice said, "You can't carry my message to the city. What a waste of my time."

"Maybe the Heralds will pay attention when they see what we do to you."

There was no way she could fight them all. She had to take out this Teetotaler (*really nailed that one, Tabitha, good job*) before he got bored and had his audience trample her. *On the other hand...* An audience this size was a lot for one person to control. Maybe too much if their concentration broke. Tabitha scooped up a broken chunk of blacktop as she ran. She spun out of an attacker's grasp, straight-armed another out of her way, and lined up her target. The blacktop was out of her hand before anyone could stop her. It flew straight and fast; this wasn't the first asshole she'd had to throw a chunk of pavement at. It clipped the Teetotaler in the side of the head just above the temple. He stumbled and fell to one knee, and the crowd followed his lead. Tabitha had a clear path. Nothing to stop her. Nothing at all.

Not until Tragicom appeared through the smoke behind the Teetotaler.

"Sorry we're late," Thalia said, dropping into crouch, "but we'll try to make this quick now that we're here."

"We *do* have other plans," Melpomene added.

Each wore a white ceramic mask. Thalia's was stretched into a broad smile, while Melpomene's was a frozen sob. The classic masks of the stage, the symbols of the muses of comedy and tragedy, Thalia and Melpomene. Only these masks were enchanted, granting their wearers strength drawn from the muses themselves.

Tabitha watched with a boiling mix of horror and rage. *They're here* now*?!* After *I did all the work?*

"Hey!" Tragicom turned to face Tabitha, and she was suddenly afraid they'd recognized her voice. *Where's the booming hero voice, you little shits? Get it together!* "I've got this!"

"Do we know you?" Thalia asked

"Yeah, what's your name, newbie?"

There wasn't time for this. She could figure out how to handle Bridget and Lyta once the Teetotaler was unconscious. Tabitha was about to move when she saw the Teetotaler smile and remembered where Tragicom had been. At a concert. In a bar.

"Get out of here, both of you!"

Tragicom cocked their heads in opposite directions. It was Melpomene who spoke. "Calm down, newbie. We won't steal your thunder."

Tabitha dashed towards the Teetotaler. Maybe she could get to him in time. She kept shouting as she ran. "That's not— How much have you had to drink?"

"What kind of question is *that?*" Thalia snapped.

The Teetotaler laughed. He already knew the answer. He'd known since they walked into the smoke. Thalia and Melpomene twitched. Their bodies went briefly slack, then

rigid. Tabitha was less than a yard away when Thalia
sprung into motion.

Thalia was fast. Really, *really* fast. That was part of her
muse's blessing. Speed, agility, and murderously perfect
timing. She cartwheeled and, supported by a single hand,
dropped her knee onto Tabitha's head. Tabitha got an arm
up under Thalia's thigh, enough to blunt the worst of the
blow, but it drove her sideways and past the Teetotaler.
Melpomene came at Tabitha from the right before she
could recover and caught her in a crushing bear hug. The
muse of Tragedy was implacable, overwhelming, and her
champion was just as strong and unfeeling. Tabitha
punched Melpomene twice in the head to no effect.
Desperate, Tabitha raised her arms in the air. *Unstick me!*
The Pixels were already ahead of her. In seconds, Tabitha's
costume became slick and frictionless, as if it was covered in
grease. Tabitha slipped out of Melpomene's grasp, hit the
ground, and leapt backwards into the water of the fountain.

The Teetotaler backed away to give his new minions
room to work. Now that he'd shifted his focus to Tragicom,
the crowd behind had gone back to being his audience.
Teetotaler didn't think he needed anything more than
Tragicom to finish her off. Tabitha feared he was right.
She'd felt powerful, unstoppable, just a few moments earlier.
Now she felt the hopelessness eating into her. Tragicom
succeeded at everything they tried. What had Tabitha done
besides argue her way out of college?

She ran through her options. She knew their powers. Knew them almost as well as Tragicom did. It was Tabitha who'd found the masks, and Tabitha who'd suggested Bridget and Lyta use them when she realized their powers were magical. She'd helped Tragicom train and ran them through the experiments that discovered the limits of their abilities. Tabitha even knew their biggest weakness: the command word that would force the masks, the source of their powers, to fall off.

Which didn't help. Without their masks, they'd be recognized immediately. Tabitha couldn't destroy their anonymity to save her own skin. There had to be another way. There had to be.

Tragicom wasn't about to give her time to figure it out. Melpomene swung behind Tabitha, flanking her. Thalia said, "If you want to run, we won't stop you."

"Real heroes are here to spread the word. Go home before you get hurt," Melpomene continued.

"Unless you want to get hurt."

Even mind-controlled, they finished each other's thoughts. *How much of you is still in there?* She tuned them out. She didn't have to beat Tragicom. Her strategy was the same: take down the Teetotaler. Tabitha feinted towards Thalia, then threw herself in the other direction. She grabbed the Teetotaler by the arm with her left hand and wound up for a punch with the other. Before she could take the swing, an arm hooked around Tabitha's own and pulled her away. Tabitha pivoted to face her attacker — Thalia — and drove a knee into her gut.

At least, that was the plan. Tabitha's knee hit at the wrong angle and slid across the fabric of Thalia's costume; a useless, glancing blow. Tabitha twisted, lost her balance, and went face-first into the water. Tabitha should have known better than to attack Thalia directly, but instinct had taken over. She knew Thalia's powers, that the masks granted more than physical abilities. The muses defended their champions, wrapped them in protective auras. Thalia's turned attacks into sudden, spectacular failures. Like a missed attack that became a pratfall. Comedy gold.

A strong hand closed around the back of Tabitha's neck. Another grabbed the back of her thigh and lifted her up and out of the water. For a moment, she was suspended over Melponene's head, still too stunned to react. Then she was falling. Through the air, back into water, and onto the cement base of the fountain.

I need to run. Why did I think I could do this? How could I think I was better than them?

The deep, wobbly echo of a foot breaking the surface of the water was followed by a hard stomp to Tabitha's back. If the Pixels hadn't been ready, the blow would have crushed her spine. It still hurt like hell. The pain snapped her out of self-pity long enough to realize what was happening. Melpomene's aura was different than Thalia's. Subtler. It had crept inside, turned Tabitha's mind inward, dragged her deepest hurt out from where Tabitha had buried it. She tried to clear her head, searched for a refuge from the memories she didn't want to face. It didn't matter. Melpomene was everywhere.

Melpomene stomped on Tabitha again, but this time left her foot pressed into Tabitha's back. She held Tabitha there under the water, her face less than a foot from the air she couldn't reach. Melpomene was too strong to fight. There was nothing Tabitha could do but let the water have her. It wasn't so bad, Tabitha thought. At least this time she wouldn't have to see her father's disappointment again. The dead, after all, were finally free of shame.

☪

The morning after Tabitha was kicked out of the last class of her college career — Advanced Biochemistry, junior year — she'd sat with Bridget on the steps of the Department of Sciences building, drinking coffee and explaining what had happened.

Not that Bridget couldn't have guessed. There'd been an argument. There were always arguments when Tabitha told professors they were wrong, or corrected stupid questions on tests instead of answering them, or changed their experiments to prove she'd found a better way. Tabitha learned early and often that professors didn't care if they were right so long as no one told them they were

wrong. It never stopped her. This time, after a five-minute
deconstruction of her professor's lecture, he'd said a simple,
"Enough," and pointed to the door. He knew Tabitha was
on probation and that the next class that asked her to leave
would be her last. He'd probably been waiting for the
honor of being the one to finally pull the trigger.

When Tabitha finished, Bridget didn't say anything.
Not even, "I told you so."

Of course, she *had* told Tabitha so. Many, many times.

"Don't need to tell every person when they're wrong,"
and, "Sometimes you've got to lose to win," and, "You'd
have anything you want, you learn to shut your damn
mouth every once and a while."

Things like that.

That day on the steps, it didn't matter anymore.
Tabitha hadn't shut up, hadn't sat quietly, hadn't played
along. Bridget didn't need to remind Tabitha she should
have known better. Tabitha was wrong, Bridget was right,
and now there was nothing to do but drink coffee and say
goodbye.

Tabitha thought about that day whenever she worked
on the Pixels. She imagined what would have happened if
she'd listened to her father's and her friend's warnings and
waited for permission to show what she was capable of
instead of demanding their attention.

She wouldn't have made the Pixels. No one would have
believed it was possible. No one would have thought her

idea was worth the time and money.

She wouldn't have spent months learning the streets of the Row, designing costumes, learning to fight. Her father would have never let her follow in his footsteps.

She wouldn't have gone out into the night to stop a delusional stage magician. She had a deli to run, and the real heroes didn't want newbies getting in their way.

Tabitha would have found a job in a lab, researched what she was told, progressed projects in inches for people with no imagination and no ambition save profit.

There, under the water, with Bridget's foot on her back, Tabitha came to the same conclusion she had every time she'd imagined that life. That life sounded awful.

So Tabitha did something no one wanted her to do.

She stood back up.

⚖

But before she could stand, she had to get Melpomene's foot off her back. Tabitha raised her arms as high as she could and punched the ground with both fists, so hard that the cement below her cracked. She let elementary physics do the rest. The force of her punch recoiled and knocked Melpomene off-balance enough for Tabitha to slip out from under her. Tabitha barely had time to stand before Thalia came to Melpomene's aid, but it was more than enough for her mind to sort through what she knew and come up with a plan. She couldn't fight Tragicom and win, and she'd never get a chance to do more than grab the Teetotaler. Luckily, grabbing was all Tabitha would need. That and a little help from the Pixels.

Get me drunk, stat. And if you let it bond with that swamp gas shit, I'm purging all of you.

Hoping to buy her Pixels a little time, Tabitha wound up a punch. A big, out-of-control uppercut that would force Thalia to dodge, aura or no. She swung, and the comedy-masked girl dropped into a split so fast it hurt Tabitha's groin just to watch. Her punch passed over Thalia's head, and her body followed its arc. She spun once, twice, three times. On the third turn, Thalia came out of the split and shoved Tabitha into the path of the now-ready Melpomene.

Melpomene caught Tabitha and leaned in to whisper. "You should have stayed down. This would have hurt less."

She felt loose and wobbly. The alcohol buzz was just enough to hold off Melpomene's aura and keep the despair from overwhelming her again. Thalia would have a field day fighting a drunk, though. Tabitha couldn't afford to get close to her again. *Maybe I won't have to...*

During Tabitha's experiments with the masks, she'd learned something about them. There *was* one thing immune to Thalia's aura.

"Do me a favor. Tell Thalia to shove her secret audition up her ass." Tabitha grabbed Melpomene around the waist. With all the strength the Pixels could muster, Tabitha twisted and heaved Melpomene in the direction of her partner. Unaffected by the mask's aura, there was nothing to stop Melpomene from colliding with Thalia and taking both down into the water together.

Tabitha moved before Tragicom could recover. She dove for the very unprepared Teetotaler and tackled him. They fell over the side of the fountain, together. Tabitha landed on top of him and pinned both of his wrists with one hand while shoving the fingers of her other into his mouth.

Now, boys.

The Pixels poured out through the tips of her fingers, as they had with Ken. This time they didn't go alone. Each carried a molecule of alcohol from Tabitha's bloodstream. She felt her head clear, the euphoria passing as the drug left her system. Then she felt something else. A kick to her ribs. And another, and another, and another. Melpomene's came slow and strong, while Thalia's fast, nimble feet chipped away. *THUDthudthudthudthudTHUDthudthud.* The Pixels were busy getting the magician drunk. There weren't enough left free to dull the blows. Something cracked in Tabitha's chest. She couldn't take much more. Still, Tabitha kept her grip on the magician.

"Get off of me!" The Teetotaler's words were barely understandable with Tabitha's fingers jammed his mouth.

"Get off of me!" Thalia echoed.

"Off!" Melpomene kicked again, hard. "Get off!"

Melpomene grabbed Tabitha around the neck and pulled. Weak from the beating and the exertion of her Pixels, she didn't resist. Melpomene held Tabitha while the magician rose and brushed off his garish outfit.

"Was that your whole plan?" he asked. His speech was slurred, and he swayed slightly from side to side. "I thought you'd at least throw a couple of punches."

Tabitha had imagined standing up after a beating, her face bruised and mouth bloody, and laughing in the face of her enemies. Instead, she felt lucky to be conscious. She forced herself to take in a deep, painful breath.

"Ever hold a microphone too close to a speaker?" Tabitha asked, and was proud of herself for managing a smile. "'Cause right now you're both, asshole."

The Teetotaler doubled over, his eyes bulging and his face pale, and screamed. Melpomene shuddered as her voice joined the magician's. Tabitha broke free of her hold, stumbled three steps, and fell to the ground. She heard Thalia wail as the feedback spread. Cries of pain rippled out through the crowd. The Teetotaler had spent hours breathing the same gas as his audience. The alcohol in the Teetotaler's blood gave that gas the key it needed, turning the Teetotaler into both sender *and* receiver. She'd hoped (*no, hypothesized*) that would short out his control. She'd been right.

One by one, the screams died off as those affected fell unconscious from the strain. The magician himself was the last to go silent, and when he did, the Row was quieter than Tabitha had ever heard. She pushed herself onto all fours, crawled to Melpomene, and placed a finger on the side of her neck. *Steady pulse. You're gonna be fine.* A pain lanced up the side where Tabitha had felt something crack. *Hopefully I will, too.*

Tabitha stood on wobbly legs and took one last look around the park. Police sirens approached from the distance. The people who hadn't been affected by Teetotaler's gas stood amongst the unconscious, their eyes all on Tabitha. Awkward, unsure of what else to do, she raised a hand and waved. Then, moving more slowly than she wished, she crossed the street and fled down an alley. The police could handle cleanup. Tabitha had a deli to run.

⚖

Tabitha slumped into a booth while Pike followed their last customers to the door. He held it open for the two men — both sober, here for whatever passed for lunch on the late shift — then locked it behind them.

Sitting hurt even more than standing. Her only slightly-healed rib pressed against the hard plastic back of the booth. Standing hurt less, but staying on her feet was out of the question. What little strength she had left was needed by her equally exhausted microscopic allies. They'd already burned through everything Tabitha ate since she got back to the deli (two Reubens, five dill pickle spears, and three bags of salt and vinegar potato chips) to replenish their numbers before there were too few left to rebuild.

"You want me to clean the cheese case for you?" Pike asked, now standing at her side. Tabitha wasn't sure how long he'd been there. Had she dozed off? "You seem pretty wiped."

Pike had been trying to baby her all night, ever since she lied and said she'd been injured in the riot. She'd fought him off so far and wasn't about to stop now. "Go home, Pike."

"Hey, it's no problem. I can have it done in like ten minutes."

"Pike. Please. Get the fuck out."

Pike held up his hands in surrender and backed away. Tabitha waited for the slam of the metal back door before allowing her head to fall onto the table. There was no way she was making it home. Maybe she could manage to crawl onto her dad's tiny office couch. Even if she did, she'd need a good excuse for spending the night at the deli. When her father called to make sure she was okay (he still kept his old police scanner and always called when there was an incident in the Row), she'd ignored the question and told him the deli was fine. Nothing about being out in the worst of the riot, and nothing about getting hurt. *Anything you can do to keep me awake while I think of a lie? No? Assholes.*

"And we have breaking news from New Caliburn,

where a riot was stopped by an unfamiliar face. Or, should we say, an unfamiliar mask. We go to Nancy Cruz for the story."

Confused, Tabitha looked up at the television. She'd turned it off, but the remote was sitting on the table in front of her. She must have hit the power button with her forehead.

On the television, a young, tired-looking reporter stood in front of the Row's park fountain. "I'm here in one of the city's most famous bar crawls where, less than an hour ago, a deranged stage magician tried to make a violent statement about the evils of alcohol."

As the reporter described the riot, the screen cut to images of EMTs treating the injured, wrecked cars, and smashed store windows. Finally, the report cut to two figures in black costumes and white, ceramic masks. Bridget — Melpomene — said, "Why did he do it? He wanted attention. They always want attention."

I get my ass kicked saving them and they get on the news. Figures.

"Though Tragicom was on the scene," the reporter said in voiceover, "they claim it wasn't them who stopped the man the authorities say called himself the Teetotaler. Is there a new hero on the streets of New Caliburn?"

The shot cut abruptly to later in the interview. Lyta/Thalia said, "He had everyone under control, even us."

"She had to fight us *and* him." Melpomene paused, then added, "It's a good thing we've got someone like that in the neighborhood. I owe her a drink the next time I see her."

She knows. She knows it was me. Tabitha was so shocked she nearly missed the reporter say that someone *did* know who the mystery hero was. Tabitha's throat tightened.

Tabitha recognized the voice before the speaker came onscreen. Ken, the drunk she'd purged of the Teetotaler's toxin. "She did something to me. Cleared my head right up, you know? Like nothin' had happened."

From offscreen, the reporter asked, "Did she say anything to you?"

"Yeah. She told me her name. She said, 'Thank The Pixel.'"

*No. No no no. Not The Pixel. Pixels. Pixel***s***!

"Who is The Pixel, and when will we see her again? Based on the work she did tonight, we can only hope the answer is 'soon.' Back to you, Bob."

Tabitha's forehead fell back onto the table. The Pixel. They named her *The Pixel*. Why hadn't she come up with a name? How hard would that have been? Tired, in pain, and annoyed, she pressed the power button again with her forehead.

Tabitha really hated the news.

Without Masks

by Rahne Ehtar

For a quarter past six in the evening, foot traffic wasn't too bad at the Roundhouse Mall. It mostly consisted of the after-work shopping crowd, those who were squeezing in a few minutes of browsing and picking up necessities before hurrying home. It was a lull compared to the regular tide of teenagers and tourists. No doubt it would pick up again before the night was through. For now, though, it was almost sedate, more in tune with a town market than a city shopping center.

Jean watched the people going about their evening routines and tried not to tap her fingers. It was the nervous energy more than the fidgeting itself she wanted to keep in check, but that would be harder to stifle. Besides, restlessness was a show of weakness. She had gotten out of the habit of indulging in those.

The seat that gave her such a good view of her fellow patrons was one of the several benches set out around the Coal Car Diner. She was enjoying the cool evening air as best she could while waiting for a co-worker to arrive, but it wasn't the wait itself that was making her nervous. She was dressed casually – that particular kind of "casual" that took some effort – and not in the uniforms she was used to, either for her regular job at Morgaine Hospital or for her "night job." That wasn't what was putting her off, either. Nor were her nerves a direct result of the date planned with the awaited co-worker, though the two were certainly linked.

Jean glared a little at the people around her. They weren't the source of her budding anxiety, but they were a very effective reminder.

She wanted tonight to go well. A simple enough wish, but she was coming to realize as she waited just *how much* she was depending on this being an evening that was, above all else, normal. It had been a long time since she'd had what she would consider a normal day, one without planning battle strategies or trying to outthink the latest maniacal villain, without sneaking into lairs or worrying if her bruises would show at work the next morning. It had been a long time since Jean had felt like she could spend some time as *herself* and not as Artisan, one of New Caliburn's many crusading capes. It had been a long time since she had allowed herself the simple luxury of enjoying someone's company, as so many around her were doing now, taking their own mundanity for granted with exquisite self-indulgence.

Jean felt she was overdue for a little mundanity. Just one night shouldn't be too much to ask for…

"Hey, there you are!"

She looked up, interrupted mid-fret. The sight of Derek Reed, co-worker of two years and current date, coming toward her at a trot relieved a little of her tension, and her breathing got a bit easier. If there was any assurance she could have asked for that the evening was going to be a normal one, Derek was it. Average height, brown eyes, brown hair that he tried so hard to style fashionably, and a dress sense that rivaled her own in terms of cluelessness, Derek was about as "normal" as she could imagine being. Being her friend of years also helped to reassure her. His company was easy, restful. Considering her own hectic lifestyle, she valued that.

She smiled, standing up. "Here I am," she agreed. "And there you are, Mr. Reed."

Derek gave her a lopsided grin, pulling up a couple feet in front of her. He was dressed semi-casually, like her, having opted for a pair of dirty-washed jeans and a dark button-down shirt. When he came close, she caught the scent of cigarettes on him. "Quitting" was what he said when she'd asked him about it once. So far as she could tell, he had been quitting for the last two years. Though to be fair, she had never actually *seen* him smoke, only ever smelled the nicotine clinging to his clothes.

He puffed a little now, catching his breath. "That's good," he said. "Phase One is accomplished; both parties are present and have made contact."

"It's a beginning." She eyed him a little critically. "But

will one of the parties survive the strain, do you think?"

Derek waved off the comment. "I'm sure you'll manage, somehow." He took a deep, theatrical breath. The resultant coughing fit had him doubled over before it was through.

"Mm-hm."

Once able to breathe, he flashed the lopsided grin again, a little rueful. "Well."

"Well."

Abruptly feeling more awkward than anxious, Jean adjusted her purse to cover a fidget. It had been a few years since she'd last made an attempt at dating. She hadn't been particularly skilled at it then, and she doubted that lack of practice had helped cure the deficiency.

Well, she'd wanted a normal night. Social awkwardness was normal, right? Just go with it and... bluff.

"Well, now we're all assembled," she said, spreading her arms as though to take in a large group. "What is Phase Two of the plan, fearless leader?"

Taking the cue, Derek held his chin, looking off into the distance, a picture of solemn consideration. "Well...our ultimate plan for the night is the consumption of a nourishing meal and the viewing of something the locals call a 'moo-vee.' But, seeing as we have arrived a little too early to begin either activity, we have some extra time." He looked back down at Jean, face overly serious in his self-mocking. "We will have to improvise Phase Two, faithful minion, while awaiting an opportune time to initiate Phases Three and Four."

She nodded, glad Derek was as playful as ever with their banter. "Understood. Have you any suggestions?"

The sober expression cracked into a smile, crumbling the fearless leader façade. He shrugged. "Since we're here, I thought it'd be nice to wander a little, kill some time before dinner. It's a first date, and first dates are all about 'get to know you,' right?"

"Like we don't already know each other after two years."

"Closer to three, really."

"Whatever. So, window shopping?"

"Don't judge me my foibles."

Jean laughed. Finally feeling relaxed, she let Derek lead the way into the mall.

♊

Wandering around and playing "get to know you" with Derek turned out to be more enjoyable than Jean had expected. The worry that had built up while sitting outside dissolved completely as they made their way through the mall, stopping in at whatever stores looked interesting, discovering things they had in common they'd never been aware of before.

For example, they had known they were both voracious

readers, a fact that was driven home by a quick stop at a bookstore on the first floor, but neither had known that they shared a penchant for young adult fiction. A stop at a hobby shop revealed that Derek was a fan of the old fashioned tabletop RPGs and a complete sap for detailed lead figures. Jean, in turn, had to be pried away from a classic *Teenage Mutant Ninja Turtles* arcade game she had fed a small fortune of quarters to as a kid. The small art gallery on the second floor was a calmer choice for both of them; Jean was partial to sculpture, and Derek gravitated towards surrealist paintings.

"I am so glad vinyl is making a comeback."

Jean looked up from where she had been flipping through CDs. In their looping, aimless wandering, they had made their way back to the first floor and come into Minstrel's Song, a music shop that was a little too proud of its own hip fashion, but which had a decent selection nonetheless. Derek had found racks of LPs, a look of rapture on his face. "It is nice," she agreed, "but only if you like the older bands. None of these new ones really sound right on vinyl."

"Agreed." Derek gave a small shudder. "Can you imagine anything with Auto-Tune under a needle?"

She echoed his shudder. "I think the turntable would rebel. *I* would. Only classics in the classic medium, please."

"Such as?" Derek was watching her out of the corner of his eye, his shifting through the albums coming to a stop.

If he were giving her a musical taste test, then Jean was ready for it. "Eric Clapton, Jethro Tull, Bob Seger...hell, throw in Queen and Pink Floyd as well. There are plenty of options for my LP collection."

Derek was grinning. "You have an LP collection?"

"I wish," Jean moved to the other side of the rack to flip through records and face Derek at the same time. "It's one of those things that I would love to start – keep meaning to – but just never gotten around to." She shrugged. "It's a big project to commit to, you know?"

"Eh, true. But *so* worth it."

As he walked along the rack, there was an almost reverential gleam in his eye. Jean wondered that this little mutual passion had never come up before. She was sure they had talked about music, it was one of those basic things that had to have been covered at some point. Had they just failed to get into favorite bands and mediums? Odd as it was, that did seem to be the case. She was sure she would have remembered finding another vinyl fan her age.

"So who's in your collection, then?"

He paused, giving the question some thought. "You had some good ones. Add in some Kansas, Lynyrd Skynyrd...and some Robert Johnson, too, though it's a little hard to find any really good quality albums of his, plus there's the whole speed and pitch accuracy thing..."

"Robert Johnson?"

Derek's eyes lit like lamps, and she learned more about Mr. Johnson, master of the Delta blues, than she ever wanted to know, from his long-lasting influence on all music ever to the legends that had sprung up around his rise to fame and early death. Since it had been the late '30s, the most popular fables had something to do with crossroads and deals with the devil.

Jean listened, smiling to herself while looking through titles and covers. This morning she wouldn't have really thought it possible, but she was actually having a normal day. She'd gone to work, spent eight hours filling prescriptions and filing paperwork, and now she was spending the evening with someone whose company she enjoyed, talking about the odd – but still normal – little things they had in common. Not a single thing superpowered or to do with the ever-present struggle between good and evil to be seen. It hadn't even come up as a topic of conversation, and to her surprise Jean realized that in all the time they had known each other, it never had been. They had never talked about New Caliburn's claim to fame, the resident capes. It was a little strange, now that she came to think about it. What with how many heroes, villains, and the little wars between them there were in this city, it was sometimes hard *not* to talk about them. Everyone had their own opinions on the various superpowered humans that walked among them, and no one had any trouble expressing them. It was like a weird hybrid of sports, religion and politics, and spawned about as virulent a strain of debate as one would expect.

But it never came up with Derek. Neither of them had ever started a conversation with anything like, "Did you hear about last night? Superhero A tossed Villain Green through the Avalon Aquarium wall. They're still looking for all the starfish."

It was a relief, actually. The more she thought about it, the more she came to decide that it was probably one of the reasons they got along so well, subconscious or otherwise. It was nice to be with someone and not have reminders of a secret identity thrown in your face at every turn.

What was the old saying about when something seemed too good to be true?

A flash of motion caught Jean's eye, making her look back. At first glance, it looked like a mouse scurrying along the bottom of the racks; small body, long tail, quick dash-and-stop locomotion. That was all as it should be, but no mouse Jean had ever seen was a gleaming silver.

She stared at the little interloper, unsure how to respond. Her instinct was to assume that whatever it was, it was hostile. It was the kind of snap decision that kept her alive as Artisan, but the thing was tiny, and all it was doing was running along the bottom of the rack, silver tail swishing. Automatic suspicion aside, there was no real reason to think that it was up to anything sinister.

The creature came to a stop at the wall, turned, and

looked up at her.

It was definitely a mouse, Jean decided, and definitely mechanical. A kind of mousebot with flat lens eyes was staring at her. It was well made; it looked exactly like a mouse save that it was quite obviously metal. It even had wiry whiskers. She wondered if they served some purpose or if they were just for show. No one she could think of made anything like this, on either side of the law. There were those who made machines, some even smaller than this one, but none to look like mice. She had no idea who had made it, if she should trust her instincts and treat it as an enemy, or if she should leave it alone, potentially the tool of a colleague.

The mousebot had yet to move, remaining unnaturally still as she considered it and her options.

She stood up, deciding to leave it alone for now. It hadn't done anything, there was no real reason for her to act. Though she would admit her decision had as much to do with Derek still standing within sight as anything else. Whatever she did would carry more than the usual risk of exposure.

Today was her day for normal, damn it.

She turned her back, deliberately ignoring the mousebot and returning to the albums. She didn't get very far before she heard a very distinctive noise: tiny metal feet on tile.

The mousebot scuttled after her, looking up at her with

what she interpreted as intense interest. Jean walked a little further into Minstrel's shelves. From the sound her ears were now attuned to, the mechanical mouse was still following.

It was getting harder to think of the mousebot as anything *but* something to be suspicious of; it was also getting harder to hide from Derek the fact that she wasn't just browsing. She caught him looking at her quizzically once, and had to pause in her pseudo-flight to reassure him. During that pause, the mouse got closer than it had before, tiny lens eyes darkening as the mechanism focused in on her.

Whatever it was and whoever it belonged to, Jean didn't trust it. As soon as Derek's eyes were off of her, she began working her way back to the farthest corner of the shop. She wanted a closer look at the rodent robot, and for that she would need some privacy.

The mouse followed her faithfully until they turned the final corner, where it darted under her foot, tripping her. Jean stifled a curse, catching herself and almost bringing down a stand full of miscellaneous odds and ends in the process. The mousebot took the opportunity to leap at her shins, metal claws digging into her pants, and began climbing up.

Jean felt a stab of panic and again smothered the urge to swear or yelp or anything else that would attract attention.

Quickly drawing on her inborn skills, those she had practiced and honed since she was a teen and which qualified her as one of New Caliburn's protectors, she wrapped her hand in an invisible protective layer and swiped at the mouse-shaped thing, already at her hips and still climbing.

She missed. The little robot kept coming, now scaling her shirt, over her belly. Her second try at swatting the thing went wide, fueled by some of the panic she couldn't quite quench. The mousebot came on unhindered, crested over her breasts, and made a final leap towards her face, glinting claws extended.

Jean's hardened hand finally connected, batting the mouse out of the air and sending it flying into the corner. She crouched, ready for it to make another charge, but the mouse moved no more.

The immediate danger over, Jean allowed herself a moment to breathe. As much as it annoyed her to have anything from her second life intruding on her day, she felt just the tiniest bit vindicated that her instincts had been right.

Miniature robots in the shape of rodents equaled bad.

She took a quick look around. There was no one in sight. Whatever noise the short struggle had made, it hadn't drawn any attention, and there were no obvious security cameras. The battle had gone unseen. Good.

Jean flicked her hand, banishing the glove she had

visualized into existence, and flexed her fingers. Her power had the potential to be truly formidable, if she could ever harness it properly. With practice, focus, and an effort of will, Jean could create objects out of nothing. Invisible and indestructible, whatever she could imagine she could make real, and they would remain physical until she willed it otherwise or was rendered unconscious. There were limits, of course, the most significant of them being her own focus. She couldn't fabricate a working bicycle, for example, unless she took the time to concentrate on every part and piece, including every link of chain. Most of her creations consisted of single, unbroken masses, because they were so much easier to create. There was also a limit on the amount she could generate, the distance from herself she could have objects come into being, and she had to be able to see where it was she was having her objects appear. But the most important limitation was herself, what she could visualize and how much effort she was willing to put into it.

What came to her easiest were shapes that were familiar.

An invisible hammer came down hard on the mousebot. It was probably already damaged beyond reactivation, but she wasn't willing to take any chances. Once completely destroyed, she scooped the little pile of scrap into her purse. She wanted to know where it had come from, and had a friend who might be able to tell her even in its current condition.

"Find anything good?"

Jean jumped and whipped around, coming to a ready fighting stance.

"Whoa," Derek held up his hands, eyes wide. "Sorry, didn't mean to scare you." He nodded at the shelf she had supposedly been looking through. "Just wondering if you'd found anything you liked."

She dropped her stance immediately, trying to regain control of her heartbeat. "Sorry, myself." She forced a chuckle and glanced back at the shelves, surreptitiously checking the corner one last time. If Derek had arrived a few seconds earlier, she would now be trying to explain something very awkward, but the corner was clean, the mousebot safe in her bag. The only explaining she had to do was why she was perusing the country section.

"No," she said, taking a breath and making it a sigh. "No, nothing very good."

If Derek noticed anything odd in her behavior, he didn't show it. "Ah, well." He put a hand on her shoulder. The heat of his palm soaked through her shirt and into her flesh. It helped ground her, bringing her back to the present moment, but it was a losing battle. Her sense of stability had been completely shaken by the scurrying shape. "The hour is getting on," he said. "Shall we proceed to Phase Three?"

Dinner. Dinner meant the date was still on. Should it still be on, when there had been a definite attack on her, and there could be more? If she were smart she would make some excuse, abort the date and head home, and then spend all night figuring out what this meant. At least it would put Derek out of harm's way. It would be the intelligent, responsible thing to do.

"Yes. Phase Three it is, fearless leader."

She'd always been noted more for her obstinacy than her intelligence.

☒

The restaurant they picked for Phase Three was nice, but still reasonably casual. It had an open floor plan and a kind of tiered setup, so that those sitting at tables in the back were three steps higher than those at the front. Potted ferns and half-walls helped to break up the space, and semi-dim lighting made it all feel more private than it really was. There were a few people that Jean could see already seated when a waitress took them to a table close to the back, on the higher tier.

Jean was decidedly twitchy by the time they were finally settling into their seats. Details of the restaurant's atmosphere were lost on her, and she was just glad they were on higher ground. She went so far as to insist on switching places with Derek so she could be the one facing the window, with her back closer to one of the dividing walls.

Between here and Minstrel's, she had seen three more of the robot mice, all keeping pace with them. One had tried repeating what the first had done and darted under her foot. Rather than trying to avoid it, she brought her foot down heavily, crushing the thing. She still wasn't sure how Derek had missed the sound but thanked her lucky stars he had.

It was nearly impossible to focus on the date as well as the possible dangers lurking. Just picking something to eat was almost too great a feat.

"Jean, are you okay?"

She looked up, attention brought back from the menu that she was studying in theory and from the shadowy corners she was scrutinizing in reality. A false smile slipped into place without her having to think about it. "Yeah. Yeah, I'm fine, why?"

"Well, it's just you've been staring at the same page for five minutes, and I'm pretty sure that's the page with the wines and spirits." His smile was strained, the skin around his eyes tense. "Are you secretly an alcoholic? Should I be planning an intervention instead of a birthday party?"

She sighed, rubbing at her eyes. "I'm sorry, Derek. I'm just... tired."

The artificial smile melted away, becoming a frown. Worry didn't suit him nearly so well as his usual buoyant mischief. "Damn. I shouldn't have made you hike around the mall after working all day."

Oh great, way to be a prick, she reproached herself. "No, no, it's fine." When he didn't look convinced, Jean babbled on. "It's just been a longer day than expected, is all, and there's a lot waiting on my plate for tomorrow. I guess I'm sort of thinking ahead, planning all that out. Now we're sitting and all..." She trailed off, realizing that she really was jabbering. "I'll try to be less distracted."

Jean tried to dismiss the residual pang of guilt over lying directly to Derek's face. It was one of the hazards of the job, and at least it was all partially true.

The frown didn't ease, however. He tilted his head. "If you're sure..."

Jean nodded firmly.

She *wasn't* sure, and the longer she stayed, twitching at shadows, the less sure she became. If the mice continued to plague her, dealing with them without anyone noticing would get tricky. She had been fortunate that there had been no more outright attacks since Minstrel's, but if they got more aggressive or more numerous, then she would have a real problem.

She scowled behind her menu, scanning through the pastas. She already had a problem, and she knew it. Some party of unknown strength and motive was targeting her, and was doing so while she was in public; in plainclothes, no less. It was very doubtful that anyone would take a special interest in her everyday self, Jean Newman, and she was certain that she was the only one the mice were

following. There were no shrieks around them, no cries of
disgust from the other shoppers. They were remaining
hidden from everyone besides her.

Artisan had a new enemy, and they knew who she
really was.

Uncertainty ate at her. She had no idea who this
enemy was, what their limitations were, what they wanted,
or how much worse the night had the potential to get. She
didn't even know if this counted as making a serious move,
or if they were just testing her out. Perhaps most
importantly, she wasn't sure anymore that if she left, Derek
would be safe. Right now all the attention was on her, but if
this enemy perceived Derek as someone she cared about,
they might harm him.

She had to stay, in case things got worse.

The waitress came back around to take their order.
Jean let Derek to go first; she had been spending too much
time looking out for mousebots to decide what to eat. So
far, she had seen none. Maybe the restaurant was too open
or didn't offer up the right kinds of opportunities. Whatever
the reason, it gave her a minute to pick out a meal.

Finding something she thought her stomach could
handle, she lowered her menu, and froze.

It was a good thing she had insisted on switching seats
so she was facing the window, that she had looked up just
when she had, and that it was still early enough that the sun
hadn't quite dipped below the horizon. If any of those

things had been different, she wouldn't have seen the object that was hurtling towards them.

In the first instant she registered the shape as a bird, in size somewhere between a hawk and a crow, flying low and directly at the window. The second instant, as the bird's wings beat down, told her the animal was actually a machine, its forged feathers catching the light of the dying sun. The next instant—

There was no time to think, no time to question if it was *really* a robotic bird on an attack or just an animal about to brain itself against the glass. There was no time to check her instincts.

Her response was instinctive but far from simple. The target was far away, moving rapidly, and off the ground. Simplest would have been to create a secondary barrier just outside the window, one that wouldn't shatter if dozens of birds crashed into it, but she couldn't see the ground outside, didn't know how tall to make it or where it should be placed. She had to target the bird directly.

She focused on the diving shape and *concentrated*.

A good dozen feet from the window, the bird seemed to slam into something that wasn't there. Its flight ceased, and it tumbled down in an arc only vaguely related to its original trajectory. There was a muffled thump just on the edge of hearing as the bird, trapped in the solid globe of nothingness she had thought into being around it, struck against the outside wall.

Jean released the breath she had been holding.

Close. That had been close, but it gave her a little more information. Whoever was responsible for the machines wasn't limited to mice, and they weren't as concerned about making a spectacle of themselves as she had thought. Neither revelation was particularly comforting.

"...Miss?"

She blinked, coming back to reality. Derek and the waitress were staring at her, the latter with a polite smile and the former with outright concern, a deep line between his brows. How long had they been trying to get her attention?

"What?"

The waitress' smile looked brittle enough to crack. "I said, do you know what you would like, miss?"

"Oh." She looked down at her menu. None of the text would come into focus. What had she decided on? "Uh... chicken Alfredo, please."

Brittle smile fixed in place, the waitress took Jean's order, collected their menus, and headed back to the kitchen.

Derek had yet to take his eyes off of Jean. Feeling self-conscious and oddly guilty, Jean took a long sip of her water, trying to shake off the tension gathering at the base of her neck.

"So..." Derek began, and at his tone Jean felt a stab of panic, the constant fear of her secret identity being unveiled surging to the forefront. Had she given herself away somehow, had he figured her out?

"You sure you're up for this, or are you going to go comatose as soon as you have a full belly?"

No, it was only more worry. She laughed, relieved, and hoped the sincerity of it would reassure him. "No," she shook her head. "I don't think I'm in danger of falling asleep any time soon."

What she said was also sincere. With adrenaline suffusing her bloodstream, sharpening every color, sound and scent, sleep was the furthest thing from her mind.

ᚖᚖ

Of course, why wouldn't *they be here?*

After the bird incident, dinner had gone quietly. They had been allowed to eat in relative calm, with no more sightings of mechanical creatures large or small, avian or mammalian.

Too much calm, the kind of calm that comes before a storm. All attempts at conversation stalled out before getting up steam. Any contribution she tried to make was too terse, too distracted, and in the end, they ate in uncomfortable silence.

Leaving the restaurant, Jean almost expected Derek to break off the date. It was hardly the fun, friendly evening it had started out as, and going on with what it had turned into only promised to make it worse. Secretly, Jean would have preferred it if he *had* broken it off, just gone home where he would be relatively safe and let her concentrate on her new problem.

She had wanted a normal night so badly. Now she itched for her metaphorical mask.

But no, Derek hadn't broken off the date. They paid for their food and moved on to the theater. Jean saw no mice trailing them and dared to hope that they might have actually left, that the evening could at least finish well—

Until she saw two mousebots darting behind the concession stand.

Of course.

No one else noticed them, neither the employees nor the line of moviegoers ordering popcorn. Jean wondered if it was because she was hyperaware or if everyone else really was that unobservant. She wondered what the fallout would be if she were to play hapless bystander and "notice" them, if that would clear everyone out and let her work on the problem, or if it would just result in chaos. It probably wasn't worth the risk, considering the number of civilians.

She became aware that Derek was staring at her. Shit, had he asked her a question? "Sorry, what?"

It bothered her seeing how much effort he had to put into smiling. "Still a little out of it, huh? I asked if you knew anything about the movie."

"Oh. Not really, no." She pretended to pick out a snack

while watching for more bots. "I just know what I've managed to pick up from the trailers. Something about a pirate king and a pirate villain fighting over magic gems… and there are aliens."

"Actually, it's all set on an alien world," Derek said, becoming more animated. "So it's really an *alien* pirate king – well, alien prince – fighting an alien pirate villain for magic gems that will give whoever holds them the power to control the seas, and therefore their world."

Jean couldn't see any more mice, but they were still some distance from the counter. Maybe when they were closer… "You've done your research," she offered. "It sounds a little contrived, though."

"A bit," he conceded. "But it could be really cool. Seafaring adventures with futuristic tech and the occasional odd creature thrown in? It could be epic."

"Or a complete mess."

He shrugged. "Nothing ventured, as they say. I'm curious how they'll mix the sci-fi and fantasy elements, and if there will be any humans at all. It would be strange to have an entire film without *any*."

"Seems like a lot of world-building is going to have to be crammed in. Is this meant to be part one of a series?" Despite her preoccupation, Jean couldn't help but be pulled into Derek's enthusiasm. It was infectious and familiar.

"I suppose it depends on how well this one does. From what I was able to find out, it's loosely based on some show from the '80s, so there's more material ready for them to use."

Derek had done a lot of reading before coming out. While waiting for their turn at the concession stand, he was able to give her a rundown on the world, politics, various species, and the protagonist's personal struggle. She was happy enough to let him chatter away; it seemed to buoy his mood.

They ordered their drinks and snack – one theater sized bag of plain M&M's, as dinner was a recent memory. Jean saw not a single mouse, even peering over the counter. The girl serving them gave her an odd look, and she ceased her inspection. Had she imagined them, then, populating empty corners of the theater with robotic mice?

It was a pleasant thought in its own way, that the worst she had to fear at this point was her own imagination. It was a fantasy that was shattered as soon as she saw the little bastards heading the other way down the hall.

As they found their seats and settled in for the film, Jean's shoulders grew tighter than ever. What were the bots up to? If anything, their moving away from her was more worrisome than following her everywhere. Out of her sight and therefore her reach, she couldn't prevent whatever it was they were doing. How was she supposed to do anything while stuck in her seat, in plainclothes, with a movie going on?

Jean fidgeted, barely registering that Derek was still

talking, waiting for the sound of distant screams.

The lights dimmed and the trailers began to roll. Her teeth creaked under the pressure of a clenched jaw. The opening credits began, a weird fusion of calligraphy and futuristic font, and she began trembling in her chair. There was no way she was going to be able to sit through the entire film, no matter how cool the space sea shenanigans were.

She leaned over, putting her hand on Derek's arm. "I'll be right back. I have to use the bathroom."

"Right now?" He looked scandalized, even in the dark.

"It's either that or you hand me an empty a cup to use."

He pulled a face and made a shooing motion for her to go. Avoiding toes, Jean left the theater as quickly as she could without breaking into a run. She had a limited amount of time unless she wanted to ditch Derek for the night, and who knew what would be waiting for her when she tracked down the mice or how long it would take her to deal with.

The hall was empty, only the sounds of movies in progress bleeding out from behind the doors on either side of her, mixing into a muted Babel. No one was in sight, either patrons or employees. That was good, and the only thing that *really* seemed to be in her favor.

She took a breath and shook out her shoulders. She had to remember that she was a civilian right now, not

Artisan. She was just Jean Newman, pharmaceuticals assistant, on a night out. If she were spotted anywhere she wasn't meant to be, she would have only her glibness to get her out of trouble.

Whoever was responsible for this, Jean made a mental note to be especially ungentle when she tracked them down.

Playing it casual in case someone did happen to see her, Jean headed back down the way she and Derek had just come. The restrooms were that way, so there should be no question why she was wandering. She'd been to this theater before and knew that after the restrooms, there was a door that led to upstairs to the projection booths and an emergency exit. She reached the turn that opened onto the main lobby, which Jean passed hurriedly, hoping she hadn't been noticed at all.

Jean slowed, every sense straining. The hall here was dimly lit, no small shapes were visible, and no telltale scuffles came to her as she crept along as quiet as possible. She paused, hand on the door to the women's restroom, debating with herself. She wasn't sure the mice she had seen had *actually* gone up to the projection booths, and if she went up, she was almost sure to be caught by an employee. How would she explain that?

She glared at the door like it was personally responsible for all of her troubles.

At the very end of the hall was the second door, its

green "EXIT" sign casting a sickly glow along the walls. Jean frowned. She couldn't think of any reason why the mousebots would leave the building, save to return to whomever had sent them. At the same time, there was no reason *not* to check first, before risking the stairs.

With one last furtive glance, Jean cracked open the exit door and peeked outside. The sun had finally set, leaving the world dark and the stars to a losing battle with the lights of the city. A bare bulb was mounted to the wall just beside the door, more to mark the exit than to actually illuminate anything. It did little other than outline the garbage and recycling bins sitting near. There were no other lights, no people to be seen or heard. The door came out at the rear side of the mall, abandoned by all save a handful of employee cars populating a narrow lot.

There was no sign of any robotic mice. She wasn't sure what she had expected, a hoard of the things preparing to swarm the theater, maybe? She snorted at herself and made to pull the door closed again.

A sound caught her ear, and she stopped. It was something small and metallic, like tiny paws striking concrete.

Jean stepped clear of the door, pausing only long enough to make sure she could get back inside once it shut.

She crouched down, searching under the bins for the source of the sound, left hand and forearm coated in their protective sleeve, hammer ready in the other. What little

light there was to be had was completely lost beneath the
dumpster, eclipsed by its bulk. Squinting, she trained her
ears forward, ready to spring back at the first sign of a
leaping body.

The sound was still there, coming nearer, though the
source was still hidden. Listening, Jean realized it couldn't
be just one mouse or even two. There were more than eight
feet striking the ground, an entire chatter of clicks coming
at her.

Visions of a metallic legion of rodents filling her mind,
Jean backed away, putting more distance between her and
the shadows just as she saw a stirring movement deep
within them.

A rush of clicks, a silver flash as the thing's hide caught
the weak light—

Something huge slammed into Jean. She had a
confused impression of wide, flat lens eyes, a plated body,
and dozens of legs all hitting her with incredible force,
throwing her back and clinging to her as the head of the
thing swung around, wicked pincers reaching for her face.

Centipede! her brain screamed.

The thing was *heavy*. It knocked her over in its charge,
only a quick twist on her part keeping her from skidding
across the concrete on her back. Once down, its weight as
well as its many pairs of legs held her there. At least as long
as she was tall, and all metal, its weight was no surprise.
More of a problem was just how determined it was to rip

off her face with its mandibles.

The only thing keeping the silver monstrosity at bay was her arm, still in its impenetrable sleeve, which she had brought up instinctively and shoved between its jaws. Jean offered a quick prayer of thanks to whichever deities it was that had granted her particular gift. Just the sight of those hooked mouth parts coming down on her apparently defenseless flesh over and over was enough to make her stomach turn, whether she knew her arm was safe or not.

Thankfully, the contraption seemed to be even less intelligent than the bug it resembled. No matter how many times it failed to snip off her arm, it never changed its strategy. Jean smashed at it with the hammer she'd managed to hold on to, but the blows, whether due to her angle or the strength of the bot's construction, only glanced off its hide.

The centipede's grip on her was getting painful, each pointed limb digging into her for purchase. If this went on much longer she wouldn't have to worry about losing her face, she would be missing chunks from everywhere else. Breathing was also becoming a concern as the bugbot's weight fully settled onto her.

The hammer was useless as a weapon, so it was reshaped into a pole. Her mid-air twist had landed her halfway between her back and her side, with the oversized centipede draped over her lower legs, then from her waist up to her face. At her knees the centipede's body slipped off and looped down to the ground. Taking care not to drop her guard as she did so, Jean threaded the pole through a small gap between the machine and her legs, and braced the end against the ground. Taking as deep a breath as she could manage, Jean heaved on her end of the pole with one hand and shoved the bugbot with the other.

The robot clung on, refusing to let go of its prey. Jean pushed harder. Slowly, the bugbot's grip loosened. She felt one of its legs rip a hole in her pants as she gave a final heave, throwing it clear.

It was back on its many legs appallingly fast, faster than she was. She only managed to get up to one knee before it had righted itself and was charging again. Jean's protective sleeve and pole disappeared as she called on a familiar shape: a shield.

She got it up in front of her just in time. Shield and centipede met with a clang, pushing Jean back but not quite to the ground again.

"No, you don't, you little shit." Metallic legs scraped and skidded over her shield, searching for purchase, for a gap in her defense, for something soft to sink its mandibles into. Jean shoved, struggling to get both feet under her.

"I don't think I ask for very much," she grunted. She seriously doubted the bot could hear at all, let alone understand, but talking aloud was a habit. "A job that pays the bills, a roof, a little treat now and then." Her sneakers ground gravel into the asphalt, finally making contact. The strain of holding off the bot made her arms tremble, but she had her feet back. "I work two jobs, ya know. One doesn't even pay, it's volunteer work. No pay, no benefits, very little in way of appreciation, and hazardous, to boot. But I still do it."

Jean was fully upright again, braced and leaning into the attacking robot, which was still mindlessly attacking the shield. It was big, complex, and strong, but thank all the gods, it was stupid.

"But you know the one thing I would *really* like?"

A hilt materialized in her hand. She dug in her toes and ducked down, keeping shield and bug as high as she could, and heaved. The bugbot lifted up, giving Jean a clear shot at its underbelly. She swung the hilt around and slipped the short blade that sprang from it between two of the overlapping plates. It was sharp, strong, and thin, all to a degree only possible when given the limits of her imagination. Her sword tore through the bug's internal mechanics, smooth silver armor no longer an adequate defense. The bug shuddered, hesitated.

"I want a fucking day off."

Jean focused on the weapon in her hand and *concentrated.*

Her creations were static once they were formed, solid and inflexible. The only movement they were capable of was the movement of many parts acting in concert. But she could, with focus, give them that flexibility while they were still in the process of creation.

In her mind's eye, she could visualize her sword stuck in the guts of the robot, paper-thin and razor-sharp. She could see it, feel it, and knew it for a sword in its very essence. With her mind, she nudged that essence, compelling it to change, but to change slowly. She told it to shift from something that was a weapon to something that moved, that mimicked life, something that was *growth*. Obeying her will, her sword sprouted shoots, vines and branches. Like live things, they reached out, tangling in gears, bending levers, tearing plates like tissue. Jean's sword became a living thing under her control, strangling and ripping the mechanical centipede from the inside.

The bugbot's struggles weakened. It gave a last pathetic whine of protest, an orchestra of breaking machinery, and slumped over her, dead.

When it finally stopped, Jean nearly collapsed underneath it. The fight had tired her, but the effort of making something that acted alive had truly exhausted her, making the sweat run down her body and every limb tremble. She hated doing that, it left her near enough to useless every time. She had to visualize every single part growing, her mind giving the object all of its animation. The moment she lost her focus, it became an inert mass. The dead weight of the centipede was just about enough to drag her back down to the ground. With a motion that required more effort than it should have, she shrugged the unwieldy machine off of her. It crashed to the concrete with a dull clang.

The world wobbled a little in front of her eyes, but she was still standing. She had won. She looked down and grinned at the dead bot.

Her mystery enemy had some cleanup to do. Like hell was she going to do it for them.

Breathing deep and dusting herself off as best she could – hoping the damage to her clothes was limited to the one rip she could find in her pants – Jean went back inside to finish her date.

ᴕᴕ

Walking back to their cars after the movie was an awkward affair. Derek's few attempts at starting a conversation were each met with monosyllabic responses. Jean was too drained to try being energetic any more, or to even really think of Derek's protective gesture of walking her to her car as ironic. Frankly, she was just glad to have someone on hand in case she fell asleep on her feet before she got there.

Once at her car, there was a pregnant pause. Jean just wanted to go home but hesitated to open the door. Derek was fidgeting beside her, and she was aware that he was psyching himself up to say something. So she waited, vague dread rising within her. She was fairly certain she knew what was coming.

Finally, looking as though he would rather be anywhere else in the world than standing next to her, he managed, "Look… I don't really know what happened tonight, but obviously, this wasn't the best date the world has ever seen. I know you're tired and everything, but it seems like something's bothering you. And I don't think it's work. So," he looked utterly miserable, "do you want to try for a second date, or would you rather give the whole thing up?"

Jean came a little more awake at that. "No, I *would* like to try for a second—"

"It's just that you seemed so out of it—"

"No, no, no," Jean stopped, tried to compose herself. The evening had gone about as badly as possible, the last thing she needed to top it off was Derek thinking *he* was the reason she had appeared so disinterested. "I'm sorry about tonight, but seriously, it was just— just me being too worn out for full engagement." She tried for a smile. "I think next time we should aim for a weekend, you know? Maybe that will help."

Derek looked at her uncertainly, the worry line back between his brows. Brown eyes, brown hair he tried too hard to style, one hand twisting the cuff of the opposite sleeve…he was the normalcy she craved so badly. "You sure?"

"Definitely." She pulled him into a quick hug, the smell of nicotine and cologne tickling her nose. After a second, he returned the embrace.

They made no plans, only promising to look in on each other on their next shared work shift. For Jean that was enough. She had plenty to deal with for a while, to think about and investigate with the shattered mousebot in her purse. Until that was done, she would have to look forward to her next taste of normal.

ᘓᘔ

Derek watched as Jean drove away, a little worried. Even at the end of double shifts, he couldn't remember ever seeing her so drained.

His fingers twitched. He wanted a smoke, but it was the habit rather than the nicotine that he craved. Besides, playing into his waning addiction would relax him, and at the moment, he wanted to hold onto his irritation.

His car wasn't far from where Jean had parked. Once seated behind the wheel, he pulled out his phone and dialed a number he'd hoped he wouldn't have to call for a couple of days. The connection rang a handful of times before finally being picked up. Derek's scowl flickered into a grin before he spoke.

"Hey, Brian, how's it going?" he asked, voice carefully careless. "No, it went fine. Say, where are you right now? ... Uh-huh, right. I'm not too far away, actually, so why don't I come down and meet you. ... No, no trouble. I'll be there in like ten minutes. And Brian," his smile died. *"Don't. Move."*

The drive from the Roundhouse Mall to the Row, a district within an easy stroll of the lake which Brian had given as his location, took less than the predicted ten minutes. Traffic was relatively light on the roads between the two places, but once in the Row itself, driving became a test of patience. As for parking! Once he found the little corner deli Brian was holed up in, he had to circle the block and half a dozen neighboring blocks before he found a space to plant his ancient Volvo.

It might have been less hassle to have just walked the eight blocks.

The deli itself – Cook's Deli, its sign modestly proclaimed – didn't have many people inside. It was too late for the daytime crowds and still too early for any of the nearby bars to be offloading their unsteady patrons. It didn't take long for Derek to spot Brian, sitting as far from the door as possible, taking an entire booth to himself. When he looked up and saw Derek, he immediately ducked his head down.

Before heading over to the booth and its shrinking occupant, Derek ordered from the girl working prep behind the counter. Her apparently permanent pout only grew more prominent at being interrupted for "Just coffee, please, black," but whatever. He wasn't in the best of moods, either.

Cradling the warm mug in his hands, Derek walked to the booth and took the seat opposite Brian. He was eating what must have been his dinner, a sandwich that looked like every kind of meat the place offered between two pieces of bread, with enough greens crammed in to constitute a small salad. It was only half-eaten, and the kid didn't look as though he were prepared to eat more any time soon.

Derek sipped his coffee and grimaced. Coffee here in the morning was fantastic, rich and invigorating with an almost nutty aftertaste. He drank too much of the stuff, really, but hey, he worked long hours. Up early, down late, you learned to take whatever kind of energy you could get. All he could really say about *this* cup was at least it was warm. Resigning himself to his unpleasant coffee, he took another swig.

Eventually, Derek focused his full attention on Brian, who gave a weak smile. "Hey, man," he said. "How's, uh. How's it going?"

Derek stared at him, letting the silence drag out, deliberately making the teen even more uncomfortable. He thought about drawing out the conversation, having Brian wait to see just how much shit he'd gotten himself into, but decided against it. Caffeine or not, he was too tired to play that game.

When Brian started fidgeting in his seat, Derek set his coffee down, dug into a pocket, and very deliberately set something small just beside Brian's plate.

"I found one of your toys."

Brian stared at it blankly, like he didn't understand what he was seeing. Next to his partially decimated meal lay a tangle of broken and mashed metal parts. It was barely a handful. Before being destroyed, it might have made something about the size of a mouse.

The boy came back to life, casting a quick look at the front counter to check if the girl behind it had noticed anything. Without anyone to serve, though, she had turned her back to the room to slice up meats for later in the evening. Brian swept the mini mechanical mess off the table, making it disappear into one of his own pockets.

"The hell were you thinking, Brian?" He pitched his voice low, also conscious of the pouting girl and the three other customers at tables closer to the front. "I told you I was taking the night off."

Brian squirmed a little in his seat, not meeting Derek's scowl.

"Was letting me have just one night to myself too much to ask?"

"I was looking out for you!" Brian blurted out, still keeping his voice down. "Sure, fine, you *say*, 'I'll take the night off,' but you *know* it doesn't work like that. We're never off the clock, and acting like we are is a surefire way of getting caught!"

"No, a surefire way of getting caught is to send your little robotic pets out in public to keep watch on me. I found that one," he gestured, "in Minstrel's. *Minstrel's,* Brian. And there were more of them scuttling around in the theater. Did you go completely insane, or have you always been like this and I just never noticed?"

"I'm not crazy, I'm cautious." He glared when Derek snorted. "I am! *Anyone* could be an enemy. I mean," he seemed to struggle for a second. "What about that girl you went out with?" He lowered his voice even further. "She could be a spy, an undercover agent for The College."

Derek sighed. "Not crazy but paranoid." He rubbed his face, and tried hard not to sound condescending. "Look, if Jean were an agent, then The College has more people than it knows what to do with, scattering them in random places like Morgaine Hospital. She's worked there for *years,* Brian. Do you think there's some long-standing threat there? That they'd leave agents there for unspecified lengths of time, just hoping they'll come across something?"

"Maybe," the teen asserted, lower lip sticking out. "Everyone needs medical treatment eventually."

Suppressing a groan, Derek took another sip of his coffee. Brian had a point, but seriously, *Jean?* It was hard to imagine someone less likely to be a cape spy. She was "normal" personified.

He had really been looking forward to a night where he wouldn't have to worry about dodging cops and overzealous heroes. He'd gotten his wish; he'd just forgotten to include his own assistant on his list of annoyances.

"So did you find out anything mind-blowing?"

"No. *Someone* went and ruined all of the bots' hard drives." The younger man scowled, obviously thinking of all the work it would require to replace the toys he'd lost during the evening. "There's no footage left to recover."

"You'd better be glad I got to the bots before anyone else spotted them," Derek said tightly. "Especially Jean, your maybe-possibly spy. The next time I go out, you and the bots are going to stay the hell out of it, understand?" He leaned forward over the table, holding the boy's eye so there would be no misunderstanding. "Try this again, and you'll be spending the night with the imps."

Brian paled and nodded, tight-lipped.

Satisfied, Derek leaned back and finished his coffee, ignoring his chastened assistant to watch the light foot traffic pass by outside their window. Ordinary people, taking their ordinary evening entirely for granted.

Next time, he promised himself. *Next time we'll have a completely normal night out.*

Notes from a Walking Tour of New Caliburn

by Amorak Huey

1.

The cobblestones are gone
but the streets still taste of gin and iron –
one sword strikes another,
our history spills
and spills.

2.

The fire started in an orphanage.
No one cared until it reached the counting-houses.
By then it was too late. This is the beauty
of flame: we are all responsible
for what rises from ash.

3.

Our past is full of _____, our present
just as _____. Some
_____ are best left unmentioned:
the year of _____,

the day we all lost our _____.

4.

Three short stories about the lake:
    1. Nowhere is colder.
    2. Nowhere is deeper.
    3. It is the wellspring of all our misery,
    all our solace.

5.

Hero is just another word
for loneliness.

6.

There are two seasons here:
winter.
And *really fucking winter now, eh?*

7.

There are so many ways into this city,
only one way out.
It makes our maps confusing
but our restaurants are extraordinary.

8.

For every Arthur, a Lancelot.
For every love, a loss.

For every life, a death.
For every beggar who starves,
a glutton who gorges.
For every square, a circle.
Another city might see this as balance
but here we know better:
each side of the coin is the same.

9.
Ink, whiskey, blood
all freeze at the same temperature.
Knowing the difference
is someone else's job.

10.
Graffiti on an abandoned boxcar:
"Superpowers by birth, villain by the grace of God."
"My sidekick beat up your honors student."

11.
They say you measure a city by its finest deli.
The corned beef is exquisite,
the pastrami worth dying for,
the tongue a bit restless.

12.
There are things about being a hero

that cannot be taught
but most anything can be learned
just as most anything can be taken apart
but not everything can be put back together.

13.
One more story about the lake:
Some day a bringer of truth will emerge from the dark
water.
Her burning blood will melt this ice.
Will end this endless winter.

Rat King

by Thomas Dorton

Pike pulled the overflowing sack out of the can. Empty paper cups and sandwich crusts tumbled on the floor as he lifted it into the air. He set the garbage down on the floor so he could pick up the fallen items, but two teenage boys walked by and tossed their trash haphazardly into the open bag, causing more trash to fall to the floor. Pike gathered all of the trash up in his arms and tried to pile them into the bag. He watched hopelessly as the bag sagged over and emptied half its contents right onto the tile.

After a great struggle, Pike tied off the bag and hauled it out to the dumpster in the back alley. He lifted it up to the dumpster's lip and rolled it in. The bag landed with a loud, wet crash. He held his arm up over his nose to block the stink and walked back inside, slamming the door behind him.

Inside the dumpster, a long pink tail was sticking out from under the garbage bag, writhing and thrashing excitedly before it disappeared under the bag, slurped up like a noodle. The enormous rat had torn a hole in the plastic and was tunneling upward through the cellophane wrappers, paper cups, and stale crusts.

Stigdäg had, in recent times, become more discerning
in his palette. Well, sort of; he still ate everything he could.
Subtleties of flavor and presentation were not his interest.
He had, instead, developed an interest in certain sandwich
remains the restaurant discarded that had a strange texture
to them. They seemed normal, but they had a vaguely sour
scent to them, almost like vinegar. And when he chewed
them and his saliva began the initial steps of digestion, the
foods became bubbly and frothy and tingled against his
cheeks. The first time he had discovered this, it frightened
him, but the more he ate foods with this quality, the more
he enjoyed the tingling, and the more invigorated he felt
after eating. His desire for these specific foods, the ones
which granted him such vigor, led him to grant himself his
name. In his mind, "Stigdäg" meant "Rat who longs for
self-improvement, that he might be a leader."

He found half of a turkey club on toasted wheat. The
bread had absorbed the mayonnaise and tomato juices, and
most of the turkey apparently had fallen off. The rat
nibbled on the bread. Standard soggy bread, though rich
with mayo tang. He would come back to it. He sniffed
around for that vinegary odor. It was hard; a French onion
soup had been spilled in the bag. It smelled delicious, but it
masked the odor he sought.

Then he found the reuben. Only a tiny piece of rye
clinging to a glob of kraut via a smattering of Russian
dressing remained of the sandwich, but it was enough. He

scarfed it into his mouth. His gleaming red eyes glowed with delight as a green, luminescent foam oozed from the corners of his mouth. His heavily matted fur bristled as he swallowed, and the muscles in his legs swelled and quivered.

Incredible, he thought. So rare is it to find a foodstuff that so quickly and so thoroughly rejuvenates the body and mind, a fire to raze the illnesses and apathies and clear room for better life.

He heard squeaks outside the dumpster. He tunneled his way out of the bag and, with a mighty heave of his hind legs, leaped to the top of the dumpster. On the ground below were four mice and another rat, a smaller brown one. He decided to practice his new trick. He squeaked down at them, though his squeak was more of a high-pitched bark due to the broadening of his vocal cords.

The mice stopped scurrying around and stared up at Stigdäg. The brown rat glanced at him for a moment before returning to her own culinary search. Stigdäg squeak-barked again. The brown rat looked back at him and squeaked angrily before crawling away from the dumpster. Stigdäg flicked his wrist, and the mice mobbed the brown rat and dragged her back to the dumpster. Stigdäg squeak-barked once more, his eyes bulging out and his gnarled yellow teeth bared, and the brown rat below committed her full, motionless attention to him. Stigdäg flicked his tail, and the brown rat broke into a rudimentary dance.

I am getting better, he thought.

ۻ

The next day, Pike was hobbling up the sidewalk to the deli. He looked up and rubbed his dry, bloodshot eyes and realized how close he was. He was taken aback that he arrived so soon, even though at several points throughout his walk he had felt intensely the tiredness in his legs, lamenting that he lived only just close enough to the restaurant to not justify the cost of a bicycle. He was then aware that he had walked the whole distance staring at his feet and had no clear memory of looking up at the traffic lights before stepping into the street. He could see from a distance a man standing outside the deli door. He was unnerved by his own obliviousness, as there were something like five to eight intersections between his apartment and the deli. He wondered if maybe it wouldn't be more beneficial to wait until he arrived at work and then smoke up in the alleyway. Then he saw the guy outside the deli again, and his heart sped up.

"Oh my god," he gasped, "I'm late!"

He barreled forward, pumping his arms in great exaggeration and propelling his legs in massive leaping steps. He pulled his keys out of his pocket and tried to pick out the one on his ring that opened the deli's front door. He stumbled up to the door and clumsily tried to shove the key in the lock. He was dizzy and a little nauseous from crashing back into reality after his stoned detachment.

"I'm sorry, sir," he said, panting heavily. "Sorry I'm so late."

The man standing by the door had earbuds in and was staring off across the street. When he noticed Pike was there, he pulled one of the earbuds out.

"You say something?" he asked.

Pike said, "I'm sorry I'm so late. I must've set my alarm wrong or something."

"Oh, I'm not here to eat," the man said. "I'm just waiting for someone. And I don't think you're late."

Pike looked at the store hours sign, then at his watch. Indeed, the deli opened at 11, and it was only 9:45.

"Oh," Pike said. His face was flushed. He walked inside quickly, hoping it wasn't totally obvious that he was high.

He turned on the lights and thought he heard something come from the back of the kitchen. A faint sound of movement. He proceeded slowly through the restaurant and popped into the back. Nothing there. He shook it off and vowed to never get stoned before coming to work again.

ठठ

At noon, a woman walked into the deli. Terry Donald was a regular but not the kind that developed a rapport with the staff. Her orders and particularities were well-ingrained into even Pike's smoky little mind. She came in so often that, when she appeared on the television news as The Pteranodon, her identity was immediately known to everyone on the Cook's Deli payroll. Her distinctive bony frame was only emphasized by her form-fitting costume, and her long, birdlike face was hardly hidden by her mask; when Pike and Tabitha had first seen her on the screen, she barely registered as a costumed crime fighter.

Pike got nervous whenever Terry came in. He wanted to be warm and friendly, but Terry was an imposing woman. She was very tall and very attractive, and her eyes seemed to speak volumes of detached disdain for deli-working scrubs. The way she so brusquely ordered her sandwiches closed off any potential for interaction. She was a tightly-wound woman, and any slip-ups in her order or attempts at socialization on Pike's part seemed to have high potential for disaster.

"Eight-inch Italian," she said. "Sweet peppers. No mayonnaise."

"Sure, no problem," he said. "Anything to drink?"

"No."

"Any chips?"

"No."

He wondered if she treated all customer service workers like this. He felt like an ATM. But for sandwiches.

"All right. Five bucks."

He started work on the sandwich, neatly laying a thin layer of prosciutto on top of a thin layer of capicola. Rather than taking two slices of provolone, he took one and tore it in half. He put on a small handful of shredded lettuce and two slices of tomato and a few sweet peppers. He also put on a couple onions, though less than he would put on a standard order. Last, he put on just the faintest amount of oil and vinegar. He wrapped it up in paper and taped the paper closed.

"Here you go, ma'am," he said.

"Thank you," she said.

She had never said that before. Not to him. She usually just said "Thanks," never adding the more personal "you." Maybe she was warming up to him, he thought. Of course, maybe he was reading into it too much. In fact, he felt that was almost certainly the case, but he nevertheless jumped on the opportunity to perhaps take advantage of a slight increase in personability.

"Have a good day," he said. His gut clenched up as he gave her a hearty smile.

"You too," she said as she turned and headed for the door.

His heart raced at her response. He watched her walk out the door. She walked with a confident stride, as if instead of wearing the flats she had on, she was wearing the heels she normally wore and stepped so confidently in. Pike wheeled around, bathing in his newfound sense of cool, feeling confident to attack the rest of the day, whatever it threw at him.

⚖

Terry walked out the door and turned the corner on the right. She looked at her watch and saw she was running later than she thought. She unwrapped her sandwich and took a bite. As she passed the alley behind the deli, she heard a rustling. She did a double-take at the dumpster. Seeing nothing, she quickly went back on her way. Then she felt something graze her ankle. She looked down and saw a mouse running down the sidewalk. She shuddered violently.

"Jesus Christ," she said. "This city is fucking gross." Her face contorted into a mask of repulsion, which only intensified when she felt another one run over her foot. And another. And another. She had never seen so many little rodents in one place before. She started to cross the road just to get away from them, but she saw the enormous black rat Stigdäg hunched over the curb, staring up at her sandwich.

"Okay, this is far too disgusting for me," she said. She spread out her arms and started flapping them, lifting into the air with her sandwich in tow. "Try and catch me up here, you little shits."

Stigdäg barked, and the mice started leaping into the

air after her. Without a good running leap, she was only able to hover a few feet, and the mice were surprisingly good jumpers. One of them snagged a tooth on her stocking, suspending from it for a brief second before the material ripped and the mouse fell, bonking her little noggin on the ground.

Terry opened her mouth wide and shrieked. A bright blue beam of concentrated sonic energy shot forth from her throat and blasted the mice, causing all of them to writhe in agony over their burst eardrums. Stigdäg climbed up on the curb and leaped high up onto Terry's back. She lost her concentration and stopped her shriek-beam, instead squalling with disgust at the massive creature trying to crawl over her shoulder, leaving black paw prints all over her jacket. She began to lose balance in the air, swaying and wobbling as Stigdäg clung to her arm and shimmied his way to her sandwich.

She is clinging to the sandwich rather tenaciously, Stigdäg thought. Her grip was so tight she clenched out a few of the peppers, which had fallen to the sidewalk. She is a fighter, a real fighter, he said. She would make a good rat.

He tried to pry her fingers apart. All he wanted her to do was drop the sandwich. He craned his neck back to look her in the eye. Her face was angry and frightened in equal measure. He bared his fangs at her, putting on a good show with lots of saliva and gnashing, hoping she would lose her grip in fear of his bite. He even bulged out his eyes for extra effect. And it worked! Her fingers sprung open and the sandwich fell to the ground. He jumped, landing on top of the sandwich.

"Goddamn it!" Terry said. She set foot back on the ground, throwing her arms up in frustration. There was no time to go in and order another sandwich, she had to return to work. But before she turned to leave, she unleashed another shriek-beam. Stigdäg, still conscientious of his foe's presence, broke for the alley, narrowly avoiding sonic obliteration.

♎

When it was safe, Stigdäg picked at the sandwich. It bubbled in his mouth, and warmth coursed through his body.

He turned to his smaller cohorts, who had limped into the alley, dazed and trying to come to terms with their newly acquired tinnitus. He squeaked to them to commend them for their valiant effort. They didn't hear him.

♎

On his break, Pike went out to the back alley and sparked a small joint. He was enjoying the cool autumn weather while they still had it. The temperatures were gradually getting colder, it would only be a matter of time before they dropped to more unpleasant numbers. When he finished smoking, he tossed the still-red roach into the dumpster. Then he heard a terrible noise come from the garbage.

The last embers had landed squarely on Stigdäg's haunches. He scaled to the top of the dumpster and stared Pike down. Pike stared back, his eyes widening as it registered in his mind what he was looking at and how angry it looked.

Pike screamed and ran back into the deli, slamming the door behind him. Tabitha was at the counter putting together a meatball sub for a customer. Hearing Pike's screams, she became visibly agitated. The customer, a short middle-aged man, tried to pretend he wasn't noticing Pike's outburst or Tabitha's annoyed facial expression. She thrust the sub at him and turned around to give Pike the evil eye.

"What the hell is wrong with you?" she said. "We got customers in here, last thing we need is someone running through, of all places, the kitchen, screaming in horror."

Wide-eyed and shaking, Pike said, "Tabitha, I saw a rat outside!"

She rolled her eyes. "So what? It's an alley. There's a dumpster. Probably gonna be a rat."

"You don't understand," he said, "it was so big!"

"How big?" she said, draining as much interest out of the question as possible.

"Uh," he stammered, trying to think of a reasonable

comparison since he didn't know the exact size in inches. "It was as big as a cat."

"How big a cat?"

"Like, a big cat."

"Garfield big or Mufasa big?"

"Garfield big. But in like the strips where he eats a lot and his stomach is swelled up to a comical proportion."

"I guess that's pretty big. But just make sure the door is closed when you come in and out so it can't get in the kitchen, and we should be fine."

"Can't we do something to get rid of it?" he asked.

"No," she said. "If it's that big, we probably won't have an issue with it just sneaking in through a hole in the wall. And if we don't absolutely have to lay out poison or traps and kill it, I don't want to kill it."

Pike nodded. She could smell the weed on him, but she didn't give it away.

"So just chill out, okay?" she said, patting him on the back. "Let the thing eat our trash if it wants, and let's go make some sandwiches."

⚖

On his walk home, Pike's high had begun to fade into a sleepy come-down. He ambled through town, his pace barely slowed when he stopped at intersections. He walked past a café with a few outdoor tables occupied by people who were soaking up the last bit of pleasant weather they would likely have until March. When he passed them, he walked a few more steps, then came to a halt. A dim light bulb came on in his foggy brain. He turned around and walked back to a woman sitting at one of the tables. She was ravenously devouring a large croissant.

"Hey, I know you," he said. "Terry, right?"

Terry looked up at him. She had massive round sunglasses over her eyes. She swallowed the wad of bread in her mouth and wiped flaky crumbs from her face. "Hi," she said.

"Did you enjoy your lunch today?" he asked. He felt lame before the words even finished escaping his mouth.

"No, I didn't, actually."

"Oh," he said. His face fell. "I'm sorry, did I mess it up? I know you like a little less oil on your sandwich than we generally put on, but sometimes I don't gauge it right and go overboard."

"I don't know," she said, thrusting her shoulders sharply upward. "I barely got to taste it. I was mugged by rats outside your restaurant."

"Oh my God," he said. "Was one of them really, really big?"

"It was fucking huge and it climbed on me. It forced me to drop my sandwich on the ground." She waved the small remaining chunk of croissant at him. "This is the first thing I've eaten in about thirteen hours. Had low blood sugar all day. Been fucking bitchy and shaky and wired because I haven't had anything in my stomach to balance out all the coffee I've been drinking." She waved her hands frantically while she talked, stabbing at the air with her bent knuckles before stuffing the last of the croissant in her mouth. "And it's just not been a good day."

Pike sighed and ran one of his hands over his hair. "Terry, I'm so sorry. I didn't even realize we had a rat until today. I wanted to do something to get rid of it, but my supervisor said that if it's outside, we're not supposed to worry about it. But I'll tell her what you said, I'm sure she'll be willing to do something."

"She better be," Terry said. "It's gross enough knowing there's rats anywhere near where you like to eat, but when they attack you and steal your food, one starts really coming up with different places to go for lunch."

"Well, don't you worry," Pike said, puffing his chest out a little. "I'll go home and make a trap big enough to catch that rat! You can come get your Italian with sweet peppers and mayo without fear of contamination!"

Under her dark sunglasses, her eyes were rolling magnificently.

"I guess that sounds creepy," he said, "but you have ordered the same sandwich at least twice a week for the last year and a half. Even I can memorize that sort of routine."

He waited a second to see if she would laugh at his self-deprecating joke. Her face didn't budge.

"But in any case, I am completely dedicated to excellent customer service, a dedication which I will further exemplify by catching that rat!"

She turned her chair to face him and crossed her legs. Watching one of her legs lift and harshly hook itself over the other mesmerized Pike instantly. "You're really going to do it?" she asked.

He nodded. "Absolutely."

"All right," she said. "You catch it, and give me a free sandwich to replace my lost one, we'll be square."

"That's only fair," he said, nodding.

"But also," she said, pointing a long finger at him, "I want it dead."

Pike gulped. "Well, see, Tabitha, my supervisor, she says that she doesn't want it to be killed."

"Oh, I'm sorry," Terry said, "was Tabitha the one who was mobbed by a gang of rodents, nearly infected by their little rat claws and teeth, and ended up dropping her food on the ground? I will not suffer another lost sandwich. I cannot have another day like today. I'm not built to run like this. I want that fucking thing dead, okay?"

Pike didn't say anything, but the way he shook made it seem like he was nodding.

"And if I come back and it's not dead, I'm going to make a call. That rat is a public menace, and I have close ties with a certain mask who I think would be more than happy to come take care of it."

Pike bit the inside of his cheek and tried to keep his eyes from rolling.

"And you know how it is with masks sometimes. Occasionally they'll make a dramatic commotion when they're taking on some villain, attracting a lot of attention from passersby. People will see that your restaurant is plagued by monster vermin. Hopefully there won't be a lot of collateral damage to the building, though that's often a side effect of the dramatic commotion."

Her eyes, so steely blue they seemed to cause a glare even after sundown , were burning holes in his own retinas. Her mouth was clenched and her arms were folded across her chest. Her legs were still crossed. He thought, in another scenario, this would be an arousing look. In one smooth motion, she uncrossed her legs and recrossed them, placing the other leg on top. No, it's arousing in this situation too, he thought.

⚖

"That girl is so unpleasant to serve," Tabitha said. "I mean, would it kill her to smile? Like, she comes in, and customers who aren't even paying attention to her get all tense."

Tabitha and Pike were both in the back of the kitchen. Tabitha was pulling containers of sandwich toppings out of the refrigerator while Pike scrubbed up silverware in a large metal sink.

"Well, we have to do something for her," Pike said. "Even if she is unpleasant, which she isn't, she's coolly aloof, but even if she was, we have a responsibility to run a safe restaurant, right? Other customers might get attacked. What if someone gets bitten and they catch the Black Death?"

"First of all, I know what our responsibilities are, Pike. This is my family business we're talking about, right? Secondly, you catch Black Death from flea bites, not rat bites, and in either case it's totally treatable. We'll think of something to get the rat out of here, but we're not going to kill it."

"I don't want to kill it," Pike sighed, "but she also threatened to destroy the deli. She said she'd come in all decked out as The Pteranodon and fight the rat and pretend to accidentally destroy the building."

Tabitha stared at him for a second, then clamped her forehead between her fingers. "Why do so many masks have to be so frickin' dramatic? Wish I could just call animal control."

"Yeah, they've been on strike for a long time."

"It's completely absurd. I mean, I know the likelihood of them ever having to deal with something like Ursatron ever again is probably zilch, but since we obviously expect them to be involved, is it really that big a deal to give them a few extra benefits?"

"Yeah," said Pike. "But I've been building a trap at home, one that should be big enough to catch the rat."

"Look at you, being all ingenuitive," she said with a small smile. Then the small smile faded slightly. "You're not working on it while you're stoned, are you?"

"Umm."

ᛮᛮ

The sun rose and poured light into the alleyway. Feeling the warm rays seeping into the dumpster, Stigdäg opened his eyes. He stood, ruffled his hair, climbed out of the trash and leaped to the ground below. He stretched out his tail and its arms, twisting his neck around until it made a small pop. As his brain closer approached full wakefulness, Stigdäg noticed a smell. Up near the wall across from the dumpster was a meatball sub. It was fresh! He scampered over to it, drooling and panting in anticipation. Even if there was no fizzy texture, there was no way a fresh, hot sandwich was getting passed up. He snatched the toasted roll in his pink paws and started shoveling the sloppy concoction into its mandibles, masticating messily and spewing marinara everywhere.

Then CRASH.

A wooden crate, with metal weights fixed to the top, came crashing down over Stigdäg, trapping it and the sandwich in a DIY cage. Pike, who had been watching patiently from a window on the floor above the deli, was holding the rope from which the crate was suspended.

"Ha ha! Caught you, you bastard!" he shouted. He scrambled down from the second floor to the first and out into the alley. He peered into the crate, where Stigdäg was still devouring the sandwich, seemingly unfazed by his wooden prison. Pike started to lift the crate up but then realized he would almost certainly lose his quarry. But what was he supposed to do? He actually hadn't thought further than dropping the crate.

"Okay, Mr. Rat," Pike said, "I'm going to leave you here until I figure out a way to more effectively box you up. Then I'm going to take you home. We can be roomies. I won't have to kill you, and Terry won't blow up the deli. All right?"

Stigdäg, having finished the sandwich, was plucking crumbs and sauce off his face and licking his fingers. He stared at Pike blankly, sensing that Pike was expecting an answer to his question. Stigdäg cocked his head.

"Aww," Pike said. It was kind of cute, in a Gollumish sort of way. He gently pushed the box against the side of the dumpster so that it wouldn't be just sitting in the middle of the alley. It didn't occur to him that neatness and organization didn't count for much in this particular spot. The wood scraped against the concrete, and Stigdäg scrambled to keep from getting his tail or feet pinched between the box and the ground.

"Now you stay there, dig?"

Stigdäg, slightly agitated, shoved hard on the wooden slats that comprised its prison and snapped them in half. He stepped over the splintered wood and sauntered past Pike, who remained still except to turn his head and watch Stigdäg walk away.

"Yo, dude, come back!" Pike shouted. He followed after the rat, but found himself tripped up by his tail and falling to the ground. Pike reached out and grabbed the large matted ball of hair in front of him. Stigdäg looked back at him, the morning sun twinkling in his eyes like new light on a pool of battlefield blood. Pike wasn't sure if rats could scowl, but if they could, this rat was scowling at him.

"Man, I'm sorry," Pike said nervously, "but I can't just let you go. I wish you could understand."

"Will you just kill it?" a voice said behind him.

Pike looked behind him and up to the roof. There was Terry, perched on the ledge in full Pteranadon regalia: the black mask strapped around the top half of her head that drew back in a long aerodynamic crest, the long-sleeved bodysuit of black spandex with unmended tears revealing scars from previous battles, the thigh-high boots with the four-inch heels that only emphasized the eternality of her legs and ended at the toes with stylized talons, and the magnificent artificial wings that splayed out when she opened her arms. All the things Pike had ever thought about how female superheroes were cruelly objectified by patriarchal comic book writers were skipped over, along with one of his heartbeats. She leaped from the ledge and floated to the ground, looking down at him with her hands on her hips. The way she looked at him with those crazy blue eyes, one would almost venture to guess she had ice vision powers.

"Hey, Terry," he said sheepishly.

"Don't call me Terry," she spat, giving him a kick. "Use my fucking name."

"Sorry, Pteranadon," he said. "Just, you know, trying to take care of the rodent problem."

"I've been watching. You're doing a shitty job."

"I've only been at it a few minutes, give me some time."

Stigdäg's face, which was technically expressionless but had a scowling intention, changed its intention to one of mild amusement at the interaction between Pike and Terry. He could have easily squirmed out of Pike's ineffective grasp, but he decided instead to wait and see how the situation played out.

"Kill it now," Terry said. "Slam its fucking head on the ground."

Pike looked at Stigdäg. Stigdäg looked back at him. Pike sat up, biting his trembling lip. He turned to look back at Terry, who folded her arms across her chest. He looked back at the rat and clenched his teeth.

"You know what?" Pike said. "No."

Terry groaned. "Seriously? That's how this is going to

go?"

"I'll make you a sandwich to replace your other one, that's fine," he said. "But I'm not going to kill this guy. If you want him killed, you can do it yourself."

"Fine. Give it here."

Shit, she called my bluff, he thought. Stigdäg started to writhe and gnash in Pike's hands. Growing nervous and excited, Pike reacted swiftly; he heaved the massive rat right at Terry's face. As the dense ball of matted fur and thrashing claws flew squealing through the air like a fuzzy cannonball, Terry let out a piercing shriek-beam before toppling over backwards with the rat clinging to her face. The beam had struck Stigdäg directly, and Pike clutched his own ears and shouted in pain. Large cracks formed in the nearby windows.

Stigdäg scratched and squirmed all over Terry's face while she tried to get a handle on him. She managed to shove him off and climbed back on her feet. Stigdäg stumbled around, clutching his throbbing head. The high-pitched ring was the only thing he could hear in his bloodied ears.

Terry dusted the fur and dirt off her face and neck. Then, her eyes wide and her teeth bared, she stepped over to the dizzy rat and lifted up her boot over his head. Pike turned away, unable to bear to watch what was about to happen.

Terry slammed her boot down.

There was a loud crunch.

The throaty squeal of agony rang through the street.

Pike looked back. Stigdäg was still limping around, clutching his head. Terry was back on the ground. The heel had snapped off her boot. She was clutching her leg and screaming. There was a bulge around her shin, something trying to protrude through the boot's thick material.

"Ah, jeez," Pike said. "Hold really still, Terry, I think your leg is broken."

"No fucking goddamn SHIT my leg is broken!" she screamed. Her face was red. She tried to suppress her tears, but a couple managed to trickle out from under her mask.

"Do you, um, want me to call an ambulance?"

"Yes, call a fucking ambulance!" Screaming spit flew from her mouth onto Pike's face. He ran into the deli to use the phone.

Stigdäg was wandering away from the alley. The ringing in his ears was fading, but no other sound was taking its place. His brain felt like it had been stabbed. Unfocused and deaf, he failed to realize he had stepped off the sidewalk and into the street in front of a car.

The car's front fender was badly dented. Stigdäg was sent flying across the street, where he landed unconscious.

⚖

Pike watched as the EMTs loaded Terry onto a

stretcher. She was hesitant to let them cut her boot off, but since the alternative was trying to pull the tight-fitting footwear off over her protruding shinbone, she relented.

"It's just they were so expensive," she said. "And I practically just bought them." She winced as the cold metal scissors trimmed open the boot, and winced again when she saw the sharp, bloody fragments poking out of her leg. She was breathing heavily.

"I'm sorry," Pike said. "I don't suppose making you two free sandwiches would make up for all this."

"No, it wouldn't," she said through gritted teeth as she was lifted into the back of the ambulance. The doors shut, and the ambulance pulled off and blared its siren.

Pike sighed. Maybe she'll come back, he thought, and one day we'll have a good laugh about all this. He pulled a joint out of his pocket and put it to his lips and lit it. He exhaled a small puff of smoke. Yeah, she's not coming back.

He looked around and noticed the rat wasn't there anymore. He peeked into the dumpster but didn't see him there either. He sighed again and pouted his lip. So much for the little furry roommate idea, he thought. He took another puff and looked at his watch. Only 9:45.

"Maybe the rest of the day won't be so bad," he said.

⚖

When he awoke, Stigdäg was in another alleyway, next
to a different dumpster. As his vision refocused, he could see
the front of the deli across the street. There was a slice of
half-eaten pizza on the ground. Gathering himself up on
his aching legs, he ambled over to the discarded slice,
grabbed a handful of cold cheese, and stuffed it in his
mouth. It bubbled on his tongue and his aches began to
fade. He took another bite, slowly working his way through
it. He looked back at the deli. His vision, now sharp and
far-reaching, could see Pike at the counter through the front
window. He took another bite.

For now, I rest, he thought, raising his little balled-up
fist and shaking it. But I'll be back.

Calculated Risk

by Kitty Chandler

"It's a calculated risk."

Prime attempted to rub warmth into her hands again, picking at her banker's gloves. In the summer, the basement kept the equipment cool enough to function, but in the winter, the inadequate insulation barely maintained the sub-optimal temperature. She could save up for one of the smaller space heaters and work out a new configuration of power cords and units, something involving one laptop unplugged at all times when she was down there.

"There would be minimal damage to the security networks. The information would be put to better use than you have the trained manpower to manage. You would have an advantage over competing interests, and I would be able to increase the accuracy of my predictions and security operations, thereby decreasing your workload."

The Chatterbox call with the supposedly anonymous federal agent wasn't going as well as she had hoped, despite the trust implicit in moving to voice chat. Implicit on his end, at least; she was using a voice overlay she had put together from a series of recordings of three actresses to disguise her age. Despite even these measures, whatever she had hoped for, she had expected this more realistic failure. In time, her arguments might have weight of repetition. For the moment, he did not believe in her skills despite her history of accurate information.

"I don't disagree, but the fact remains you're not authorized or cleared for any of this. At least, I assume you aren't. And you won't identify yourself..."

"And you haven't discovered my identity, which should qualify me for one of your highest security clearances," she pointed out.

"Still. You'll have to go through proper channels. We appreciate everything that you've done, but..."

"Thank you for your time," she sighed, and disconnected the call before he could reject her inquiry in more words than necessary.

Rashida scribbled down some notes anyway and taped it to her main monitor as three more people came into the chat room where she spent most of her time. The flow of conversation would adjust, and she needed more resources to monitor it until she could determine what it would adjust to.

The chat room was her focus tonight. Not the main focus but the central focus, taking up the largest monitor for the moment. On her left-hand side, the mouse and switcher box connected to three different computers, each with a widescreen monitor left, right, and above. The center computer was its own, separate unit. In an emergency, she could detach it and take it with her and have all her most vital information and settings; the other three were just for research.

Tonight, her research took her onto the popular social networking site Agora, first looking for activity patterns and phrase repetitions that matched her profiles, and instead tripping over an imminent crisis. One that might not require significant assistance but at least merited attention.

She pulled up a message window for Misha Aleksandrov's Agora profile. He had posted an update within the last five minutes and was therefore most likely to be within her reach. *Is something wrong with Amanda? She sounds upset.* A short conversation ensued.

Misha didn't take much persuading, which could have been boredom or could have been that Amanda had been exhibiting signs of stress in a face-to-face environment to which she didn't have access.

Maybe I'll swing by, see how she's doing, Misha concluded.

And that closed out that ticket. She moved Amanda's Agora page over to cover half of the lefthand screen; she'd monitor it for updates as the night progressed. To be fair, nighttime noises were most often just raccoons or the occasional stray cat, but Amanda had been complaining about her ex-boyfriend showing up unexpectedly at her place of work, among other locales, for the past seventeen days. By her calculations, that meant he had been harassing her for approximately two to three times as long, allowing for escalation and the fact that he was a known offender with three prior arrests for violent crimes. Precedent both abstract and in her closed case records indicated there would be an incident of violence within the next two weeks. But it wouldn't be tonight.

Until the next emergency required her attention, she could conduct her long-term investigations with only a periodic glance at the monitoring station. There were three supers she was tracking on a regular basis at this point, correlating their activities with identifiable persons in the immediate vicinity and pulling all names that appeared more than twice. Those names went onto a short list of individuals who would have reason to have prior warning of any incidents requiring unusual intervention. She had only once located a likely candidate for an individual super's day-to-day identity on the first try, but over time and with information gathered about the suspects, she could at least narrow it down to a handful of candidates. That information was only kept on her central computer and behind the tightest firewalls she could devise, for security purposes. The only people likely to find out about her more illicit information gathering were her parents, if they came downstairs and looked over her shoulder.

Not that they had any idea to do so. Her mother might suspect what she was up to. Her mother had started it all in the first place, anyway.

When she was eight, her mother had taken her into the

family office and told her some things about her family. In a guilty and hushed tone, and only after telling her that she couldn't tell her stepfather any of this. Which, after Rashida had thought about that, explained a good part of the guilt.

She had told her about a person called Resonance, whom Rashida had heard of in magazine articles and retrospectives, and who turned out to be her own mother. Months before she was born, Resonance had retired. Rashida didn't need a calculator to figure out why, but she said nothing when her mother lost her nerve in the middle of their conversation and asked her not to look into any of it, to forget it had happened, they would discuss it another day. That day never came.

Which was fine. Rashida started a savings fund the next day for her own computer, where she would control the information and didn't have to worry about her parents looking over her shoulder as she searched for the truth about her family history.

She spent the next year tracking down her biological father and his public identity. There were limited candidates based on the available information, but the problem was narrowing it down from the dearth of new information. In the course of attempting to do so, she discovered patterns of behavior which seemed to fit other individuals her mother described as old friends. Another, connected pattern of events turned it into a database of potential supers. Their contact information. Or as close as she could come to it; obviously attempting to dismantle the carefully constructed layers of secrecy would be met with resentment at best and outright hostility at worst. If it came down to discovery, she did have her security protocols and a final scorched-earth program that would wipe all related data. Her monitoring and reporting programs would give any curious interloper more than enough to deal with, in that case.

Monitoring meant the chat rooms and message boards quartered on that screen, and an endless scrolling litany of the same social patterns. She had chosen four based on the fact that they seemed to hold a representative proportion of local high school students and young adults, one of the most volatile populations of the city and the population which most concerned Rashida at the moment. She knew of at least two separate occasions on which undercover operatives of either local law enforcement or federal organizations had attempted to infiltrate the online chat, only to be discovered, spending several fruitless weeks trying to listen in on conversations that were deliberately kept from them. It was how she had made contact with the federal agent whose assistance she periodically sought.

Rashida had decided to participate to a greater degree after an assault investigation was dropped due to lack of evidence, evidence which she found in abundance in the hidden, mirrored chat rooms the investigating officers clearly knew nothing about. As anonymous tips could now be delivered over the Internet, she spent some time analyzing the behavior of the chat room residents to sort out which were boasts and which were boasting confessions of actual misdeeds. An illicitly acquired photo recognition program gave her an additional advantage, at least in narrowing down the field of suspects and potential victims. Over the course of a year, she built or traded for her setup, till she had an appropriate number of monitors and CPUs to handle the full load of all her crawler programs for both information and safety alerts.

☡

Tonight, those alerts were quiet. With scattered individual exceptions, the city was not under siege, not from any problem that needed a less frazzled pair of eyes and hands to sort through. She relegated observational duties to periodic checks and follow-ups, and went back to assigning resources to a heater, or some extra computing power, or more efficient heat retention in her irritatingly cold, underground office.

☡

Upstairs was bright enough to make her squint when she came out of the basement. She considered again bringing more lights into her workspace; contrary to the popular stereotype, it wasn't actually an advantage to be lit only by the pale screens of her monitors. On the other hand, she didn't want to take up too much electricity, and she was pushing it with as many CPUs as she had to begin with. Plus the hypothetical heater. She would look into non-electric means of heating the basement, Rashida decided. She didn't need to heat the entire area, just her workstation, which took up only half the space. And if she could make use of the ceiling beams and hang curtains, it would make more efficient use of what heat she could find by containing it within an area.

"Are you going to stare at those all night or put them on the table?"

Rashida jumped. "Sorry, Momma." She'd gone into one of her states again; she was normally better at multitasking than that. And setting the table was her job. Plates and glasses, flatware and napkins. She had half-formed impressions that this had been a bigger table, once upon a time, with more people, but she guessed that had something to do with where they'd lived before Marcus.

"Marcus might not be in till late, tonight," her mother added, and Rashida turned on her heel in mid-stride, grabbing the third plate from the table. "He's got a lot of paperwork to sort through."

Her hand hovered over the glasses as she tried to work out which of several possibilities that meant. Requisitions seemed likeliest; she hadn't seen anything on the police blotter that required an extended incident report, although there were always forms to be filled out for applying for leave or transferring to another post. However, no one in the house had spoken of a vacation, and she didn't remember her parents talking about him changing jobs.

He didn't have to stay late very often now; that was one of the reasons they'd agreed he would switch to robbery/larceny, so that he could be home more.

Rashida kept setting the table, moving slower, slower to step out of her mother's way as she fixed a plate for Marcus to put in the oven for later.

"Don't worry," her mother smiled, wrapping an arm around the girl's slender shoulders as she walked past. Rashida yelped, tugged backwards without warning. "He's putting together notes for someone else to pass a case along, nothing terrible."

"Oh," she nodded, and sat down.

If her mother wasn't worried, that eliminated the possibility that there was some cause to worry, about which she had not been made aware. Therefore, there was no logical or practical reason to worry, and her sense of unease was entirely a result of psychological scarring from whatever had happened when she was four years old. She had been far too young to maintain clear memories of the incident, but emotional memories were always to be accounted for. She allocated a greater portion of her attention to the physical activities she was conducting, such as sitting down and eating.

Upon review, going over the checklist of things she had yet to do tonight three times was a strong indicator that she was more compromised than she had thought. Rashida shook her head and firmly shut away all crisis-management-related tasks until Marcus got home.

"Rashida." Her mother gestured for her hand for the grace.

"Sorry."

Dinner was quiet. She kept her eyes on her plate and her mind as still as it could be. The part of her that acknowledged she had a social obligation to be a good conversationalist and daughter, and apprise her mother of her current activities, kept up a running conversation, while her leftover resources processed ongoing problems. Her mother knew, both with a mother's instincts and with the perceptions that had made her famous before Rashida was born, that she didn't have her daughter's full attention. But they were all used to this by now.

She was down to chasing the last few bites of roast across her plate and trying to collect all of the gravy when the door opened. "If anyone asks," Marcus announced as soon as he was inside, "I'm not at home, you don't know where I am, I'm out at a bar with the guys."

"All right," Mother came up to take his coat and hang it in the closet, with his briefcase beside, because if she didn't, he would leave both somewhere he wouldn't remember them in the morning. "Should we ask what happened?"

"Well, I shared all the data, all my reports and everything. Ooh, brisket?"

She smacked his fingers away from the plate. "You can eat at the table with everyone else. You shared your reports...?"

"Pretty sure he didn't hear a word I said. I'm going to go back in tomorrow, and he's going to want to sit and talk over each case for three hours. Wouldn't mind so much if he didn't keep asking questions I already went over with him. This what it's like to be you, kiddo?" He glanced over at Rashida, who grinned at him.

"Often."

She liked Marcus. He had come along at a time when her mother was deeply unhappy and had made their lives better, which was as much as she could remember. She had clearer memories of his presence in recent years: the day he had gone with her to tour the local high school and told her afterwards that if she wanted to go to a private school, all she had to do was say so. He had been the one to argue for letting her set up in the basement and giving her privacy, and he had been the one to argue against her seeing a therapist.

Rashida liked that he didn't worry about her or how she was doing. Her mother, she thought, worried that she was doing a bad job as a female parent. Guiding her daughter through the social labyrinth of what was expected of her as a young black woman growing up in the city. Rashida understood the risks, and she understood her mother's concern but found it unnecessary.

She stayed in her basement because that was where she was useful, and if she was there she wasn't out in the world, which was dangerous and full of mean, awful people. She did her schoolwork, participated in two approved-of extracurricular activities, and kept her parents from worrying about her investigations by simply not telling them.

⚖

Homecoming approached. Rashida's days filled with even more noise, most of it rumors, and with dodging questions from her mother and a couple of her teachers about whether or not she had any intentions of going. Prime's nights were filled with Agora pages of dresses and long paragraphs with poor punctuation and sticky caps-locks about who was going with whom, who could be relied upon for sexual activities, and where everyone was going to go drinking afterwards. Less common, but still up from normal levels, were discussions about dinner plans and social groups arranging the sharing of entertainment resources. Those, she filed away in a separate document to be cross-checked with peripheral participants in their social circles who might need nudging towards less risky homecoming activities.

As a result or perhaps as a side effect, everyone else in the city seemed to be going berserk at the same time. Two muggings within fifteen minutes of each other occupied her attention for as long as it took to direct three social media accounts to that location, at least two of whom maintained close connections with certain supers. Five anonymous tips then called in the muggings to the local police office, courtesy of her voice overlay database. If they could maintain a regular and visible patrol for the rest of the night, it might keep that area calm. A second screen was devoted to pictures and Agora pages detailing an event as it happened in real-time, an event she was sure would result in behavior regretted the next day.

"Rashida." Her mother stood at the top of the stairs but didn't come down, by prior agreement. "Don't forget your bedtime."

"I won't," she called back. She had an alarm set to remind her, and one to warn her fifteen minutes in advance. After the second night she had stayed up too late, she had programmed her computer to freeze and save any in-progress data collection until she logged off and went to sleep. There was no point in decreasing her functionality unless it was a major emergency.

Although, if there was any night to throw her a

genuine, major emergency, it would be this one. Amanda's ex-boyfriend was causing trouble again, and Rashida had had to take over one of the woman's friend's computers to open her latest panicked journal entry. A few minutes later, the police tip line got a text about a suspicious person in the area lurking at windows and making noise. With luck, one of those two approaches would prove useful.

Reports of continuous brown-outs on the east-side power grid were also troubling, given that there had been a recent break-in at the plant which serviced that power grid; there was also an increase in reports of fluctuating water pressure at two separate apartment complexes, but she barely had time to pay attention to that, let alone allocate anyone to respond. Building management would have to take care of that.

Footage of girls in compromising positions had appeared on several networking sites at once; Rashida knew they were barely a year older than herself. That went to federal channels as an anonymous complaint and was closed. And there was a sharply increased proportion of violent or aggressive text messages belonging to numbers on her list of gang members or suspected gang members.

"I should be old enough to drink coffee," she muttered. Though she had a large bottle of next to her, which would improve her functionality and cool her body at the same time. One long drink later, she could focus properly again. Several of Amanda's friends were offering comfort and assistance, suggesting the situation could be downgraded to an every-ten-minutes check.

What the hell is going on out there? user RedTwo posted. It was the first posting in over two minutes. The chat room had slowed down some.

"What are you talking about?" Prime muttered and typed at the same time, then double-checked the brown-outs. No major loss of power for any duration longer than seven minutes. Backup power supplies would be flickering on and off, no major hazard.

Don't know, heard gunshots. Going to the basement.

Good for tornadoes, too, someone added. Several other comments scrolled by, offering sympathy and support in capital letters with, more punctuation than a page of dialogue needed. Text-based manifestation of what would be tonal shifts and hand movements if all parties were physically present. This was escalating past the ability or, more likely, the willingness of the police to deal with.

Social sites flew by as she searched for someone of the right age range and skill set to deal with the problem, and who could be reached immediately. The list was thin; everyone was busy with their regular duties, and the hazard of the age range she was searching within was that the bulk of them tended to be part-time at best, still occupied with the business of identifying themselves and building their lives. Very little of that involved the sort of rescue operations she needed.

She might have to expand outside her first-choice parameters, risk sending in someone who was outside the age range of the aggressors and who thus had less experiential empathy and relevant instinct, dropping the likelihood of success. She finally found Hercules "Hal" Pyle (username SonOfAGun, which she privately felt was a little too on-the-nose) coming in from dinner. His father would have been better, but surely he had learned some useful tactics, and according to her files, he had marginal experience. Localized.

She knew where he was. She didn't have to forward on many of the casually desperate messages. Just a couple sufficed before she got his attention.

I don't know if there's anything you could do, she sent. *But if you can, or if you know anyone.* Getting his father in on it would also be acceptable.

His reply came within five minutes. *I don't know. I'll see what I can do.*

Thank you. She'd monitor the situation, but for the moment, that ticket was closed.

⚖

The next morning, Rashida slept in until the last minute. Even so, she found it difficult to wake up, and while she was awake through most of her classes, she had a headache which made it difficult to concentrate. Food and drink helped, but not as much as she would have liked for Ancient Civ II.

The television was on the news while she had lunch. Normally, she ignored it in favor of eating quickly and leaving to do other things, but today she was too exhausted to make an efficient job of it. She slumped over the table with her head propped in her hands in between bites, listlessly scooping beef stew into her mouth. Her chin hung over the bowl because she was too tired to aim. She shredded the mediocre biscuit into what was left of the stew and stirred the bits around with a spoon. When she heard the name of the street on which the gang fight had been building, she looked up with a frown. She'd set someone on that. The ticket was closed.

"...here where the bullet penetrated the wall of the house, straight through to where Carlos Estes was doing his homework. Lucky for him, he'd stepped out to get a snack."

Rashida's spoon hovered over her bowl as she tried to reconcile this new information with what she knew to have happened. The calls had begun around six-forty-five in the evening, extended past nine, and then she had tasked Hal to deal with it. According to all of the information she had been able to gather, he was the son of Helios, and he had at least inherited his father's penchant for dramatic rescue and salvage, even if it was somehow unclear whether or not he had inherited his abilities. That ambiguity nagged at her when she had the time to look at it more closely. Right now was very nearly the opposite of having time to look at anything closely. Helios had engineered ceasefires. A three-street skirmish over gang territory should be well within Hal's reach.

The news broadcast ended without repeating the most important points and recent updates. She would have to find out some other way.

"Hey, are you all right?" Abby King, who usually took the lunch table after Rashida was done with it, looked at her curiously. "You feeling sick or something?"

She felt feverish, and her mind functioned at less capacity than she was used to, but explaining that to her fellow students never worked out well. "I'm just tired," she said, dumping her dishes on the conveyer belt on her way out.

The computer room was too crowded. She went out onto the benches in front of the English classrooms to look. Her knees drew up towards her chest so her tablet could rest on her thighs, heels balancing on the edge of the bench. She looked barely old enough to be in high school in the first place, let alone for the severe expression on her face.

The news wasn't good. No one had died last night, but that was more due to the timely intervention of the police than any de-escalation of violence that was supposed to have occurred before they needed to be called in. "This isn't right." She resisted the urge to pick up her tablet and shake it like an eraser-board. As though that would change the past. "You weren't supposed to..."

What had he done?

Police bulletins were sketchy. They knew heated words had been exchanged due to disturbance calls earlier in the evening; Rashida matched that to the texts she remembered finding. There was a confrontation big enough to warrant mention in the subsequent report, it sounded like several of the gang leaders were there. There were enough members of both groups present that words escalated to brief hand-to-hand violence, then they separated for half-an-hour. Then they returned with guns. It took no real effort to extrapolate what had happened after that.

The confrontation was key. The meeting, the supposed defusing of tension, had instead escalated into armed conflict.

"You are the goddamned son of Helios," she shouted, frustrated, face flushed and unable to apply rational thought to any of this. "You were supposed to fix this!"

In the next second, she ducked her head and hid her face in her tablet. Few, if any, people knew Helios' other identity, let alone that he had a son. He was one of the few identities she was certain of, primarily because of Hal's involvement and the similarity of their approaches. The high profile nature of Helios' activities didn't hurt, though, allowing her to correlate time and location data, plus speech pattern matching, until probability outweighed any doubt. That would only mean, however, that he would protect the identity of his son even harder. On his own, Hal had had a few good cases, but that didn't mean he was well known enough for a student in high school to be shouting about him in the halls.

No one was out, though. She was late to class; everyone had gone inside already, which was why no one was there to hear her blurt out things better left unsaid. Rashida scrambled to get moving, hoping the teacher would forgive her for being late one time all year. Her focus was slipping. She couldn't allow her focus to slip. She couldn't afford to make another mistake like last night.

ᚯᚯ

"Hi Momma I'll be downstairs until dinner just let me know when it's ready." The words came out rapid-fire and punctuated by her bookbag dropping to the floor by the basement entrance.

Her mother turned a full circle as she tracked Rashida's movements past her and down the steps. "It'll be ready in ten minutes!"

She pretended she hadn't heard. She'd come up in fifteen minutes, having just figured out what her mother had said, which should be within the span of time it would take for her parents to realize anything was wrong. At least, she hoped it would take only that long to confirm and correct her error, or set such corrections in motion.

After the fact, she had the luxury of collecting more information and putting the communications flying back and forth into context. She was no longer sure the situation would not have de-escalated on its own had she not sent Hal into the mix. All parties involved knew each other well enough to have a more accurate idea of when they were posturing and when they were in earnest. They might have de-escalated themselves. No one wanted a firefight in the same neighborhood where they lived and worked.

Rashida hadn't arrived at any good conclusion by the time her mother called her again for dinner, so she didn't try to eke out those extra five minutes. Marcus was there, too, and they settled in for dinner.

"How was school?"

Routine question, to which she gave a series of routine answers which sounded hollow and obviously false as she said them. A brief discussion about her Ancient Civ studies led to her getting lost on a mental tangent of the gang conflict, and why Hal hadn't been able to defuse it.

"Rashida..." Marcus prodded, gently and smiling. "Hey, what's up?"

"It's nothing," she lied. Not even a good lie, but she sat up, remembering something. Marcus had been in charge of crime scenes, in other supervisory positions. "Have you ever, um." This would require careful phrasing. Perhaps she could word it convincingly to imply that she was working on a group project which was not proceeding as well as expected. "I mean, you're kind of in charge of a group of people, everyone has their job to do, and you make sure, you give everyone the jobs you think they can do...and then the person who has the easiest task commensurate with their skills..."

Across the table, Rashida's mother mouthed "commensurate" with badly concealed amusement. Any other night, that would have been normal, but tonight it grated as a reminder that Rashida couldn't interact with people in the same way others could.

"...not only completely fails his assignment but makes the whole project worse?"

Both her parents grimaced. Her stepfather set his fork down and leaned back in his chair. "Well. For one thing, no matter how much you think someone might be able to handle their job, people just have bad days. Sometimes people screw up. Sometimes people make mistakes. On top of that, maybe there's something about this assignment that's harder for him that you don't know about. You know, a lot of guys don't talk about things that are hard for them, 'cause they don't want to look weak when they're trying to impress a young lady."

"Marcus..." her mother interjected, less amused now.

He shrugged. "I'm just saying. It's true. And there could be a lot of reasons. Talk to the kid, see what's going on with him. This assignment have to be done today?"

"The sooner the better," she muttered at her plate.

"Why don't you get on to your Secret Lair and do it, then. We'll be up here with dinner when you fix whatever's bugging you. You need any more help, you come ask, 'kay?"

She threw her stepfather a grateful smile, an "Okay!", and cleared her stuff to the kitchen counter so she could bolt downstairs before her mother raised any objections. Which it looked like she was going to. At some point, most likely before college, she would have to explain to her mother exactly what went on in her basement. Not tonight. Tonight she had other problems, problems with bullets, and she meant to get a long ways away from those problems before she did any explaining to her parents.

ᛟ

"I think she's taking more after her father."

"In more than just looks, you mean?" Marcus teased, before glancing up and seeing her face. "Okay. What do you mean?"

"I mean..." Alyson sat down at the other end of the table, sighing. Then got up to pace around the dining nook. "I don't know what I mean. I'm also starting to think I shouldn't have told her about her, uh. About my family." Her irritated look drew the line of separation between her daughter and the rest of her family.

Marcus leaned back again and considered this for a moment or three. "Which parts are you thinking you shouldn't have told her?" he asked, his quiet way of asking what she had told her daughter. Their daughter. Rashida was as much his as she was hers, he was the only father she'd ever known.

But there were some things she'd never explained in detail to Marcus, and to her immense relief, he'd never asked. Everything to do with her previous life, everything that was a little bit out of the ordinary. How she'd gotten the money to set them up in this house and herself in her job, how they paid for the private school Rashida went to. It was all neatly tied up in the box marked Family, which he hadn't tried to open. Alyson had gifts. She used those gifts at work, she might have passed those gifts along to her daughter, or might some day in the future. And that was that.

"I don't know, I just..." She spread her hands, let them flop back on the table. Twisted her fingers around each other. "She wanted to know where she came from. She was eight, too young to know all the details, but I told her a little of it. About my family, and how we come from..."

He waited, eyebrows raised. "Money?"

"Privilege," she said, drawing it out into three unhappy syllables. "Power? Something like that. My father dragged us up from, well. We weren't poor. But we didn't have much to spare, and he always said we were meant for better. He dragged us up from that, we didn't even know how until we were close to grown."

Marcus got up when the coffee started to bubble and burn. "And you told her this, what he did, when she was eight? And now you're thinking that might have been a mistake?"

She untwisted her fingers long enough to push herself up from the table and look at the basement door, tucking her hands under her arms. "I don't know. I think maybe...not telling her about her father's family might have been a mistake."

Saying it that way might have been a mistake as well. The same ability that gave her unusually acute intuition into the way people worked and talked to each other gave her sensitivity to the slight sting her choice of words left in her husband. But how else, really, could she say it? Every other way seemed too impersonal, too clinical. This wasn't a science they could point to and say, this trait comes from these sequences. Not yet, anyway. Give it a few more morally bankrupt researchers, and she had the feeling that might change.

"It's the technical aptitude," she said finally, as he passed her a cup. She wrapped one hand around it for warmth, dunking a biscuit in and stirring with the other. "I wonder if I should have told her. Her father's family always was technologically brilliant, but it came with some, well. Side effects."

"Like what she's going through now." He sat back in his chair, sighing.

"Exactly." Even though he didn't know all of it. And she didn't know how to begin to tell him, after all these years. "I think it might have something to do with, I think it might be affecting her judgment. And I don't know if she, or we, I don't know if we'd know about it, or if we should even be worried."

He reached over and plucked the coffee cup out of her hand. "I've changed my mind. You need this less than I do." He gave her back the biscuit, though, which she nibbled on while treating him to a pouty mock-glare. "It's too late to think about things like that now, anyway. You go to bed, I'll be up soon. We'll talk about it tomorrow. Maybe we can all sit down, talk about it this weekend. Whatever's going on with her, it's not going to get fixed or get worse overnight. You're worrying about it, and it's making you more upset that you won't tell me what's really going on."

In the end, Marcus went to bed before her, only because they were trying not to fight. She had to tell him, she knew, and soon. If her little girl was growing up this fast, she would have to tell him the full story of why she had to stay away from her family, why she had rejected everything, all of it.

Not tonight, though. Please, God, not tonight.

She reviewed all the footage she could find for the rest
of the week. Most of it was compiled by cell phone
cameras, but there was a security camera outside of a
jewelry and pawn shop that had a decent quality recording
of approaching members and bystanders, and another
ATM camera around the corner. Between that and
reviewing the logs of text messages, Rashida was able to
extrapolate a rough sequence of events and most of the
salient details.

Hal had taken a compassionate approach to the
situation, appealed to their empathy for each other as fellow
human beings. What he had failed to take into account was
that they had no empathy for each other. Their conflict, at
least in the case of the most charismatic members, had
progressed to the point where they perceived each other as
enemy first and human second. She had seen this behavior
exhibited in countries where active conflicts were taking
place, but this was the first time she had had to apply it on a
localized scale.

But he was an older boy and had been to school and
learned these things. Not to mention he was the son of one
of the greatest superheroes in the world. How did he not
know this? For that matter, how had he not managed to de-
escalate the situation by the use of physical force when all
else failed?

Rashida circled around that thought several times

before succeeding in pushing it away for another day. The immediate problem was the increase in tension and hostilities. No arrests had been made as yet. Although they knew something had happened, there was no proof who had fired which shots, and the bulk of those bullets were likely too mangled to derive a ballistic signature and match. Even if they were able, there was no guarantee that the name on the gun registry, assuming it was registered, was the same person who currently held and used the gun.

The police couldn't, or wouldn't, do anything about this, and she had no alternative resources she could delegate to the task. And, she decided, sitting back in her chair, she shouldn't delegate resources to this anyway. This had been her mistake. She would fix it.

Sorry about that.

She caught the message on her next sweep, closing some things that were temporary research and opening new tabs. She left it there till she had finished and closed two more tickets, by which time there was a second message.

I didn't think it'd go that bad. I tried to talk them out of it. I'm really sorry.

A third one appeared while she was watching.

Is there anything else I can do? This one had a frowny face appended to it. She wasn't sure what that meant in this particular context; she assumed it was an expression of remorse.

She didn't know, herself, how she was going to fix it, let

alone what he could do. The tabs rushed past as she searched for either a suggestion or something she could handle, something she could fix at the moment. Hal's father was in Pakistan putting down some rebel skirmish, she saw. The headlines made it sound so easy.

Or was it that easy?

Rashida slumped back in her chair, reading that article more carefully. She had old articles about her mother to cross-reference it with, to plan the optimal approach. Between the two of them, they had negotiated several peace treaties, and she hadn't studied the details nearly as well as she should have. She had trusted that whatever abilities they possessed to organize peace were inherent to their superhuman natures, and not something acquired with time and training. That might have been a mistake. It would also account, now that she took the time to think about it more critically, for Hal not being able to pacify the situation the other night.

But it would also make it that much more difficult for her to correct. She would need to plan for contingencies, run scenarios, anticipate responses, and apply solutions herself. And, she reminded herself, it wasn't as though there was anyone else available. She'd looked once.

Hal had stopped sending messages. Possibly he had logged off, but a quick check of his activity disproved that. She had to consider what to say to him very carefully, and before that, she had to come up with a plan. Which would

be the harder part. They responded to strength, she would
show them strength somehow, but she would also offer
them terms which they could accept. She wasn't
demanding much of them, after all. Which someone should
have explained to them, that and how this was more
profitable to them in the long term than engaging in an
ongoing war with strong potential for escalation into fatal
violence.

That. That could be her chief argument, cost-benefit
ratios. But she had to phrase it in a way they would
understand. Which would take some days of planning. She
had to say it with enough strength backing her that they
would listen to her and consider her displeasure at their
calculations. And that would take Hal.

⚖

By Friday morning, she had devised a rough sketch of
a plan. She spent that evening refining it and going over the
details with her new partner. Saturday afternoon was soon
enough for implementation. She would meet him at the site
and they would proceed from there. First, she had a
shopping trip.

"The hell do you need all this stuff for, anyway?" her
contact asked. "How old are you, twelve?"

She knew she came across as older than her age within
text-based media, but she had miscalculated how young she

appeared to people outside her family and the school. "I'm fourteen. Do you have it?"

He handed her the paper sack of weapons she'd purchased, and she passed him the savings she'd accumulated for a heater or another computer. Now it would go to fixing her mistake. Disappointing, but she'd have to learn not to make such mistakes, and her frozen fingers would remind her.

"So, what are you gonna do with all this?" he asked her again. She glared at him.

"Don't tell anyone about this," she snapped, and moved along.

She met Hal at the corner grocery that was also a taqueria and bookstore. The distribution of weapons went less smoothly than she hoped. "What? Are you..." Hal looked up and down the street for someone else, but everyone had hidden indoors, away from the bullets. "You're *twelve!*"

"I'm *fourteen*," she sighed, distributing her share of the weapons. The knife went into a sheath tucked behind her belt, in case she was trapped with her hands bound behind her, and a razor blade tucked into one sleeve for similar circumstances. She had pepper spray in one pocket and mace in the other, and the final weapon had to be a gun. If all else failed, if Hal was incapacitated, she would be able to defend herself effectively with a gun.

Hal didn't like the gun. He wore a half-mask over his

lower face and a crested helmet on top, giving him the appearance of some metal band's idea of a knight. To her surprise, she could still read the disapproval in his face. "Who the hell are you going to shoot with that?"

"My attackers," Prime shrugged. "If I have to. I don't intend to have to, I intend to leave the show of force to you," she elucidated, with irritation at his slack-jawed staring. "Let's go."

Silence delineated the conflict zone, and a complete absence of anyone not in gang colors. Those who were sitting on front steps or walking along the sidewalk, leaning on cars, they all wore some sign of gang affiliation, and they all stared at her. Not at Hal, at her, which might be to his advantage but put her squarely where she had planned and where she least wanted to be: in the spotlight. Most of them stared with scorn, some with curiosity, all with varying degrees of gaping from the well-disguised to the blatantly incredulous.

"I want to speak to the person in charge of the SSC." It sounded far more like she was a fourteen-year-old girl trying to be an adult than she wanted, but until she grew another few inches and a couple of years, she was stuck with what she had.

No one said anything. Of course not, because no one took her seriously. They took Hal seriously, but she spoke first and she looked the most out of place.

The one who stood a little apart from the others now

stepped toward her, glancing once at Hal before visibly deciding she was their spokesperson. "What's a kid like you want with the head of the Crew?" he asked, in that syrupy voice her most hated teachers in elementary school had used. She reviewed the plan and kept her calm.

"Are you the person in charge?"

"Shouldn't be out here by yourself like that, girl," he drawled, extra swagger in his step as he came closer, hands in his pockets and pants hanging down. "Didn't you hear? Was a lot of shooting last night."

"That's far enough," she told him. He was surprised enough to stop. Behind her, Hal's body language shifted to a more stable yet alert stance, his face still unreadable behind the half-mask. "I want to see your boss."

"Maybe I am the boss, little lady," he smiled. "You ever think about that?"

Rashida looked at him. At the trio behind him sitting on the steps of the apartment building, at the person coming down the street beyond him. In the reflections of the windows on the apartment building, she saw three more people coming up from the other side of the intersection, behind her. Hal shifted, one foot at a time, to turn a full circle and take account of everyone now on the street. Focus. This required focus on both their parts, him for the physical danger and her watching the body language and attitudes, the balance of probabilities. Pay attention to that, not the roaring in her ears or the chill down the back of her neck.

She made her voice cold and authoritative, like her mother when they'd tried to put her in the mandatory study skills class. "You are not in charge. If you were the boss, you would not be the first one to speak, since your job is to determine who is safe enough and important enough to meet with him. I would guess that your boss is the person you looked at before coming out to meet me, and to whom you and your associates are now looking, as you have no idea why a fourteen-year-old..."

"Fourteen? You're not fourteen. Gotta be ten or twelve, tops!"

"...why a fourteen-year-old is attempting to hold a conference with you. Particularly a fourteen-year-old who appears..."

Right on cue. One of the two gangers coming up behind her tried to grab her as she watched his reflection in the window. She stepped to one side as he reached, brought her left hand out of her pocket, and aimed it high. Maybe a degree or so too high, but the spray dripped down into his eyes regardless. Dull thuds, and then a crunch, drifted up from where Hal had been standing, and her second attacker screamed and hopped away on his one good leg, swinging his arms wildly. She raised her voice to be heard above the screaming and took two steps closer, as her attacker tripped into Hal's arm-bar and fell sprawling.

"...to have incapacitated one of your soldiers."

Several of them--all those still standing--shifted a hand under their coats. She had to recalculate.

Now she had their attention. First she had amused them, then she confused them, and now she had established herself as a threat. Not a very harmful threat; as long as she kept the gun in her pocket, they would, too. Everyone could be civilized here. All she'd done was pepper spray the one attacking her, and he'd tried to grab her first. Hal had immobilized the other two with some form of unarmed combat, but they still focused on her, presumably putting him in the category of bodyguard. Bodyguards were allowed to use unarmed combat as long as no weapons were drawn and they didn't advance beyond the range of their protectee. Both of those factors indicated they were not a threat.

The crew, and particularly the leader, had to be asking themselves now, though, if she had brought only one soldier with her, what he was capable of. And she was too young and too small for them to see as anything but a child. Not the driving force behind any invasive action into their territory. They had to be asking themselves what it was that she *did* want. In another second, they would ask her outright.

"Little girl looks like you, comes out here, she usually wants something else." The young man who came down the steps had a deeper voice, looked as though he was in his thirties. She'd done some quick research on the alleged upper leadership. This one had been running the gang for five years and showed no signs of weakening his grip any time soon. He was also the oldest leader they'd had since the gang's inception nearly thirty years ago. Old enough to have seen several changes in leadership in this and other crews. If she could make him a rational argument, he might broker a peace negotiation. If she could provide him with incentive.

A humanitarian incentive hadn't worked, so she would try something else.

"I want you to negotiate a ceasefire with your opposing number, the Locos Rotos. I want you to control your people so that there is no repeat of the incident earlier this week."

He laughed, for the benefit of his crew, if the tightness in his facial muscles was a standard indicator. "You think I don't control my people?"

She made a point of glancing around at them while she calculated which response would have the best outcome. Behind her, Hal made a derisive noise and stepped up behind her, folding his arms over his chest. "If the ceasefire is to be successful, you will need control of your people. I have your opposite number on speed dial." She pulled out her phone with her left hand, making two others twitch when she reached into her pocket. "You can either talk to him, negotiate cessation of hostilities, and the both of you restrain yourselves from further displays of profligate violence..."

"Pro-what?" someone asked.

"...or I can call your opposite number, offer him the same deal, and tell him that he is receiving this same deal after you and several of your soldiers were assassinated by a twelve-year-old girl." Hal cleared his throat again. "And her bodyguard."

The street was deathly quiet. Her throat felt hot, sore and hot, as though she'd gotten strep again. And she knew they were being watched by more eyes than just those on the street right now. A show of force had to be the best option. It was the only leverage they had when the South Side Crew didn't know them from a bullet hole in the wall.

"You said you were fourteen," the boss said.

"Your soldier thought I looked twelve."

He nodded, glancing around at the nearby buildings. At the windows. Then at them. "You..." he pointed a finger at Hal. Prime felt the world grind to a halt as she recalculated the probabilities. "I know you, don't I. Saw you earlier, you came around right before the shooting started."

She spoke up before Hal could, calculating that the odds of success were better if she did the talking, although only by a small margin. "My intention was to secure this ceasefire without bloodshed, but if that's what it takes, we are prepared to eliminate the threat by any means necessary." Two guns came out, but the leader gestured them to keep their firearms lowered. "By any means necessary" was a good phrase, carried weight and associations with people who had a lot more force at their disposal than she did.

"By any means necessary." He took another step towards her. "You government, girl?"

Prime kept her eyes on him and didn't say anything.

He looked around the street, and she knew he was looking for snipers. Moving curtains, red laser dots, some sign that she had other people backing her up, causing her to be this confident, because if it was true and he was about to be ordered around by a fourteen-year-old girl, he would lose control of his men. He would lose all face.

"You ain't normal, are you?"

Prime stepped one foot out to assume an at-ease stance, holding up the phone so they could all see her pushing the button. "Prime..." Hal said, wary and on edge, but she held the phone against her palm and held up a finger to silence him. She couldn't let him control the conversation any more than she could let the leader of the SSC.

"What am I telling him?" she put the phone to her ear. "This is Prime. Put Carlos on." She pulled her shoulders back and her head up, she'd seen Marcus call on his authority as a police officer often enough to know how it was done. "Well? What am I saying?"

For the first couple seconds, no one moved. Prime pictured it in her head, the possibilities spinning faster and with more volatility than she had ever tried to control. The odds that they would all walk away with nothing vanished quickly, replaced with teetering even odds that the SSC leader caved to her bluff, or that he called and something very nasty happened to her and Hal for making him look scared of a little girl. Her internal clock ticked down the seconds she had before they realized she wasn't on the phone at all. She had to make decisions, find the precise words that filtered those probabilities down to the ones she wanted. This wasn't staring at a computer screen. This was real. And so were their bullets.

Suddenly, she understood her mother better. Wanted to tell her she was sorry, so sorry.

"I'm here. Where are you?" Prime waited, building the other person's speech in her mind. She didn't know the cadence of the man's voice but she could approximate. The Rejection Hotline chattered in her ear. "Never mind. The deal's off. He won't go for it."

Murmuring started. Hal came up behind her, and even she felt the unease pouring off of him in waves of sweat and nervous motion. "Prime, what are you..."

She covered his mouth with her hand. "Your window has closed," she told the hotline, hung up, and switched phones, looking at the SSC leader and ignoring the guns now pointed in her direction. "Yours is still open. Do we have an arrangement?"

He waited long enough for her breakfast to rise up into her throat, but he took the phone. Snatched it out of her hand. The number was pre-programmed in the display, and it was the right cell phone number, she'd checked earlier. "What's your stake in this, anyhow?" he asked, lifting the phone to his ear. "What're you here for?"

"The next generation," she told him, without explaining what that meant.

⚖

Negotiating the ceasefire took until after dinner, and by the time she got home, she was grounded for the rest of the weekend with limited computer time for the next two weeks, for staying out all day and worrying her parents half to death. That was fine. The basement was cold, immediate problems were resolved, all she had to do was check in with everyone now and again so that they didn't worry. She was starting to gain a greater appreciation for how other people might worry. A more intimate, emotional appreciation. Relations with Hal were strained. She checked in once a night, sometimes he replied, but they didn't talk about what had happened.

Three days later, Marcus was working late again, and her mother gave her permission to pick up their dinner at the deli on her way home from school. After the phone call, and acting on impulse as she hadn't done in years, she sent Hal a message to meet her there. For all she knew, he was upset with her enough to start a fight, but it was a public place and there would be at least a few people in the store itself. It would be safe.

"Placed an order over the phone?" she asked, looking around. The late afternoon light was streaming through the windows, coloring everything in warm yellows and oranges. She spent so much time in the blue-white light of her computer screens, it felt strange. "Yes, that's it, thank you."

Outside the deli, there was a young man, looked like a senior in high school, pacing up and down in front of the door. He did look a bit like pictures and footage she'd seen of Helios, accounting for the half-mask he wore to conceal his younger face. Similar body type, hair, movements. They were both broad in the shoulders, though the lack of padding and armor shrunk him somewhat, giving him a leaner, more gymnastic look. Not a bad look on him, she realized. It felt more natural to him than the armor he had clearly based off of his father's.

"Hey, can I get a, one of those small almond thing...yeah, that one." Her mother would forgive her not coming home with exact change, or she would explain. As explanations went, this was more benign than the one for her weekend antics.

Rashida came out and sat down on the curb far enough from the door that customers could go in and out without obstruction. "Bought you dinner." She passed him the pastry.

He looked at it. "This isn't dinner," he said, sounding like both of their mothers, or so she assumed. Looking as though he didn't know if he wanted to eat it or not, he broke off a piece and started to nibble after a second.

"Close enough."

They sat in silence until she felt enough time had passed for him to welcome the sound of her voice. "You did good the other day."

He grunted and didn't respond. She generated several other conversational openings, all of which she discarded as useless for the short amount of time she had. Bluntness would have to work. "I calculated the approach for maximum surprise," she explained to try and make him feel better, edging closer and lowering her voice so as not to be heard distinctly above the street noise. "They didn't expect someone of my age, with a gun, to speak to them of advantages and, um. Maneuvers. Taking you along implied that either I was not the only such person allied against them, or that I had greater resources and someone even worse behind me, after I reminded them that the leader rarely steps in first."

Hal nodded, as though he thought pretending her words made a difference would help her in some way. He brushed crumbs off his fingers, then his pants, and said nothing.

"Police intervention had already failed, indicated by the lack of subsequent investigation into several attempted murders and the lesser counts of discharge of a firearm in a residential area. Lack of a police presence suggests that they either feel intervention by law enforcement is neither possible nor effective, and thus the authorities who should be protecting the interests of the civilians in the neighborhood were derelict in their duties and it...all factors indicated a sudden shock from the outside would be the most effective remedy." She trailed off; even that explanation sounded mechanical and useless.

He nodded again and still said nothing. His hands rested in front of his knees, one wrist folded over the other.

"You shouldn't feel bad," she straightened, clutching the bag close. "I didn't do a very good job of this, either."

Now he spoke, with the hoarse and sticky sound that came from swallowing several times. She knew from experience. "You got the peace treaty. Ceasefire, whatever. You got them to stop shooting the place up, I couldn't even stop them from starting it in the first place. And you're fourteen."

She smiled. "Everyone assumed I was twelve."

He dropped his head and made a noise she guessed was a choked-back laugh. "I don't think even a super twelve-year-old could have pulled that off. *I* couldn't pull it off. And, you know, I'm..."

"An adult?" she asked, with dry awareness that even an eighteen-year-old would use that line on her. "A super?"

"*No*," he growled. "Because I'm Helios' son and I should be able to do this. I should be able to talk down two local gangs without having to follow the lead of some kid."

"That's a ridiculous idea. A fallacy. And no offense taken, by the way," she added, shaking her head irritably and dropping her voice again. "I'm Resonance's daughter, and I can't negotiate my way out of being grounded, let alone..." she was going to say, negotiate a peace treaty, but she had, hadn't she? Rashida looked down at their dinner, which was getting cold. "I have none of my mother's talents. I think I'm supposed to, but I don't."

Hal turned and looked at her, actually looked at her instead of in her direction, for the first time since she'd come out of the deli. Bits of pastry flake still clung to his mouth. "You're *Resonance*'s daughter? The one who, the same Resonance who was our representative in the Baltics for three years? Who negotiated the hostage situation in the school? You're her kid?" He yelped the last word, then looked around to see if anyone was paying attention. No one was. Hal stayed silent for a minute-and-a-half while Rashida chastised herself in every way she could for outing herself and her mother. "I didn't even know she had a kid."

"It's not common knowledge, and for good reason," she told him. "I would appreciate it if you..."

"No, yeah, I know, Dad told me the rules, don't tell anyone, don't let anyone know. Unless you absolutely have to. Sometimes not even then." He nodded. "And, I guess. Thank you for telling me?"

"You're welcome." The courtesy stood in for whatever she should be saying that she couldn't think of right now.

Social protocols had no dictates for this, though they provided her with a number of handy escapes she didn't think she should take right now. "But I'm not my mother, you know. I mean, I'm not like her. I don't do... My ability at social interaction is limited. I don't think like she does," she found herself saying. "I can think and understand things, I mean, I'm not stupid."

"I didn't say you were..."

"But I don't know how to cover the distance between social protocols and their implementation." She held her hands at a considerable gap. "I suspect there is something broken inside my neural pathways or my limbic system. I have a heightened ability to intake and process information beyond human norms, but I am incapable of..."

Hal chuckled. "Of not sounding like a robot?"

It took her a second to place her response as irritated. "I wasn't going to put it like that, but. Yes. I'm not my mother. Sometimes I wonder if she..." The bag crunched under her hands. "If she wishes I were more like her, easier to understand."

"I know how that feels," Hal muttered. She believed it more than she would have thirty minutes ago.

It had been thirty minutes, hadn't it? She was going to be in more trouble if she didn't get home with dinner. "I have to go," she told Hal. "I expect I'll see you online. It was good to meet you," she added, realizing that not only was that one of the expected and approved-of social interjections, but that it was also true. "Maybe we can arrange to see each other again?"

"I think I'd like that," he nodded, though clearly he wasn't sure of what he was saying. She could either convince him that she was in earnest, or she could let it pass without comment and wait for a signal from him that her contact was welcome outside of the Internet. For that matter, now that she'd offered the invitation, she wasn't sure, herself, whether or not she wanted to make contact. Social interaction with someone who wasn't accustomed to her differences. It was a daunting prospect. "Are *you* sure about that?"

Social interaction had to start somewhere. She was Resonance's daughter, even if she had very little of her mother's abilities. Maybe he could relate to that.

Rashida lifted her chin and nodded. "I'm sure."

Spring Memories

by C. Gayle Seaman

Pink snow swirls around me
As the late spring breeze off the lake
Dances among the cherry blossoms,
Sending petals floating to the ground,
Like confetti after a parade.
Spring in New Caliburn
Is my favorite time of year.
It's not just that everything is fresh and new
Before the hot, humid summer descends on us,
Or that my daughter was born in the spring.

Spring is when my childhood dream came true
And my life changed forever.

Growing up in New Caliburn
Meant being surrounded by superheroes –
And villains.
Some kids would pretend to be Helios
Or MeltMan or The Contractor.
One of my friends even wanted to be Nekomata
With the head of a tiger.

Me, I didn't want to be a superhero –
I wanted to be a sidekick.
Not just any sidekick, of course,
But a sidekick to my favorite superhero –
Piecemaker.

And the spring I was twelve
My dream came true.

Twenty years later,
Every detail is still etched on my mind.
The air was sweet
With the subtle scent of camellias
As I walked down the Row that windy, sunny day.
I hadn't a care in the world,
And was daydreaming of adventures with Piecemaker,
When I heard a loud bang.
As I ran towards the sound,
I caught a glimpse of yellow and black
That had me stopping in my tracks.
Turning my head to the side street,
I forgot everything else.
I stared at my hero
Striding quickly down the street past me.
Running to catch up,
I arrived at the car accident just behind him.

The woman in the driver's seat was dazed
And the baby in the back was wailing.
The cause of the accident was clear.
Standing in the middle of the street
Was The Contractor,
One of Piecemaker's most determined opponents,
Looking large and intimidating
In his black armor.

The driver had obviously swerved to avoid hitting him
And run into a tree instead.
It was probably just as well
As she may have done more damage to her car
Had she hit the armored villain.
He must have been lying – or rather standing –
In wait for Piecemaker.

After a quick look at the car and me,
Piecemaker faced his enemy calmly.
I was mesmerized until I heard my hero's voice for the
first time.
"Hey, kid," he called," I need your help."
They were words I had been waiting to hear
All my life.

"Anything," I replied,
Hero worship in my eyes.

"Can you get those people and yourself to safety
While I deal with The Contractor?"
Of course I could –
I would do anything for my hero.

"Yes!" I shouted and ran to the car.
The woman was already struggling
With her seatbelt,
But she was obviously in shock
And worried about her baby.

Secure in my belief of Piecemaker's ability to win
any battle,
I helped the driver out of the car
And propped her against the trunk
While I crawled in the back
To unfasten the baby from her car seat.

Once I had the baby out of the car,
I steered the mother to sit on a curb
At a safe distance
And stood back to watch
My hero in action,
Still cradling the baby.

Pieces of metal from The Contractor's armor
Were flying around him

As Piecemaker used his talent
To take it apart.
Almost as quickly,
The Contractor reassembled them.

For a few minutes
They seemed to be evenly matched
But gradually I could see pieces of metal
Spinning around The Contractor
That he was not fast enough to incorporate
Back into his armor.
Piecemaker's speed and experience were winning out.
I could see the strain
On The Contractor's face
As he tried to keep up.

Suddenly it became too much for him
And as pieces of his armor exploded
Around him,
He turned and ran down the street
In just his underwear,
Followed by small pieces of his armor
Flying after him,
Biting into his head and back,
Like dozens of angry bees,
Until he was out of Piecemaker's range.

My hero watched till he was out of sight
Then turned to survey the accident.

Sirens heralded the arrival
Of emergency vehicles
And soon people were swarming about,
Attending to the driver.
As they put her on a gurney,
Piecemaker walked towards me.
With a "Thanks, kid"
And a clap on my shoulder,
He strode off.

I wanted to run after him,
But I was still holding the baby.

For the next six years,
I looked for him everywhere I went,
Longing to help him out again,
But it was not to be.
The year I turned eighteen,
Piecemaker got a real sidekick –
Crashtest – who had superpowers of his own.

Me, I left New Caliburn for med school,
Married my childhood sweetheart
And had a daughter.

I returned to the city to practice medicine.
I may not have superpowers
But I can still help people like Piecemaker does.

Did, I guess I should say.
Apparently he retired,
Although Crashtest is still around.

My wife and I bought a place on the Row.
And when I have a day off, like today,
I take my daughter to Cook's Deli for lunch,
Where we work our way through the expansive menu
And the big guy behind the counter
Gives us a friendly wave,
Always pleased to see us.

Innovation

by Arlo J. Wiley

After all these years, he still felt it. He still felt the same pull he'd felt as a boy, the tips of his fingers practically humming with excitement. When his dad had passed out for the evening, bottle in hand, his mom sitting at the back door, staring, waiting for something — for what, he never knew — he would climb out his window and run the block-and-a-half to Dad's shop. Frank, the mechanic who on occasion drove Dad home, would always leave the side door unlocked. What he liked best about Frank was that Frank never asked any questions.

Walking into the shop was like crossing a magic threshold. All those gleaming automobiles, those beautiful machines. He would take cautious steps toward the first car, lifting the hood as gingerly as he could. He would place his hands on the engine, his whole insides shaking, vibrating with energy. He made the engine roar to life. He didn't even need a key. He had no idea how he was able to do what he did, where this...gift, he guessed it was, had come from. But he knew how it made him feel: strong, powerful. Special. Like flipping a switch, he would shut the engine down, close the hood, and move on to the next car.

It wasn't just the cars. Sometimes he would experiment with the lights and the generator, testing his boundaries, seeing just how far he could go, playing with motors and fuse boxes until it was light out and he remembered he had school. He'd run back home, catch the bus, and sleep through every class. Those were the days Charles Strewski remembered most fondly.

It wasn't long before he moved on to something even more exciting, with a higher chance of risk; namely, grand theft auto. All he had to do was press his hand to the wheel, feel that wonderful little buzz, and the car was his. He sold the cars to the chop shop on 42nd, which was a decent living until he made the mistake of stealing from his dad's shop. He went to jail and never spoke to the old man again. Those were the days Charles wished he couldn't remember.

Growing up, Charles never gave much thought to heroes. The only time he'd ever see one was when his grandfather took him into the city for a Merlins game. One of them would fly overhead, smiling and waving as the audience cheered. Charles would clap along with everyone else, but soon he stopped to think: why didn't they ever show up in his neighborhood?

Behind bars, his interest grew. It wasn't just the number of petty thieves and pickpockets he encountered who had been put away by tights — as the old man would have called them — though that was astounding. There was another inmate, a young man whose record read Tyrell

Woods but who preferred to go by the name Professor Innovation. He was doing time for stealing scrap metal from several area businesses, but his ambitions were much grander. It turned out Tyrell was something of a wunderkind, capable of building complex machines a car thief like Charles couldn't even comprehend. The only problem, and it was a considerable one, was that he couldn't quite get them to work.

When Charles heard this, he smiled. "I can help you with that."

That was the first time Charles had told anyone about his gift. Tyrell was ecstatic. One day out in the yard, Tyrell told him he was a superhero. Charles had taken a long drag on his cigarette, thinking about the phonies he'd seen soaring high above the football field. "No," he said. "I don't think so."

Tyrell would spend hours showing Charles the designs in his sketchbook, one wild contraption after another. They looked like the work of a madman. This one would crack all the safes on Main Street at the same time; that one could commandeer every car in a 25-mile radius. Charles couldn't believe *this* was the guy he'd shared his secret with.

"You can't get any of these to work?"

"Some of them, for a little while."

"How long's a little while?"

"Five minutes."

"Five minutes?"

"Tops."

"And then what?"

"Then they sort of just sputter out," Tyrell laughed.

So there they were, two young men who had made great promises to one another: Charles that he could bring Tyrell's machines to life; Tyrell that his machines were even capable of life. Through some kind of cosmic miracle neither man had ever witnessed, it worked. Tyrell would build the craziest thing you could think of, like a robotic spider that could drill through walls and shoot steel nets like webs. And with one touch, electricity coursing through his fingertips, Charles would turn them into real, functioning machines.

They lasted a hell of a lot longer than five minutes, too. In fact, they lasted as long as he wanted them to. One more touch and they'd go clanking back to the floor. Charles never much cared for the preachers his mother had dragged him to every Sunday — fat and loud, all of them — but a phrase came back to him: "The Lord giveth and the Lord taketh away." Had a nice ring to it.

When they got out of the joint, they found there was no reason to start off small, not with such ambition and God-given talent. Why waste their time on gas stations and liquor stores when Tyrell could drill right into a bank vault and Charles could cut the alarm before it went off? They even stole spandex from a nearby factory, running it through Tyrell's sewing machine so they could have proper costumes.

Tyrell was, of course, Professor Innovation. He had the initials "PI" emblazoned across the chest of his outfit. "It's cool because it's like the number!" Charles had no idea what Tyrell meant, but he laughed anyway.

Charles found the naming process a little trickier. He went through dozens of potential alter egos. Electron. Zapper. Lightbulb. Light*switch*. The Human Battery. Battery Ram. When Tyrell suggested that Professor Innovation could use a colleague with similar academic inclinations, it suddenly came to him: Doctor Battery. He even swiped a big prop battery from some supermarket display; Tyrell reinforced it and turned it into a backpack. With the battery slung over his shoulder and bright yellow goggles strapped on over his bright blue mask, Charles Strewski felt like somebody for the first time.

Those were the best days of his life.

ᚯᚯ

$374.62.

Charles took a quick glance at the fistful of cash before stuffing it in his pocket. It represented the end of an era. Not the Doctor-Battery-and-Professor-Innovation era; that had ended long before. No, these were the last few hundred dollars he'd earned during a brief stint with a second-rate inventor named Toolbox. He had deposited his share in banks all across New Caliburn under various aliases. Tyrell would have been impressed with how he'd pulled it off, had the two of them still been on speaking terms.

He gave the teller a curt nod and made his way out of the bank, head down in case anyone noticed him. It had been years since he'd put on the costume, but he had knocked over, or tried to knock over, just about every banking establishment in the tri-county area. The thought that anyone would be able to recognize him even without the spandex made him jittery.

As he stepped out into the city's frenzied hustle and bustle, worse now that the first snow had fallen, he was reminded of something else that gave him the jitters: the cold. He'd have to buy a coat with this money, as much as he didn't want to part with any of it.

It had been years since Charles had been in this part of New Caliburn, but he remembered his way around well enough to find the secondhand clothing store. As he paid for the coat, the face of the girl behind the counter registered a look of pity at the whiff of near-homelessness he gave off. It lasted only a moment. Charles left before he could do something he'd regret.

The cold was slightly more bearable, but it still bit right into him. He'd have to find a place to stay, and soon. He'd confronted his (former) landlord that morning about the prostitute who lived next door — he *knew* what the stream of men going into and out of her door meant, he could hear *exactly* what it meant through the wall — and after a few choice words, all involved decided it would be best if he got the hell out of there.

When he looked up, Charles found he had wandered into the Row. A certain animosity left over from childhood stirred in him; if he walked another few miles, he'd find himself in front of the house he grew up in. There was a wide gulf between that neighborhood and this one. The people who dined at the restaurants or shopped at the frilly boutiques which made the Row "the Row" probably never even thought about those floating above the poverty line mere minutes away.

His stomach, on the other hand, felt no such animosity. A sandwich was a sandwich. After a quick inspection of the available options to determine which might be cheapest — the burger joint seemed a little too proud of its organic potatoes, the bistro called itself a bistro — he settled on the deli at the corner. It hadn't been there the last time Charles had visited the Row. The simple name, Cook's Deli, underscored the functionality of the place. It didn't look out of place next to all the other shops and eateries, but everything in it seemed to have a purpose. There was nothing ostentatious about it.

Charles walked in to a modest crowd, the lunchtime dregs. He ordered a ham-and-turkey sandwich on rye from the man behind the counter — who was affable and large, inasmuch as Charles paid attention to those things — and found a remote table in the corner where he could sit and think.

Think about what? He knew what he needed to think about: where he was going to stay, what he was going to do for money, what his next move was. Should he leave New Caliburn? Could he? If he couldn't find work, would he have to steal again? Even if he could leave, where would he go? Once he got wherever he was going, then what?

He was an adult, he knew right from wrong. He knew he'd made some bad decisions. When he'd stolen his first car, he knew that was wrong. When he'd put on the costume to become Doctor Battery, he knew that was even worse. What choice did he have, though? He'd been chased into a corner, trapped, nowhere to run. His dad was the one who'd started it, the drunken fool, always three sheets to the wind when his boy needed him. Then there was his mother, who sat there and let it happen, she always let *everything* happen right under her nose. He shook away those thoughts. He'd made a kind of peace with them after his second jail stint. Nothing his folks could do now; six feet under, both of them.

Then there was Tyrell. They were supposed to be partners. "Doctor Battery and Professor Innovation," that's how they were always billed. Never one without the other. On the one occasion they'd had to sign a ransom note, that's how they'd signed it. Charles assumed this meant they were in it for the long haul, to the bitter end, or at least until they both wound up in White Oak. It turned out his assumption had been wrong. Oh, they'd had a good run; ten years, a handful of successes, what felt like a hundred plans foiled.

It was incredible they'd never been caught. The masks would leave them scurrying back to their "lair," which was really just a basement with a couch, but they were never busted. A few times, they'd made it all the way to the paddy wagon, but Tyrell had planned for that eventuality.

(Charles hadn't been as lucky with Toolbox, who had a penchant for making deals with the mob behind his back.)

Eventually, Tyrell grew tired of their best-laid plans being undone by idiots who could punch better than they could think. He was convinced he could go legitimate, get into a good school, become an engineer, anything other than what they'd been doing for the last decade. Charles didn't hesitate to remind him that Professor Innovation was nothing without Doctor Battery, that nothing he created could work without Charles' touch. Tyrell didn't respond to that kindly. It escalated from there. Things were said which couldn't be unsaid.

One day, Charles went to the lair only to find a note which read, "There are better things out there. For both of us."

There are better things out there. For both of us.

Charles had sped over to Tyrell's house. He was gone. Packed up, moved out. Charles broke in and started an electrical fire just in case Tyrell had any second thoughts. The ground was scorched.

He balled up the sandwich wrapper, threw it in the trash, and left.

ᴥᴥ

"No, no, man, I'm tellin' you, these freaks, with them it's like a—"

"A what? A conspiracy?"

"No, man—"

"What you're saying, it's a conspiracy. That's what it's called."

"C'mon, don't write me off as some right-wing nutjob, man. One of 'em's even in the White House!"

"You have got some serious problems."

These two had been going at it for at least 20 minutes. Probably longer; they were already in the thick of it by the time Charles walked up to the door of the tenement house. He knew they didn't call them tenement houses anymore, but he couldn't help it. That's what it looked like: intimidatingly tall, made of crumbling brick, so old and decrepit he was sure it must be condemned.

As he waited for the superintendent to meet him, Charles leaned against the railing and watched the two men entrench themselves deeper and deeper in their argument. The pale, blotchy one, the one with stringy hair who clearly hadn't gotten his fix in days, was passionately against superhumans in general. So passionate, in fact, that his eyes bugged out each time he made what he must have considered a salient point. The other one, who looked like he could knock Stringy over with one touch, showed remarkable restraint in not doing so.

"You've bought into it just as much as everyone else. It's all staged, man."

"What's staged?"

"All of it. The quote-unquote 'good guys,' the quote-unquote 'bad guys,' none of it's real. It's an illusion, a…a bedtime story for the people of America."

"Really. And what would be the point of that?"

"To distract us from what's really going on!"

"Like what? What is really going on?"

Stringy cackled. "Nobody knows, man! We're all too distracted!"

"You're telling me the Lake Superior attack was staged?"

"That is a *classic* example! All those tights coming together to fight a common enemy for the first time? Classic superhuman propaganda."

"Yo, my grandfather served in the Lake Superior attack. National Guard. Boots on the ground. He was there."

"See, man, they got everybody duped. Mass brainwashing."

Considering his gifts, Charles had his own thoughts on the matter. He knew all too well how real the "good guy/ bad guy" dichotomy was, he just happened to disagree with the labels. Whenever some world-ending space god happened to descend from the heavens with the intention of setting mankind ablaze, sure, that was a villain. And the cape who soared across space to throw him into the sun's core? He was a hero. In that instance.

What about the cape who pummeled the guy who was just trying to get by? Not everyone has the privilege of gainful employment, especially with a rap sheet. At least the guy robbing a bank or stealing some valuable gem does it for a reason: to pay the rent, to take care of his family, to do the things a man is supposed to do. What excuse did the "hero" have to trounce him over and over again for years just for doing what it took to survive? What great evil was *he* stopping?

There was one hero in particular who had been determined to hunt Charles down at every turn. His arch-nemesis, Piecemaker—

"You the one lookin' to rent?"

Charles turned around to see a man who could not have been more different than the building he managed: short and round, with a bespectacled baby face that didn't quite convey the meanness he hoped. "Yes, I am."

"We've got a few spaces open. You do stairs?" He did. "You can do a hundred bucks a week?" He could (at least for now, though he kept that to himself). "Lemme go get the key, I'll be right back."

"Do you need I.D., or...?" Charles had a wallet of fakes prepared.

"Long as I get a hundred bucks a week, I don't care who it's from or how you got it. You don't ask me no questions, I won't ask you none."

It was an arrangement Charles could respect.

As the superintendent toddled inside to retrieve the key, Charles' attention turned back to Stringy and Muscles. Stringy's head was about to explode.

"It's like, it's like...it's like you're a child! You understand what's goin' on, you know what's up, you just wanna pretend you don't so you don't have to face facts, man! Just because you don't want it to be true don't mean it ain't!" Stringy was raving at this point, his eyes damn near rolling out of his head.

"It's cool, man," Muscles said, trying to talk him down. "It's cool. Chill. Just a difference of opinion, that's all."

"It ain't no difference of opinion when I know the truth and you don't! You're blind, man, and the worst part is, you wanna be blind! There's nothin' else I can say to somebody like that, man!"

Stringy threw his hands up in disgust and walked away. He didn't get far; he made it to the street corner before he stopped, as if something clicked in his brain. He stared at the ground and started pacing back and forth, lost in thought or something like it. After a few moments, Muscles shook his head and walked up the steps. As he passed, he slapped Charles on the shoulder.

"Don't worry about him." Muscles shook his thumb at Stringy, still pacing. "He gets that way sometimes. Lord knows I shouldn't egg him on like that. It's sad. You know how they get."

Charles nodded.

"Anyway, welcome to the building."

⚖

The space he was paying $100 a week for wasn't even as big as the room he'd had as a boy. Still, it was something. He didn't have many personal affects; he picked up some old clothes from a storage locker and folded them in a pile, neat as he could. He put the pile on the floor and laid his "new" coat on top. The bed that came with the place was stiff as a board, no sheets. He sat on it with a worrisome creak and surveyed his 150-square-foot kingdom.

The one thing he could give the place was that none of the other tenants gave him any trouble. It was clear that none of them wanted to be there; when he passed someone in the hall, their shoulders were often hunched together, eyes on the ground. Charles wondered if there was anyone there who *wasn't* a criminal.

Sometimes at night, he would see Stringy sitting on the

doorstep, strung-out or shaking depending on how well the day had gone. He would occasionally stare at Charles, wide-eyed, but Charles doubted he was seeing him.

During the day, Charles walked the snow-covered streets looking for employment. His résumé hadn't been updated in a good 15 years, and even then, he'd only held a few brief jobs. His dad's shop when he was a kid, a restaurant on the Row where he'd bused tables in high school, a dive bar out in Ashwick. His record didn't exactly help. He often made his way back to Cook's Deli, served either by the big, friendly man or a young girl who bore such a striking resemblance to him she must have been his daughter.

When he was too cold and exhausted to continue, Charles would come home — he guessed that's what he was supposed to call it — and lie in bed, staring at the ceiling, thinking. His thoughts were always the same: his mother, his father, Tyrell, and on occasion (when he felt like reminding himself just how low he could sink), Toolbox.

And Piecemaker.

There were others who had given Charles and Tyrell grief, like Captain Action or Monsieur Monocle, two-bit masks no one except for the most ardent of hero worshipers would recall. If you asked any kid who their favorite superhero was, they would probably say Helios or The Actioneer, never Piecemaker. Still, Piecemaker was a real superhero, complete with annoying sidekick and roster of do-gooder buddies he could call on in a pinch.

It had started routinely enough. Charles and Tyrell were in the middle of making off with a priceless diamond recently acquired by the Caliburn Historical Museum. The fools on the city board had somehow deemed it wise to make the diamond the centerpiece of one of their Fourth of July floats. Doctor Battery and Professor Innovation were determined to show them just how foolish they'd been.

After weeks of planning and construction, Tyrell built a small two-person vehicle fit for subterranean travel and equipped with a drill so they could make their way to the surface. The plan? They'd follow the parade's path through the sewers, then drill their way up through the street, directly in front of the float, before snatching the diamond and making a speedy getaway. Which is exactly what they did.

As parade-goers fled in terror and the mayor scrambled to contact the Heralds, Charles and Tyrell were sure they'd gotten away with it. This was their biggest heist yet, their first major success. They'd caught the city unawares during one of its most public celebrations. This was a message to any and all citizens of New Caliburn: *Doctor Battery and Professor Innovation are out there, and you never know when they'll strike next.* Then the vehicle fell apart.

Piece by piece, nuts, bolts, and metal fell around them in a series of deafening clangs. Soon enough, they themselves fell to the ground. (It took weeks for those scrapes to heal.) Charles looked up to see what the hell was going on; a gloved fist made contact with his face, knocking him sideways. Standing before them was Piecemaker, hands on his hips, striking the boring old triumphant hero pose. His costume was checkered in yellow and black, which after several years Charles figured out was supposed to represent a construction sign. Because he could deconstruct things. Or something. What it made him look like was a big bee.

Tyrell turned to confront Piecemaker, but he too was swiftly knocked on his ass. As Piecemaker gave Tyrell a punch in the gut, Charles leapt at him, only to be thrown to the ground again. This went on for several minutes before Tyrell grabbed the diamond, throwing it as far as he could. Piecemaker raised his fist, ready to pummel Tyrell further into submission, when he saw a crowd rushing toward the diamond. With a heavy sigh, Piecemaker ran after the gem.

Seizing this window of opportunity, Charles and Tyrell hurried off, jumping down the nearest manhole and trekking back to their lair, this time on foot. None of the other masks they'd encountered had this kind of power; for all they knew, the others had just been disgruntled beat cops in spandex. Piecemaker was different. For the rest of their careers, Piecemaker haunted them, often showing up out of nowhere to dismantle their plans with maddening casualness. By the time Charles teamed up with Toolbox, Piecemaker had gained the kid sidekick. Also, he could suddenly fly somehow. It made him even more annoying.

Each time Charles had almost been caught, it was Piecemaker who had been responsible.

Charles and Tyrell were helpless to plan against Piecemaker's interference. They asked around some of the underground villain clubs about any weaknesses he might have, and the only thing they came up with was that he couldn't break apart simple one-piece objects. Simple one-piece objects were not Tyrell's area of expertise. At every turn, they watched Piecemaker shatter their dreams. In his heart of hearts, Charles knew that if Piecemaker hadn't dogged them so tirelessly, Tyrell would have stayed.

He knew that.

When Charles emerged from his second stretch in jail, Piecemaker was nowhere to be found. The word was that he'd retired, as if he was just allowed to give up and go back to hiding in the shadows. If Charles ever found him, he'd kill him. He knew that too.

⚖

Babyface, as Charles had taken to thinking of his new landlord, took the stack of twenty-dollar bills and hid it away in a desk drawer.

"Pleasure doin' business with ya," Babyface said in a tone of voice which in no way indicated pleasure. He'd rattled off the same cliché last week. Charles wondered if he even realized he was saying it.

Charles nodded and smiled. "I'll see you next week."

The words came out with a measure of confidence Charles didn't feel. Two weeks' worth of rent? $200. Lunches at the deli, dinner where he could find it? If not $100, close to it. Unless something changed, he was going to be sitting in an alley, jingling a cup, this time next week.

As he walked down the hall to his apartment, he heard footsteps behind him. Frantic, bumbling footsteps. Without even turning around, he knew who it was. He turned around anyway.

Stringy was twitching, scratching. It had been a bad day.

"Hey, man," Stringy said, voice shaking nearly as badly as he was. "Hey."

"Hello."

"Hey, man, you, uh, hey, can you help me out?"

"What do you need?" Charles knew where this was going.

"You got any, uh, any money I can borrow, man? I promise, I…I promise I'm good for it, I swear, right hand to God. Not much, even, just like, I don't know, you got a twenty?"

"I'm sorry, I can't spare anything right now," Charles said. He turned to the door, hoping Stringy would get the message and scamper off.

"Hey, man, I know things are tight, so, so, like, just… just ten, how about ten, can you spot me ten?"

"No, I'm sorry."

"C'mon, man, please, help me, I need your help." Stringy was in Charles' face, those wild bug eyes darting in every direction.

"I told you. I can't."

Stringy's demeanor changed. Gone was the pleading; in its place, righteous indignation. "Hey, man, what the hell is wrong with you? You're gonna look me in the face, somebody who needs help, you're gonna look somebody like that in the face, man, and tell 'em they ain't worth your help? They don't fuckin' deserve it?"

Charles felt a rage bubbling up the likes of which he hadn't encountered in years. As calmly as he could: "If you don't move, now, you'll wish you had."

Stringy's nose pressed against his.

"What was that, man? Huh? You go around threatenin' folks who need your help?"

"I told you."

Charles placed his hand on Stringy's neck. For the first time since they'd been talking, Stringy stopped shaking. "The fuck are you doin', man? Get your hands off me!"

It was true that Charles couldn't shoot bolts of electricity from his hands, nothing fancy like that. His gifts were really only of use when it came to turning things on and turning them off. However, there was one other thing he could do.

Stringy shouted in pain and stumbled sideways.

"What...what was that?"

Severe static shock, that's what. Stringy's eyes were wider than Charles had ever seen them. It was almost comical; he had to suppress a laugh.

"You...you're—"

"Don't bother me again."

Stringy stared at him for another wordless moment, then ran as fast as he could in the other direction. Charles found it hard not to smile as he unlocked his door.

⚖

Another day, another string of rejections. No one wanted to hire a thief, much less a thief with limited job experience. He tried restaurants, he tried fast food joints, he tried gas stations. Nothing.

So Charles again found himself, defeated, at the corner table of Cook's Deli. He had become a post-lunchtime figure. The big guy behind the counter smiled and said, "Let me guess: turkey-and-ham on rye, plain?" He even threw in a complementary bowl of soup.

Charles would have refused such an offer of charity, but he didn't think the man did it out of pity. When he said he wanted to thank him for being a loyal customer, Charles believed him. There was something genuine about him.

He ate his sandwich and soup — potato cheddar, better than anything he'd had in a good long while — and looked out the window as dozens or hundreds of shoppers hurried up and down the Row. All rushing to find that perfect gift, the perfect shiny bauble for acquaintances they saw once or twice a year. The meaninglessness of this ritual had always bothered Charles. It seemed obscene, almost.

When he'd had enough, he turned his attention to the guy behind the counter. He had been talking to a younger man for some time now; whoever this young man was, it was clear they knew each other. Maybe his son? If the guy had his daughter working here, perhaps this was a family affair.

Charles had an idea.

He got up from the table and approached the counter. The guy saw him walking up and told his friend he'd meet him at his table. Then, to Charles, "How can I help you?"

"I wanted to ask—" Charles hesitated but pressed on. "Are you hiring right now?"

"Not today, but we might need some help around the holidays. Tell you what, soon as we're hiring, I'll let you know. What's your name?"

"Charles."

"Nice to meet you, Charles. My name's Carl." Carl chuckled at the rhyme, then reached over by the register for a notepad. "What's your phone number?"

"My phone…isn't working right now. But I'm sure I'll be around."

"I'll just tell you face-to-face, then. Does that work?"

"It does."

Carl broke into a large grin. "Excellent. I'll be sure to let you know, okay?"

Carl held out his hand. Charles shook it. He walked out of the deli feeling more optimistic than he had in some time, though he was keenly aware of how light his pockets were.

☌

Charles didn't want to do what he was about to do. Part of it was a wish to, as Tyrell had said that horrible day, "go legitimate," to aspire to something greater. That was certainly part of it. Most of it, though, was that he simply had no desire to go back to prison, maybe for the last time.

What choice did he have, though? That was the question he always circled back around to: *What choice do I have?* The answer was, as it usually was, that he had none. It was this or nothing, for the rest of his life nothing. The thought echoed in his mind as he pushed open the door.

It was a crummy place, even if one allowed a convenience store a certain amount of crumminess. A quarter of the overhead fluorescent lights blinked on and off, casting a surreal glow on rows of canned food. The walls looked like they'd been painted when Charles first went to jail, proudly displaying the ravages of time. It was one in the morning, before the after-hours crowd would invade its aisles, so the place was empty save for the sleepy kid behind the register.

Charles could see the security camera in the corner, above the beer cooler. No one had made an effort to conceal it. He had a decision to make: go through with this, not caring that he would be filmed, or risk waking the cashier by crossing her line of vision and tapping the camera off? It would have been so much simpler if he could have zapped it from the doorway, but his gifts had their limitations and this was one of them.

He decided to chance it. Even if the cops deigned to look at the footage, who's to say they'd be able to pick him out of all the other hooded crooks in the city? Who's to say they would care?

Charles approached the cashier, who made the smallest effort to look up from her tabloid. "Can I help you with something?"

"No."

He shot his hand out, gripping the cash register. The drawer popped open, a dollar bill fluttering to the ground. He leaned over, grabbing handfuls of cash. The cashier's delayed reaction kicked in. "What the fuck?"

Out of sheer bewilderment, she grabbed hold of his wrists and tried to pull him away. Charles gritted his teeth. "Let go, young lady."

"Fuck you!"

Charles sighed, and then the cashier was yelling out in

pain, stumbling back against the cigarette case. As Charles shoveled the last of the money into his pocket, she shouted, "I'll call the cops, asshole!"

"No. You won't." He short-circuited the phone.

"Have a nice evening," Charles nodded to her as he walked out of the store, quickly but calmly. He was surprised by how easily it all came back to him, though he supposed he shouldn't have been; like riding a bike.

The cashier, calling after him: "My brother knows the Heralds! The Actioneer's gonna kick your ass!"

She whipped out her cell phone and turned to the young girl who had emerged from behind the row of snackfood, carrying an armful of candy bars. "Did you see that shit? For real, though, my brother has got the Heralds on—" The girl ignored her, hurrying out of the store. "Hey, you have to pay for those...fuck it, whatever."

The girl ran out onto the sidewalk, watching Charles as he walked into the distance. She followed.

⚖

The bundle of cash, now smoothed out and folded, was tucked away neatly in the top corner of his otherwise empty closet. He placed the scant pile of clothes next to it in case anyone happened to take a look around.

Sleep came easier to him that night than it had in weeks, and when he woke up that morning, it was with a newfound sense of hope. He could do this after all.

Charles slipped his coat on and walked outside, down the steps to where Muscles was smoking. His and Stringy's morning routine had already reached the point where Stringy was on the street corner, pacing and staring, staring and pacing.

"Morning," Muscles said, eyes still on Stringy.

"Good morning."

"Where you off to today?"

"I'll probably just take a walk, get a sandwich."

Muscles nodded, took another drag, and turned to Charles. "Hey man, I'm sorry for the way he's been acting."

"That's okay."

"The stuff he's been saying, it's…it's unforgivable, is what it is. His mind's all confused. Probably doesn't even hear the words comin' out of his mouth."

Charles smiled, wondering if they had reached a point in their conversation where it would be acceptable for him to walk off and go about his business.

"If it's true," Muscles said, "that you really are, you know — what do they say — 'superhuman,' I want you to know that's fine by me. I know a lot of people think they bring trouble to neighborhoods like this, but that was never my train of thought."

Charles' smile faded.

"I never had a problem with supers, the ones in capes or out of 'em. They're just normal folk. Done a lot of good for this world, too. They got the bad apples, but so do we."

"Is that what he's been saying?" Charles felt that rage welling up inside of him again, at himself for showing off, at Stringy for forcing him to, if he had just—

"Look, man, you don't got to tell me. Either way, it makes no difference."

Charles turned his back to Muscles and muttered a terse thank you, walking as fast as he could, his mind running. It occurred to him that he might have to do something about Stringy, though what he didn't know. Muscles believed Stringy, though Charles doubted many others would take the word of a junkie at face value. Maybe scaring the bejesus out of the kid would do him some good, get him to shut his mouth. Then again, it was entirely possible Charles was overthinking this, maybe there wasn't reason for worry, maybe this was nothing, maybe he was just being paranoid, maybe he was still on the adrenaline high from last night.

A voice called out to him.

"Sir?"

It was a young girl's voice. Charles looked up to see he didn't recognize his surroundings; he'd been so lost in thought, he'd just kept walking, no destination in mind. A mostly empty parking lot sat on the left, a row of old industrial buildings on the right. Downtown nowhere.

"Excuse me, sir?"

He turned around. The girl, who couldn't have been

more than ten, was bundled up tight in a ratty old coat. Next to her was an older boy, a teenager, no coat. The cold didn't seem to faze him. Charles wondered if he was about to be mugged. Wouldn't that be ironic?

"Yes?"

"Sir…sir," she stammered. The boy — her brother? — leaned over and whispered something in her ear. Then, "I saw you in the store last night."

Charles froze. He waited for the girl to say something else, but it was clear they were waiting for a response. He cleared his throat. "Are you going to call the police?"

"No. No, sir. I wouldn't do that. I…we know who you are."

"Oh, you do?"

"You're—" She hesitated again, and the boy piped up: "You're Doc Battery."

Charles had never been outed before. He didn't know what he should say, if he should say anything at all. The best course of action would be to laugh these children off, make them feel like imbeciles for even suspecting that he could be anyone other than who he appeared to be. Which was…which was what, exactly? A down-on-his-luck drifter?

Charles approached them. For their part, they didn't even take a step back. He placed a firm hand on the boy's shoulder. "Did the police send you? Do you have anyone listening?"

"No."

Charles looked him right in the eye. "You know what I can do to you, boy?"

"Yes, sir. There's no cops, just us."

"It's *Doctor* Battery. I always hated when they shortened it, like I was a cartoon character." Charles let go of his shoulder, and the boy's relief was visible. "What do you want?"

"We're in a gang."

"A gang?"

"It's not like that. We don't have, like, guns or anything. We know computers. We build stuff. We've always looked up to you and your, uh, your colleague. We're the Innovation Gang."

Charles' heart stopped. He was touched, maybe more than he'd ever been. But he also knew they wanted something from him, and he wasn't in a particularly giving mood. So what he said was, "You picked the wrong name."

He turned away, but the girl stopped him. "Sir... Doctor. When I saw you in the store, I knew it was you. I had to go after you. You're our heroes. You and your friend. If you could help us, maybe teach us or something, we would—"

"We would be very grateful," the boy finished. "You don't have to take it, but here's my number."

The boy held out a torn piece of paper with a phone number carefully scrawled across it. Charles took it from him with some reluctance, then jammed it in his coat pocket.

"Good luck with your science project, kids."

⚖

Sleep wasn't very restful that night. Charles tossed and turned, waking every hour or so to wipe the sweat from his brow. When he saw it was getting light outside, he sat on the edge of his stiff, uncomfortable bed for another few hours, fading in and out.

He got dressed, hoping it was late enough in the morning for Babyface to be in his office. Charles walked down the hall and knocked; after a few moments, Babyface opened the door, straining to look up.

"How are ya," Babyface said, not a question but a statement.

Charles walked in, money in hand. "Here's the rent."

Babyface took the money, locked it away in his drawer, and took a seat. Charles waited for the "pleasure doin' business with ya," but it didn't come. Instead, there was an odd silence, as if something very important was being left unsaid. Finally, Babyface said, "I've been hearing things."

"What kinds of things?"

An unhappy smile creased Babyface's lips. "Super things."

"What do you mean?"

"You've heard what Pete's been sayin', haven't you?"

"Pete?"

"Pete, the pale kid with the hair. You know, the druggie. You ain't real good with names, are you?"

"I haven't heard anything."

"Sure." Babyface didn't believe him. "Look, like I said, the kid's a druggie. He's so hopped-up on that shit, he probably doesn't remember his name any more than you do. And as a general rule, I don't put an overabundance of faith in what comes out of a hophead's mouth. So he walks in here, ravin' that you, I don't know, 'shocked' him? I don't even know what that means. Anyway, I pat him on the back, tell him I'll take care of it, and send him on his way. That's the end of that.

"Then the cops come by. Not the regular cops. You know the ones. They're askin' if I've got a Charles... somethin'-or-other...livin' here. I tell 'em the name don't ring a bell. Then they show me a photo, it's grainy, from a security tape. If I squint my eyes, hell, it might be you. It might be lil' Sally Anne down the street, too. Then they say the clerk, she said the guy 'shocked' her, he might be dangerous, keep an eye out. I thank 'em for their vigilance or whatever the hell, they move on to the next bum."

Another heavy silence. Charles stared at Babyface, his feet propped up on his desk, hands draped over his gut. Not looking Charles in the eye.

"And?"

"*And* I feel the need to remind you of the agreement we

made the day you came here. You don't give me no trouble, I won't give you none."

"I haven't done anything." Charles could feel the tips of his fingers tingling.

"This? This qualifies to me as trouble," Babyface said. "Look, if you got powers, if you want to pretend like you're a supervillain, robbin' five-and-dimes? That's your thing. It's a free country. And I got the freedom not to be associated with that kind of trouble."

He knew the answer, but Charles asked anyway. "What are you going to do?"

"I'm gonna ask you to take your things and get the hell out of here."

"I gave you my money."

"I'll consider it a thanks for not throwin' you over to the cops." Babyface swallowed with a little more difficulty than normal.

Charles took two steps forward and placed his hands on Babyface's desk. He saw a foot twitch. Babyface was still trying to act as if he hadn't broken a sweat, as if he was still in control.

"If they told you I'm dangerous, if that's what you think, you're taking an awfully big risk, aren't you?"

"Yeah? What's that?"

Charles leaned forward, so close he could smell the awful gel Babyface kneaded into what little hair he had left. "That I won't destroy you."

They locked eyes. Babyface didn't know how limited Charles' gifts were. He could frighten him into letting him stay, but there would be no reason for Babyface not to turn around and call the police. Charles would have to leave, stuck trying to find yet another place to stay.

He removed his hands from Babyface's desk, slow enough to give the impression that he was still considering whether or not to annihilate the little man where he sat. Babyface sat glued to his seat, unable to move.

Charles slammed the door behind him, hoping Babyface had just crumbled to the floor in a sobbing heap. He entered his apartment one last time, not allowing himself a moment to look around; after all, there was nothing to see. He put on his coat, grabbed the clothes pile, and took the money.

He hurried out of the building, hoping he would see Stringy, hoping he would have someone on which to take out the anger that was making his head pound, but he didn't. He stood on Stringy's favorite street corner, wind whipping around him, and realized it wasn't just that he didn't know where else to go. He didn't know if he *wanted* an elsewhere to go.

Charles stood there for several minutes, eyes shut tight, listening to the traffic rushing past, clutching his belongings, alone in the world.

He remembered the phone number in his pocket.

⚖

After he made the call, Charles hung up the payphone, sat on the rusty bench, and waited. And waited. It was some time after four o'clock when the truck pulled up.

The boy he'd met the day before opened the passenger's side door and stepped out.

"C'mon. Get in."

This was Charles' last chance to say this was a horrible idea, that he didn't know what he was doing, that he should get as far away from these kids as possible. He didn't. Instead, he climbed inside the truck, squeezing in between the boy and the slightly older boy behind the wheel (if he was old enough to drive, it was just barely).

The boy's name was Ricky, the driver's Simon. They didn't ask why he'd had a change of heart. If they had, Charles wouldn't have told them.

Beyond a few murmured greetings, the drive to the Innovation Gang's lair was silent.

Charles thought it charming that after all these years, there were still kids going around calling their hide-outs "lairs." It was an old warehouse — which, to be honest, was what he and Tyrell had always wanted — which showed signs of heavy water damage. It was easy to see why it had fallen into disuse.

Still, the kids had made it their own. A number of card tables had been pushed together, one right next to the other, at least a dozen computers resting on them, all connected. There was a shelf stocked with computer manuals and books on coding, among other things Charles had no understanding of.

What caught Charles' eye most of all were two full-color print-outs of Doctor Battery and Professor Innovation, hung on the wall with the least water damage. He remembered one of the pictures clearly: a photo snapped during the parade heist, showing him and Tyrell at the height of their powers, parade-goers scurrying as Tyrell sat behind the wheel of the drill-car and Charles clutched the diamond. It was the one and only time they'd made the front page of the *New Caliburn Observer*. The next day, he'd felt an illicit thrill buying a copy.

The other picture he didn't recall as clearly. He could tell it was closer to the end of their partnership. They both looked exhausted, running from a newly-robbed bank to the waiting arms of some giant robot thing Tyrell had built. Piecemaker had undone that one too, no doubt. How did these kids find these? Was this what you could find on the Internet? What else was out there?

As Charles took everything in, Simon began typing away at one of the computers, so fast Charles was amazed. Ricky called, "Ed! He's here!"

There was a dull hum, and Charles turned to see a garage door rising. Behind the door was a sophisticated workstation, a long, expansive desk with at least half-a-dozen monitors attached. Surrounding it was a veritable scrapyard's worth of metal. The little girl from before came running out, a grin stretching across her face.

"Doctor!" she exclaimed, and held out a hand. "My name's Tasha."

Charles shook her hand, so fragile in his.

"It's nice to meet you again, Tasha," he said.

Behind Tasha, the man Ricky had called Ed followed. Compared to the others, Ed really *was* a man; he must have been in his early 20s. It was plain he was the leader of the group. Upon seeing Charles, he broke into a smile just like Tasha's. So *he* was her brother.

"Doctor Battery, sir," Ed said as they shook hands. "It's a pleasure to meet you. As you can see, we've looked up to you and Professor Innovation for some time."

"That's…flattering," was all Charles could think to say. "To be honest, I'm surprised anyone remembers us."

"Please." Ed sat in a folding chair behind one of the computers, motioning for Charles to do the same. Ricky and Tasha slumped against the bookshelf, Simon still typing away. "There are other supervillains. We…do you mind being called that? 'Supervillain'?"

"I prefer Charles."

"Charles. Sorry. We know there are others who are better-known, who have given rise to waves of imitators. We're not interested in that. We don't want to be a bunch of knock-offs, the five-hundredth generation copy of The

Pulverizer."

"I never liked him."

Ed laughed. "Me neither! He's so *boring*. All he does is punch things! You and Professor Innovation, though…you were different. You were clever. Professor Innovation…the things he came up with, they were incredible."

"He was a genius."

"Yes! A genius! Exactly. And you, without you, none of it would have worked. You were the *power*!"

Charles wasn't sure how to take this. Before yesterday, with the exceptions of Tyrell and Toolbox, he had never confided his identity to anyone. To suddenly be surrounded by…fans? Admirers? It was remarkably freeing. It also felt like he was about to vomit.

"Thank you," he muttered. "Like I said, this, all of this, it's flattering. What do you want from me?"

"Sir—"

"I know you want something. And that's okay. In your position, I would too. What is it? Do you want me to sign autographs? Show up at your fan club meeting?"

"This *is* the fan club meeting," Ricky said from the corner.

"This is all of you?"

"Yes," Ed replied. "This is the whole Innovation Gang, right here."

"I guess I expected…I don't know, I hear the word 'gang' and I don't think of four kids and their toys."

"We're more than just that. We want people to know who we are. We…sir, we want you to teach us."

"Tyr— Professor Innovation, he was the one who built everything. He was the genius. I was just the battery."

"You were out there for years, though. We've read, and I don't know if this is right, but…you were never caught, were you?"

"No. We never were."

"That's amazing. The fact that you were able to do that…we want to know how you accomplished that. Please, sir. Tell us what you know. We want to learn."

Charles leaned back in the folding chair. He feigned as if he was mulling it over. He'd already made his decision, it was just a matter of how long to tease it out. He felt their eyes on him, watching, waiting, filled with anticipation.

"Okay. It's a deal."

Ed clapped his hands together. He thanked Charles. Ricky, too. Tasha wanted to shake his hand again. Even Simon looked up from his computer. Charles could get used to this.

⚖

He tried not to let on how impressed he was by them. When he was their age, shit, he was still handing cars over to chop shops. He knew how to turn a computer on, he used the one in the library every now and then. That was it.

The world had changed without him noticing.

These kids, though, they were like…he didn't even know what. He wasn't sure he had a word in his vocabulary for how smart they were. They made what he and Tyrell had done look like child's play, which he supposed it was. Grown men dressed up in spandex going around with robots and flying machines and laser beams? That was childish, wasn't it?

The Innovation Gang ate it up, though. As Ed explained, "That's part of the reason we love what you guys did. Today, everything is so *serious*. It's not fun anymore. I bet you anything, I can go outside, walk around for two hours, and see at least three different superhero battles. And they're all gonna be the same: a bunch of idiots crashing through office buildings and blowing up fire hydrants or whatever. We want to make things fun again."

For a day or two, as they showed him everything they knew and everything they'd done, Charles wasn't sure what he could teach them. He was a petty thief and they were little scientists, all of them. As long as they revered him, he could get whatever he wanted from them. For now, it was a roof over his head. Later? Later would depend on what wisdom Charles could impart.

One thing became evident: the Innovation Gang didn't have a plan. They were ambitious children, coding software, designing computer viruses, building remote-controlled devices that could hack radio signals and police scanners, but that ambition lacked focus. Charles knew he wasn't a great thinker, but if these kids wanted to make a name for themselves? He could probably nudge them in the right direction.

They showed him the videos they'd watched hundreds, thousands of times. There were old news reports, grainy film footage, blurry home videos bystanders had taken with their camcorders. In each one, there were Doctor Battery and Professor Innovation, riding in on some elaborate apparatus, stealing cash or jewels or other valuables. In almost every one, they were stopped.

"You guys got beat up a lot, didn't you?" Ricky asked.

Tasha hit him. "Shut up, Ricky!"

Ed stepped in. "I'm sorry, Charles—"

"No, no," Charles said, patting Ricky on the shoulder. "You're right. It's true that Professor Innovation had a great mind. We did a lot of clever things. Our crucial flaw was that we could never get away with them."

Charles pointed to a computer monitor playing a video of one of his and Tyrell's schemes being foiled. "Pause it." Simon tapped a key, and the video stopped just as a musclebound figure descended on the duo. "Look. Do any of you know who this is?"

Tasha struggled to think of his name. "It's, it's—"

"Of course. It's Piecemaker. Your guys' arch-enemy," Ed finished for her.

"That's right," Charles said, leaning in to get a good

look at that buffoon's stupid bee costume, his sneering face. Then he stood back and looked toward the children. "Let me ask you a question. Simon, who's your favorite superhero?"

"I, uh—" Simon floundered, and Ed stepped up to apologize again: "I think Simon knows more hackers than he does masks."

"Okay." Charles turned to Ricky. "How about you?"

"I mean, it's gotta be Helios, right? He's the best one."

"And you, Tasha?"

"The Actioneer! I played all his games."

"Something you have to understand is that what you're doing might put you in direct conflict with one of your heroes."

"I mean," Ricky sulked, "I didn't say he was *my* hero. Just of all the heroes, he's the best one."

"More than likely, though, the heavy-hitters, the tights in the front ranks of the Heralds, they're not going to pay any attention to you. The Innovation Gang? Unless you shoot a rocket at the moon, they're never even going to learn your name. The ones you have to worry about are the second-string capes. Simon, back the video up."

Charles watched as the video rewound, as Piecemaker flew back up into the sky and he and Tyrell ran backwards into the museum. "Okay, right there. We've just stolen... well, I don't remember what, but we've just stolen something. Play the video, Simon. Look at us. We're totally vulnerable. Tyrell could build things, I could turn them on. That's all. Right there. Piecemaker falls right on us. There's nothing we can do to stop him. Look — oh, it still hurts watching it — with one swipe of his hand, that machine Tyrell spent weeks on is just a bunch of scrap. My powers can't take on Piecemaker, and we're not fighters. We're plenty good at running, though, and that's why he never caught us."

They watched more videos of Piecemaker reducing Charles and Tyrell's plans to nothing. A favorite refrain of Piecemaker's, as he kicked their asses, was, "Not today!" And the thing with his hands on his hips, Charles had almost forgotten how irritating that was. Piecemaker did that in damn near every frame where he wasn't slapping them around.

"I don't want to dampen your enthusiasm. I want you to succeed where we failed. None of you have powers, do you? I didn't think so. You're going to have to be very careful. Think of what you can do to evade the heroes. Plan ahead. We were young and stupid. You're young, but you don't have to be stupid."

Charles drilled them on what they would do if they got into a tussle with a mask, where they would run, if they could think of any of the hero's weaknesses. He tried to branch out and use members of the Heralds, as well as B-list masks he remembered from his time in costume, but more often than not, he came back to Piecemaker.

Watching those videos had rekindled his hatred of the man, and he couldn't resist the temptation to run through fantasy scenarios with the children where they escaped his grasp or even won against him in battle.

He slept in the warehouse, as did the kids. Tasha, sometimes accompanied by Ricky, would go out to forage for food and candy. Charles felt a momentary pang of worry about two children running around lifting food, but they were tough. They hadn't chosen this life, but they were going to survive it. Charles would make sure of that.

Once they had obsessively gone over every video they could find and run through every scenario Charles could think of, he determined they were ready to get their toes wet.

"Another mistake Tyrell and I made was not starting small. We started hitting banks as soon as we'd made our costumes. We probably lost something by swinging for the fences right out of the gate. What do you think would be a good starting point?"

He was surprised that Simon was the one who spoke up. "You know, I've actually been working on some code. It would be for drones, you know, like…"

"I know what a drone is."

"Right, right, yeah. It's a targeting system for small drones that would let them see where people's wallets are, in their pockets or their purses or whatever. Then that drone would release two even smaller drones that would go in and extract the wallet and bring it back. We wouldn't even have to have the drone fly back here, it could just go to some drop point we set up or something."

Charles had to smile. Never in a million years would that idea have occurred to him. It was clever. More importantly, it wasn't the kind of thing masks concerned themselves with.

He turned to the others. "What do you all think? Does anyone have a better idea?" No one did. "Is this what you want to do?" They nodded. Charles could tell Ed was trying to contain his delight. "All right, then. Let's get to work."

⚖

The work came slowly, but that was good. Slow work was careful work. Simon wrote various programs, if that's what they were called, fingers sweeping across his keyboard. Ed drew up plans for the drones while Ricky gathered scrap. Tasha made sure they had food. Charles offered to go with her once and almost did, but Ed decided against it. If anyone was looking for Charles — and he hadn't given them any reason to think beyond *if* — it was best the Innovation Gang keep a low profile.

He marveled at how well they worked together. Ed teased Tasha the way older brothers did, and their dynamic seemed to affect the whole group. They were a family.

Charles would have felt like an outsider, but Ed had been so welcoming, and the others followed suit. He was one of their idols. He didn't know how to respond.

One night, as the others slept, Charles helped Ed with his blueprints in the garage. He didn't know much about this sort of thing, but he followed Ed's lead the best he could. When there was work to be done, Ed had a focus that was almost scary; nothing could disturb him. When Ed took a moment to catch his breath, Charles asked something he'd been wanting to since the first day.

"Have you ever tried to reach Professor Innovation?"

Ed ran his hand through his hair. "Professor Innovation? No. We only found you by accident, remember."

"I haven't seen him in…I don't know how long. It's been years. We didn't exactly part on good terms."

"No?"

"We wanted different things, that's all. It happens."

"I wondered. But I didn't want to ask you anything before. Didn't want to be pushy."

"No, no. I don't want you to worry about that. It's… hard for me to say this, but…I appreciate this. All of it. I never expected anyone to know who I was."

At this, Ed smiled. For a moment, at least, he was speechless. Then he said, "You know, if you have any information, we might be able to find Professor Innovation."

"His name is Tyrell. Tyrell Woods."

"I'll talk to Simon, see what he can find. Let's get back to these plans."

Ed turned away, but Charles touched his arm.

"Thank you."

Ed smiled again, and they resumed work.

⚖

Charles wasn't sure how long it had been since they'd had food that didn't come from a can or out of a wrapper, so he thought he'd take Tasha and Ricky to lunch. Ed was tough to persuade, but he was in serious focus mode; Charles told him it was the least he could do, and Ed relented. The three of them piled into Simon's truck — the boy had given a half-hearted nod when Charles asked if he could borrow it, not looking away from the monitor — and Charles drove them down to the Row.

"Have you been through here before?" Charles asked.

"Oh, yeah," Ricky replied.

Of course they had. If you were looking to steal food, clothes, anything, the Row was the place to go.

Charles found parking nearby, and the three of them walked to Cook's Deli. Charles ordered three of his usual, and they took his favorite seat in the corner. On the way to the table, they passed the big guy (*Carl*, that was his name), sitting at a table, again in conversation with his younger friend.

They ate their sandwiches quietly. The kids looked uncomfortable being out in the open.

"Do you like your food?" They nodded. Tasha said, "Thanks, Doctor," and Charles ruffled her hair — something he had never done, something he'd never wanted to do — and reminded her to call him Charles.

When his friend had left, Carl waved to Charles and walked over to their table, hands resting on his hips.

"Charles! Haven't seen you here in a while."

"Oh, I've just been busy," Charles said. "You know, with the holidays." He gestured to the kids, as if that made sense.

"Are these yours?"

"My, uh, my niece and my nephew. Say hi, kids." They both gave an unsure "hi."

"Nice to meet you," Carl said. Then, away from the kids, in a hush: "About that opening we were discussing, I'm sorry, we're already at capacity. I didn't see you, and well, we had spots needed filled."

"You know, I actually found something else."

"Good! Glad to hear that." The boom returned to Carl's voice. "Well, I'll leave you three to your lunch. Let me know if you need anything."

Charles assured him they would and Carl walked away. As he did, Charles felt a shudder of recognition. He didn't know why. He'd always thought there was something reassuring, even somewhat familiar, about Carl's kindness, but this was something different. He grew uncomfortable, and he had no idea why. Had he met Carl before?

Carl stepped behind the counter and greeted another customer. Charles watched him, studying his movements, his face, the contour of his jaw, his giant, oversized hand opening the cash register—

It snapped into place with frightening clarity.

Charles couldn't move.

He started shaking.

Tasha and Ricky stared.

How hadn't he realized it before? It was so obvious, especially after watching all those hours of video. He was angry and terrified and lightheaded, sick to his stomach. He had allowed this man to serve him food? He had asked him for a job?

"Kids, kids, we have to get out of here. Right now."

Ricky put down his sandwich. "But—"

"Right now."

The screech of metal on tile as Charles pushed his chair back was almost unbearably loud. He grabbed Tasha by the hand, yanking her from her seat. Ricky took another bite and ran after them.

"Have a nice afternoon!"

Charles couldn't say anything until they were back at the truck. The kids hadn't asked any questions, either. He stood there, leaning against the truck, in a daze, out of breath.

Tasha took his hand. "Doctor, what's wrong?"

"The…the man in the deli, the man who talked to us, he's…" Charles swallowed, hard, his throat sore. He opened his eyes. "That man is Piecemaker."

��

The door slammed against the wall. Simon shot up, tripping over his chair. Charles, still shaking, was surprised to discover that every step he took was actually connecting with the floor below. The kids followed, sheepishly.

"Ed!" Charles shouted. "Ed! I need to talk with you! Right now!"

The garage door went up, and a wary Ed emerged. "What? What is it?"

"I've found Piecemaker."

"What?"

"Piecemaker. I know where he is. I know *who* he is."

"Are you sure?"

He went over everything, commanding Simon to play the videos with Piecemaker over and over again, each time pointing out a different nuance of speech or movement.

"You're a hundred percent sure this guy is Piecemaker?"

"Absolutely."

"Then let's get the son of a bitch."

Any plans to pick pockets went right out the window. Ed and Simon began drafting new ones, and Charles made sure he was involved. He had relished his role as mentor, but this? This was *his* mission.

Ed went with Charles to the deli; as soon as he saw Carl, he knew he was Piecemaker. There was no denying it. Charles waved and smiled and shook hands and looked in Carl's eyes and thought, *I am finally going to beat you, to show you how worthless you truly are, and there's nothing you can do to stop me.*

They spent half their time at the deli, watching Carl's daily routine, scouting the place, learning what they could of the security system. The other half they spent hard at work in the lair, drawing diagrams and going over holes in their plans and talking things through again and again and again.

It was decided they'd put too much time into the drones to abandon them completely; moreover, they could be useful as a distraction. After closing, when Carl was still cleaning up and putting everything back in order, Tasha would knock on the door, yelling for help. Carl, ever the naïve do-gooder, would open the door, and in would come the drones, pilfering from his day's take. As Tasha dashed away, Carl would disassemble the drones and run after her. Tasha would lead him to an alley, where...

Where what? That was a matter of some debate. Ricky suggested they could put a live wire on the snow-covered ground and let Charles fry Piecemaker…that was quickly put to bed. (*Where were they going to get a live wire? Wouldn't that fry the rest of the gang, too?*) Ed thought maybe they could build some sort of machine to capture and imprison Piecemaker, but Charles dismissed that.

"No, no. Do you know how many times Professor Innovation and I tried something like that? We need something that's going to work."

The plan they settled on was a dangerous one, but it seemed like the only practical option. On a Sunday evening, the Row's least crowded night of the week, Tasha would lure Piecemaker into the alley, where — armed only with planks of solid wood or some other simple weapon Carl wouldn't be able to defend against — the five of them would attempt to bring him down in a brawl. Five armed assailants, one defenseless, plainclothes mask? They were willing to bet on those odds.

As Ed was putting finishing touches on the drones — there were a dozen of them, all told — he asked Charles for a favor.

"Would you bring these online for me?"

"You want me to?"

"I could do it myself, but…it wouldn't feel right. I want you to do it."

"I would be honored," Charles said, and he was.

One by one, he tapped the grey, metallic drones, watching as they blinked to life. It had been so long since he'd been a participant in the act of creation, he'd almost forgotten the accompanying rush. Almost.

"Two days, man," Ed grinned.

In two days, what Charles had been dreaming of for years would become a reality. There was just one thing that bothered him.

"Did you find anything on Tyrell?" he asked.

Ed took a moment to respond. "We did. I tried calling him, but he didn't pick up. No answer."

"You called him? You found an actual phone number?"

"We did, yeah. I would have mentioned it to you, but given your history, I thought maybe I should call first."

"Where's the number? I'll call him. Even if he doesn't answer, maybe if I left a message, he'd call back. This is so important, and I feel like if he could just be a part of it in some way—"

"Yeah, of course. I'll have Simon look it up again tomorrow, okay?"

"Sure, sure."

Sleep came easy that night.

⚖

It was the day before *the* day, the big day, the day of days. Charles' whole body was a live wire, bursting and buzzing with energy. He and the kids ran through the plan a few more times. Simon sent the drones on a test run; they worked perfectly. Everything was ready. There was only the waiting.

Charles despised the waiting.

He decided to go for a walk. He deserved a day to himself, to clear his head and reflect on what he was about to do. After tomorrow night, he wouldn't just be another nobody walking the streets of New Caliburn. This was his last opportunity to take it all in from a ground-eye view. He may as well take it.

The cold was fierce, but it didn't bother him. He couldn't even feel it. He walked past the shitty old tenement house, wondering what he'd do if he happened upon Stringy; hell, he might even thank the poor bastard. He walked through the neighborhood he grew up in, but only briefly, not wishing to invite unpleasant memories to intrude on such a pleasant day. He paid tribute to his childhood home by relieving himself on the front lawn.

After a few hours, he felt rumblings in his stomach and realized he needed food. Where else to go but his favorite lunch spot? One last sandwich for the road, as it were. Charles walked into Cook's Deli in a jovial mood.

"Carl!" he exclaimed, waving.

"How are you this afternoon, Charles?" Carl asked.

"I am — what's the word? — *splendid*. I'm splendid!"

Carl laughed. "What's the occasion?"

"Oh, I always get sentimental around this time of year."

"Got anything special planned?"

If only you knew. "Just a family get-together."

"Sounds good to me. You having—"

"My usual? Yes, I am." Carl made the ham-and-turkey on rye himself, and Charles asked, "How about you? Do you have anything special planned?"

"I'll be here. Figured we may as well stay open for Christmas, maybe give out some free meals to those who need 'em. You know, the holiday spirit and all that."

Of course you would, wouldn't you? "Of course."

"We do what we can. My daughter works here—" Charles had been right. This opened up new and exciting possibilities for what they could do after tomorrow. "—so I'm hoping she'll join me."

How obnoxiously sweet. "That's very sweet."

Carl shrugged that away — so modest — and handed Charles the sandwich. "Enjoy."

"I always do!"

He did. In fact, the only thing he regretted about this whole affair was that he wouldn't be able to enjoy any more of Carl's sandwiches. A small to price to pay.

Charles finished his sandwich, and on the way out, he made sure to wish Carl an exuberant, "Merry Christmas!" With that, he was on his way, consumed in thought. Pure, electrifying thought. He pondered what he would do after his victory, whether he would kill Carl on the spot or take him prisoner, hold him for ransom, lure his daughter into their trap, see if that snot-nosed sidekick would show up to rescue his hero.

He thought that would be best. Better to make him suffer, to let him know exactly what he had done and the price he would be paying for it. Charles was keeping this all to himself, of course; he had become something of an honorary member of the Innovation Gang, but from now on, it would be Doctor Battery and the Innovation Gang. Considering everything he'd done for them, he was sure they wouldn't mind.

These thoughts made Charles giddy. So giddy, in fact, he realized once again that he'd lost track of time and place. It was dark now. He had better get back, especially if he planned on calling Tyrell. Oh, what the hell, even if it was after midnight, he'd still call him. Charles wanted him to know what was about to happen.

When he arrived back at the lair, Charles discovered it was later than he'd thought. The only light was the soft glow of a computer screen running various lines of code. Ricky and Simon were bundled up in their sleeping bags, fast asleep. There was no sign of Ed or Tasha; Charles assumed they were holed up in the garage, hard at work on any last-minute changes.

Charles figured he would knock on the garage door, let them know that he was home, and offer his assistance if they needed it. As he approached the door, he heard muffled sobs. Tasha? As he got closer, he heard Ed speaking to her in a soft voice.

"You know why we gotta do this, right?"

"I know. But he's so nice."

Was she having second thoughts about leading Piecemaker to his doom? Charles found that somewhat charming.

"I know he's nice, sweetie," Ed said. "But you knew this was gonna happen. We gotta do this for us. Why are we here, huh? Why do we do what we do? What have we always said?"

She sniffled. "So people respect us."

"That's right. This is about respect. We take down Piecemaker, what are we gonna get?"

"Respect."

"See, you got this. We're not gonna get any respect, though, if we're sidekicks. Nobody likes sidekicks, right?"

Charles stopped.

"You know I'm right," Ed continued. "If we ride in on his coattails, it's not gonna be Ed and Tasha and Simon and Ricky anymore. We're gonna be…I don't know, Doc Battery and the Battery Kids. Do you want that?"

A pause, then: "No."

"No. I didn't think so."

Charles pressed his ear against the garage door.

"You're right, he's been nice to us. He's helped. But we gotta do this without him or nobody's gonna respect us, ever. Everything's packed and ready to go. So I need you to get some sleep, we're gonna get up and bright and early, right? Just the four of us, okay?"

"Okay," Tasha said, quiet, small.

Charles felt the electricity pulsing through his body. With a hum, the garage door opened.

There was a brief moment which seemed to last an eternity, as the garage door lifted on Tasha and Ed, frozen in horror. In that moment, Charles saw the looks on their slack-jawed faces, their frightened eyes. The old anger returned to him. It burned in him with a new purity. It was all he could feel.

Tasha and Ed stood staring at him, saying nothing.

"Well?" he spat. "*Well?*"

"Charles…Charles, listen, I don't know what you heard or what you think you heard—"

"You don't have the right to call me that!"

"Doctor—" Tasha croaked.

"*Doctor.* That's right."

Ed took a tentative step forward. "Look, uh, Doctor, look, we can talk this over."

"Talk? There's nothing to talk about. I gave you *everything*, and this is how you treat me? I taught you everything you know. I gave you Piecemaker. I gave you Tyrell's name! You—" Charles paused. "You never called him, did you?"

Ed's silence was damning.

"How long have you been lying to me?"

"I didn't call him. You're right. Hear me out, though."

"How long?"

Ed said nothing.

"Has it been this whole time?"

"This…this was a mistake. It's not personal."

"Do you even call yourselves the Innovation Gang?"

"No, we—"

"Do we even mean anything to you? This whole thing, worshiping at our feet, that…was that an act too?"

"I'm, I'm so sorry. Tasha saw you that night, and we had no idea who you were, we looked online, I remembered Professor Innovation from when I was a kid and starting out, and we figured—"

"You figured you could what? Use an old fool like me? Toss me aside?"

"We wanted to learn from you. That part was true." Silence. "I only did what I thought I had to. For my sister. For my friends."

Charles stepped toward Ed. Ed took three steps back, no idea what to do. All cleverness and ingenuity had abandoned him.

Tasha was crying, harder than before. Charles reached out toward the trembling Ed, who was probably going to join his sister in bawling any second now.

"Please, no!" Ed shouted, throwing his hands in front of his face, as if that would help.

Charles grabbed one of the drones and short-circuited

it. An arc of electricity shot from the drone in his hand to the eleven others, each one popping, smoking, going up in a hail of sparks. He wasn't sure he'd ever done anything like that before.

He turned to Ed and seethed, "Be glad this is all you're getting, boy."

Charles turned to see that Ricky and Simon were awake, sitting up, their eyes stretched wide in almost as much terror as Ed's.

"You all think you're so smart, don't you?"

He placed his hand on one of the computers, thinking of all the information they had stored in them, all the hard work that had gone into programming and coding and everything else. He fried one, then another, then another, until they were all sizzling, blackened husks.

Charles looked at the four of them, gathered together now, nothing more than scared little children. He decided to impart one last bit of wisdom.

"Let this be a lesson for you, children. Never trust anyone."

He left them then, Tasha's sobs echoing in the empty warehouse.

☪

He couldn't think straight. His mind was a jumble, a series of conflicting thoughts vying for dominance. One word blared loudest in his head, and that word was

Run.

It didn't matter where, not as long as it was out of New Caliburn. Out of the state, even, away from anywhere remotely connected to this place, away from this life. Money. He needed money. The hundred or so dollars in his pocket was good for now, would get him on the road, but it wouldn't last long. He needed money, and he knew where to get it.

The walk there was interminable; no more losing himself in thought, losing track of time. He was acutely aware of each minute that passed, of every mile he walked. With every step, he grew angrier and angrier, so angry he felt like he was about to pass out. He started seeing spots in front of his eyes. That only made him press on harder.

By the time he reached the tenement house, Charles wasn't fully in control of his own body. He felt possessed, a pawn sliding across the chessboard. That was fine. He didn't care.

He took the steps two at a time then pushed open the doors with a great heave. The noise would have been enough to wake every tenant on the floor. He made his way to Babyface's office; it was locked. No matter. He kicked it. Again, harder. Still it wouldn't give. He stepped back, charged the door, and slammed into it with his full weight. With a crack, the door swung open.

Charles went straight for Babyface's desk, but when he

tried to pull the drawer open, he found that it too was locked. He pulled again, and again. It wouldn't budge. He cursed, loudly. Babyface sprinted into the office, clinging to the robe he'd thrown on.

"What the fu—"

It took Babyface a moment to realize what was happening. He wasn't able to keep his cool this time. "Get the fuck out of here! You're not welcome here! You get the fuck out of my office!"

Babyface made the mistake of approaching Charles; Charles grabbed him by the arm and shocked him. The little man careened into the wall, falling to the floor.

"Hell'd you do to me?" he moaned.

"Where's the key?"

"Fuck you."

Charles took a step toward him, and Babyface crumbled. "Stop, stop, it's under the desk."

Of course it was. Why hadn't he looked there? Charles searched under the desk and felt the key, taped in place. He ripped it free and unlocked the drawer. He wasn't sure how much was there. A few hundred, at least. That was good enough for now. He took the cash, throwing the key at Babyface.

"Son of a bitch," Babyface muttered. "You won't—"

"I've heard that one before," Charles said.

There was an electrical outlet on the wall next to Babyface, two cords running from it. Charles crouched down next to Babyface. "I want to thank you for your assistance."

"What are you—"

Charles shushed him and took the cords in his hand. They began to smoke. Babyface was shouting something else, but Charles didn't listen. He held onto the cords until they were so hot he could feel his skin burning. He let go. They burst into flame.

Babyface was screaming, the fire spreading. He tried to regain his footing, but he was shaking too badly; he toppled over again, crawling on his hands and knees away from the flame.

Charles had been so focused on the task at hand that he was surprised to see a crowd gathered in the doorway.

Someone shouted, "There's a fire!"

"Yes," Charles laughed. "Yes, there's a fire."

The whole floor was suddenly gripped with panic. It wouldn't be long before someone called 911, and he needed to be gone when they did. Charles moved through the crowd, toward the door, when he saw a face out of the corner of his eye. A familiar face.

Charles was on Stringy so fast, the kid didn't know what happened to him. It took his wild, rolling eyes a few seconds to lock onto Charles', to realize who was pushing him up against the wall.

"Yuh…you!"

Charles wrapped his hands around Stringy's neck. A

new wave of anger washed over and through him, through every fiber of his being. He was looking right in Stringy's face, but he wasn't seeing him. He wasn't seeing anything. He could feel the electricity, clearer and more powerful than he could ever recall. He had always had that buzz, that gift, but for the first time, he felt how strong he could be if he pushed himself. His body was a lightning rod.

A voice was calling to him. Shouting for him. He couldn't tell whose it was. It was...a friendly voice, he thought. Familiar.

Tyrell?

"Let go of him, man! Let go!"

He was back in the moment, panting, gasping for air. He had to remember where he was, what he was doing, and... the voice, he realized, belonged to Muscles. Charles turned to Muscles, who was urging him to let go of Stringy, too scared to touch him. Without a second thought, Charles shot his arm out, hitting Muscles, and turned his attention back to Stringy.

Charles was startled to discover he was electrocuting him. He had never done this before, never knew he was *capable* of doing this. Stringy's tongue was lolling out of his mouth. The kid was making strange, terrible noises Charles had never heard.

He could feel it, could feel the rush. He was this close to squeezing the life right out of Stringy's body.

Charles threw Stringy to the floor with a thud. He was

twitching badly. But he was still alive.

Charles ran through the crowd, out the building, down the street, running, running, he kept running.

⚖

The car wasn't new, he didn't know the model, it had more than a hundred thousand miles on it. It didn't matter. Charles was exhausted. He couldn't walk anymore. He placed his hand on the door and the locks popped. Once he was inside, he pulled his same old trick, hand to the wheel. The engine started, and he was off.

It would be easy to keep going, not turning back, all the way out of New Caliburn. He couldn't, though. Not when what he'd been dreaming of was right there, in his grasp.

That was why Charles found himself pulling up in front of Cook's Deli. He sat for there several minutes, his breathing heavy, his pulse quick. This was it. This was it, then he was gone. He'd never set foot in New Caliburn again. He expected there to be some bittersweet feeling as he reflected on this fact but there wasn't.

He got out of the car and walked to the deli's entrance. Just for fun, he tried the door. Locked, of course. He'd come upon a lot of locks tonight. Then he began banging on the door.

"Carl! Carl!"

Charles shouted his name several times before a shadow emerged from the dimly lit kitchen. When Carl realized it was Charles banging on the door, a look of friendly confusion crossed his face. Charles savored it.

"Charles? Are you oka—"

Charles blasted the locks open. The door flew off its hinges. He stepped into the deli.

"Hello, Piecemaker," he said.

It was plain to see how stunned Piecemaker was, standing stock-still there in the middle of the deli. Charles didn't hesitate to lash out at him. Piecemaker blocked the hit and went to punch Charles in the gut; Charles jumped back, out of the way. Charles still wasn't much of a fighter, but this was an older, slower Piecemaker he was dealing with. Back in the day, Charles wouldn't have stood a chance of dodging that blow.

Still, he wasn't going to win this fight with brute strength, and he didn't have any planks of wood on hand. Charles dived behind the counter, hiding in the shadows. Piecemaker turned the lights on, but Charles reached for the wall switch and burnt them out.

Piecemaker grunted. "Charles, why don't we just sit down and talk this through? If you need help, I can help you. We're friends, aren't we?"

Charles stifled a laugh.

Then he heard something scraping against tile, followed by the familiar clinks and clanks of Piecemaker disassembling an object. So much for that friendly chat. Piecemaker was still the lunkheaded hero he always had been, and now he had a weapon. Charles sat crouching behind the counter, listening. Playing the waiting game.

"Why don't you come out from behind there? Let's talk."

Charles listened for any hint of movement. There was a whistling through the air. He stood up and jumped out of the way, just in time to avoid being bombarded with pieces of chair. Piecemaker charged, and Charles reached for the countertop behind him, searching for something, anything. What he found was a griddle.

He yanked the cord out of the socket, sent a wave of electricity through the griddle, and held it up as a shield. Piecemaker's forearm struck the hot surface of the griddle and he recoiled.

"Isn't this a little silly? We're gonna throw down with sandwich makers?" Piecemaker said, still trying to find some levity in the situation, still not taking Charles seriously enough.

"You're right," Charles said, throwing the griddle to the floor.

If there was ever a time to push himself, to see just how far he could go, Charles knew this was it. He ran for Piecemaker, just as Piecemaker threw his hand up, breaking the griddle into dozens of tiny pieces. He flung the hot elements at Charles, but Charles dropped to the floor and

Piecemaker diverted them safely to the counter.

As Piecemaker turned to face him, Charles leapt at his old enemy, knocking him to the ground. He tried to pin him there, but he simply wasn't strong enough; Piecemaker flipped him over, knee pressed against his chest.

"Okay, you're done," Piecemaker said.

"No."

Charles could feel the power again, rising from within. Electricity shot from his fingertips, taking hold of Piecemaker. The hero tried to break free, but he had made the mistake of letting Charles get away all those years, and Charles wasn't about to do the same.

He started to…not black out, but he was seeing spots again. Seeing nothing, really, feeling only his rage and his power.

That was when Piecemaker broke free, struggling to his feet in a daze. Charles was not going to let him off that easy. Charles stood, balls of electricity forming in his palms. He stared at Piecemaker, who still had one knee on the floor, still steadying himself. Charles allowed all his anger and rage and hatred and disgust to the surface. They formed a weapon in his mind.

Charles had always wanted to feel like this. To be strong, to be powerful, someone worthy of being feared.

A pot of water came flying from the kitchen, splashing all over Charles. He suddenly knew what it must feel like to be short-circuited. He was snapped back to the present, confusion washing over him. A terrible vibration shuddered all through his body, forcing him to his knees. The electricity in his palms fizzled out. He even felt a slight shock. That was new.

Piecemaker waved his hand, and the pot's handle whipped around to hit Charles in the face. He fell to the floor, shivering. He was so weak he could barely move.

Piecemaker approached him in silence. He sat on the floor next to him.

"What are you going to do now? Hit me some more?" Charles sputtered.

Piecemaker didn't say anything, but he helped Charles into a sitting position. Charles leaned against the counter.

"You don't even remember me, do you?" he asked.

"You're Doc, uh…Doc Battery."

"*Doctor* Battery."

"Right, right."

"I'm surprised you remember me."

"Kind of difficult not to. There were a lot of names and a lot of faces back in those days, but only one of 'em wore an outfit that ridiculous. And I'm including my own." Carl gave a small laugh.

"Do you think this is funny?"

"Do I think you attacking me unawares in the dead of night at my place of business is funny? No. Not particularly." Piecemaker took a good look at him. "So the whole 'loyal customer' thing, that was a ruse?"

"Not the whole time."

"How'd you figure me out?"

"I was the first?"

Piecemaker repeated the question.

"Because I'm better than you," Charles said, "and I finally proved it."

"Huh." Piecemaker shook his head and stood up. "Well, I'm sure you know what comes next."

"Do I get to ask *you* a question?"

Piecemaker thought for a second. "Sure. One."

"Why…this?" Charles gestured feebly at their surroundings. "Why did you leave?"

"It's a simple thing," Piecemaker said. "I'm on the other side of 50 now. I'm old. Spent too many years runnin' around in tights pretending I wasn't. It was way past time for me to move on."

"I wasn't afforded that luxury."

"It's not a luxury. It's a choice. We all get the same one."

"You know nothing about me. You know nothing about my life, the choices I've had to make, you sniveling—"

"You even know what that word means? 'Sniveling?' Had it yelled at me for years and never thought to look it up until after I opened this place." Piecemaker sighed. "Look, I'm not gonna beat the shit out of you. I know I did before. Probably more than I had to at times. But I'm different now. You're gonna get locked up for a good while, but you know what? When you're locked up in there, you're still going to have that choice, the same one everybody gets. It'll still be yours to make."

Charles took in what Piecemaker had said. He was embarrassed for the man. "After all these years," Charles said, "I expected better of you than that…that sentiment."

"Sentiment's not so bad, you get used to it." Piecemaker picked up the phone behind the counter. "I'm gonna call some friends of mine."

"How do you know I won't tell the whole world who you are?"

"Charles, they probably care about me as much as they do you. You want a sandwich?"

⚖

The 'friends' Piecemaker called were members of the Superhuman Task Force, or whatever they called themselves. The super cops. Charles was disappointed he didn't get to meet one of the Heralds.

They asked him who he was, what his powers were, how long he'd been active, all things he was sure they could have looked up in their files once they knew he was Doctor Battery. Still, he played along, the obliging lapdog, answering every question he was asked.

Charles relayed the sad tale of the Innovation Gang — no, that wasn't their name, he wasn't sure they even had a name — and gave up their whereabouts. He presumed they would wind up scattered to the winds in foster homes, perhaps jail for Ed. They knew his secret, but who could they tell? Who would believe them? Who would care?

After all the questions, Charles was told a judge would likely sentence him to time in White Oak, which is what he'd assumed. He had never been locked up for costumed crimes, but he had heard all about White Oak. Kind of hard not to when you ran in his circles. The giant tree out front (one of the world's oldest, supposedly), their goal to reform inmates instead of punish them (it was a *reformation center*, not a *prison*), its famed non-violence (he wondered how that worked; magic, probably).

So this was the life Charles had to look forward to. Talking to a bunch of shrinks in a flowery reformatory where he couldn't shock anyone even if he wanted to. He had come so close.

Charles was transported from the interrogation room — he had been blindfolded both on entering and exiting — to one of the hybrid jails while he waited for sentencing. Much had been made of these hybrids: instead of spending more taxpayer dollars on a super-prison for those waiting to go to super-prison, city officials had decided to throw the low-level supers, the ones who weren't deemed a threat, into cells with regular folks.

Even after all of this, Charles was not deemed a threat.

He was put in a cell with a man who had been in and

out of jail his whole life; no one told him that, Charles could just tell. He had short, dirty brown hair with a thick beard and numerous tattoos. Charles didn't ask what he was in for. He didn't care. The man grunted in his general direction, but that was all that passed for conversation.

Charles did what he usually did in situations like this, which was think. He was surprised that the thoughts he encountered weren't as despairing as he expected. All he could think about was how close he'd come to defeating Piecemaker. He relived their encounter over and over again, electrocuting him, how glorious the power—

"Fuck you smilin' about, buddy?"

Charles looked up to see his cellmate fixing him with an untrustworthy stare. Charles got up from the bed, even more uncomfortable than the one at the tenement house, and walked over to him. The man took this as an affront to his territory.

"You want to know?" Charles said.

"I asked, didn't I?"

Charles leaned in close and whispered, "I know who Piecemaker is."

"Who the hell is Piecemaker?"

Charles laughed and headed back to bed.

"I said, who the—"

Charles spun back around and punched the man in the face, electricity crackling along his knuckles.

"*I* know. *You* don't." He kicked the man in the gut.

"Remember that."

Charles sat back down on his bed and resumed thought, his cellmate coughing up blood on the floor next to him. You know, this might not be so bad. He may not have physically defeated Piecemaker, but he was the only one who'd discovered his secret identity. In that regard, he had bettered him. If he could get through his time at White Oak, hell, they'd teach him how to use these gifts he didn't even know he'd had. Piecemaker would still be out there. The whole world would be waiting for him.

Charles Strewksi considered, for the first time, that the best days of his life may be ahead of him yet.

Delilah by Proxy

by Alyssa Herron

Large milk with ice. For here. Sesame bagel. Sliced. Not toasted. To go. I'd given the girl behind the deli counter the same order almost every day for the last six months. Always the same girl. Never the man I'd been coming to look for every day since I first walked into Cook's Deli. He wasn't here again this morning. So, like I always did, I grabbed my two straws and drank my milk and waited. I hadn't seen him yet. As I drank, I watched the older men staring at me. I stared back, dared them to blink first. I knew that my shaved head and boy-girl body and clothes jacked with their morning. If I was able to put them off their lox, so be it. Even better if they were supers. Nothing made me smile like making a super squirm. But he wasn't here. So, I pitched my milk and carried out my bagel. Well, her bagel.

Outside the deli, I headed toward downtown. Our apartment was just a few blocks from the deli. Figures it took me almost the entire two years since he set up shop to figure out who was running the place. I guess he deserved some credit. No one else in the place seemed to know who he really was. But then, maybe no one else almost had him for a stepfather.

Our apartment was small. Not wholly lousy but not wholly decent either. My mom had made it nice with a few tricks and fringes and fluffs, but when she got sick, it turned into form and function. Who needed end tables and buffets when there were hospital beds and potty chairs to be had? We were beyond frugal but fabulous. We were stage four lymphoma.

"Joyce," I said, as I came through the door. "How's tricks?"

"You get my bagel?" she asked.

"Mom, when have I ever not gotten your bagel? How are you going to sit there and not eat it if I don't get your bagel?"

"I feel okay today. I think I'll have some," she said.

Sure she would. I climbed up on the bed next to her and handed her the deli bag. She was so small. A frame where a person used to hang. I rubbed my head against hers, my nubby scalp against her slick-smooth one. She pulled the bagel out of the bag and started, tearing bits out of the middle. She could only eat the doughy flesh on the inside. The outer skin was too hard for her to tear through.

"He wasn't there," I said. She nodded and chewed, wrapping her arms around the layers of sweaters and blankets that covered her body.

"Of course he wasn't," she said.

"Nurse should be here at noon. I'll be at the store if

you need me. Okay?"

"Amanda?" my mom sighed. She would tell me she forgot. She didn't forget. Before getting sick, at least. So I needed to think she was intending to forget.

"Vit, mom. You know my name is Vit. Has been for years."

"I know, honey. I forget. Can you bring me in some water before you go? And take the rest of this for your lunch." She handed me the bag from the deli, where she had dropped crumbs and chunks of her bagel. The other half laid in the bottom under the seedy debris, untouched.

"Sure, Mom." And she laid back down, curling into the pillow.

A few hours later, I stood behind my own counter at work, chewing on my mother's stale bagel leavings. At least it was a counter for now. The guy who owned the store had talked about enclosing the register, and me, behind a plexiglass partition. The concern being more for the register. To give some separation. I never had any trouble. The boys left me alone. The girls came on to me. Not the gay ones. The young, dumb ones who think it's hip to flirt with the dyke in the sex store. Like the old guys at the deli, if you make strong enough eye contact, they always back down. Partition aside, the place would probably be closing soon. No one bought hard copies of porn any more. I was supposed to organize a website a while ago, but like I knew how to do that. Make them come in and buy their junk in person. It was pretty empty, so I left my crunchy dough and went to stock new titles in the back. In places like this, in towns like this, the specialty titles are kept in the back. Here it was behind a purple curtain with a blue stripe. The ones who look for titles back here will ask in an empowered way, "Anything new behind the cape?"

I really, really hated when they said that.

Behind the cape is the superhero merch. Cosplay porn, for the most part. But some of it is the real thing. Old supers who couldn't hack it as civilians, so they dropped their spandex to their ankles for a few dollars. I wouldn't watch it, but I saw who did. Like those two idiots. Young boy showing off his date, as if I didn't see his memory lock vibrations from across the room. And he tried all the time. A new boy every month, and he always tried to walk out of here with a few free DVDs and a flogger. Get your merch online like everyone else, freak. Always shocked when I made him pay. Yes, jackass. These are the droids I'm looking for. Whatever you need to tell yourself. Pay me, you bum. Or better yet, go try that jacky magic trick on someone who wasn't part super. Itchy with irritation, I left them in the weirdo room and got back to my counter.

It was starting. I could feel it, and it was more than irritation from those two. Just past midnight and I wanted to claw off my scalp. The blue hearts on my arms and legs started to burn, and the skin around them sweated in films. That's how it worked for me. This miserable compunction to knit their hearts together, fill them up, and stop any real feeling from bleeding out. My very chromosomes begged me to do it. Half of them, to be biologically accurate. I got the tattoos to make sure they never could.

I learned what I could do pretty early. Third grade. Valentine's Day. The shy boy with the enormous glasses and perpetual dry cough, and the girl who played violin. I knew they would finish high school never having spoken once, and I knew they'd be better together. Some people just are. Good things would come from it, I could just tell. I didn't have to craft up a phony card and hide it or have her find his stolen spectacles. I just put my hands on them one day at lunch. Right one on her, left one on him. They looked at me like I'd just called the teacher an elephant ass. Then they looked at each other and haven't stopped since. I'm counting on their kid to cure cancer. Too late for me, but maybe someone else. After that, I thought I could make the world better by tying up all the romantic ends. I didn't want to, but I was drawn. It pushed out from my insides, from under my skin and even from the follicles of my hair. Like something reaching out to connect. But when it come to the most important romantic end, my mother, I couldn't. That was the last time I'd scratch that genetic itch. Never again. Finally, Kid Wonder Balls came up for air with his boy du minute and pulled me from my own cellular tug-of-war.

"Hey, thanks for the suggestions. Really excited about

these. See you later," he said. Carrying his three space-wrestler movies and a vibrating miniature cowboy hat, he and his friend headed for the door. While I didn't have a partition, I did have a remote door lock. He turned when the door wouldn't budge.

"Forget something?" I asked.

"I'm good on toy cleaner," he said. And then the fool tried again. If they only used their powers for good instead of stupid.

"Sixty-two seventeen, Cowboy," I said. It didn't take lasers or tractor beams to get him back in line to swipe Mommy's card for me. I smiled and waved, but I could tell by his friend's face that the Rockin' Roy's Ten Gallon Haymaker might need to wait for another night.

I looked around the store, expecting to pretend to vacuum and leave, but I couldn't. Although I didn't see her come in, there was suddenly a girl in the corner. She looked around, wide-eyed and keeping a few steps back, just in case something jumped off the shelf to shake itself at her.

"Help you?" I asked. She didn't scream, but did the quick scared-mom-vocal-breath intake. "Sorry."

She was cute. If I was into that sort of thing. But I wasn't. And she was mute. She shook her head and ran out of the store. I considered it for a second, then locked the door behind her and clawed my hands through my hair. It was always long enough by this time of the early morning that the tips in the front curved right into my eyeballs. Time to go home.

My mom was breathing unevenly, barely making a dent in the couch where she had "accidentally" fallen asleep. She hated the hospital bed. So did I. I grabbed a pillow from a chair and laid on the the floor, flopping my hair out of my face. It had grown to my chin since I left the store. Just like it did every night. Ignoring everything else in the room, I went to sleep.

I woke up a few hours later with my mom's heel in my sternum. She was halfway off the couch. My stupid hair was halfway across everything.

"Mom. Come on. Let's get going." I walked with her into the bathroom and hoisted her into the tub. Today, there was only minimal groaning and skin damage to either of us. Something no one tells you: start with an empty tub. As the water ran, and I finally settled her in and started washing her back, she petted my hair.

"You'd be so pretty. You were, you know. Such a pretty girl," she said.

"I know."

"Your dad had red hair. Did I ever tell you that? Not on his head," she said, icking me out as only moms can. "His head hair was brown. His beard was red. He never let that grow in either. I thought he was handsome in a beard. It made him look worldly. Like Hemingway."

My dad was a drunk calico. Great. That's not what I remembered. Maybe she was thinking about the one after him. Or the dozens after that one. Or the last one. Or maybe Carl. Who knew? I started taking off the dermal skin layers, and she bristled.

"Sorry," I said, but kept scrubbing with her loofah.

"I care about people, " she said.

"A lot. Maybe this being sick is just the awning for that shit-shop of caring."

"It's cancer, honey," she pandered.

"And superheroes don't shoot that, right? They only fire good things on bad guys?" I asked. Nothing to say to that one. "I haven't ever seen Carl at the deli."

"I asked you not to do that. That's my old stuff."

"But they have the best bagels."

She pushed me off and pulled herself out of the tub.

"Stop it," I said.

"You stop it, Vit," she said, with as much strength as her eighty-five pounds could muster. "All the grown-up girls here get to make their own mistakes." She walked out of the bathroom, limping, dripping, and naked. I let her go.

I drained the tub and plugged in my razor. The hair that got wet during the bath clogged the motor a bit, so I pulled as I shaved. Strands of red hair the length of my arm fell to the floor. I gathered them up and threw them in the garbage. I'd thought about selling it once or twice. It still might come to that.

At the deli, the line was longer than usual. Some race was jamming up the streets, and the boys and girls in tights and neon bras stood in line for water and bananas. The girl did her business behind the counter. The clerk. The Daughter. His daughter. We were both little kids when her dad and my mom got together. Then got apart. The supers were good at disappearing, I'd give them that. Her name was Tabitha. And not one of these bouncing racers knew or seemed to care who was selling them their designer water. I gave her the same practiced and intentioned eye contact I had perfected. She was impervious.

He wasn't there today. Her dad. He had just left. I could feel it. How is it I never got here to see him? I was late and Mom had an appointment. I left, squeezing through the pack with only two elbows and the slightest of hip checks to some impossibly skinny guy in pantyhose who was leaning on his kid's stroller. I'd have to go without my milk today. That probably meant something in a separation-attachment sort of way.

My stomach growled, loud enough that my mother in her patient's gown on the table and the doctor beside her both looked over at me. I shifted in my seat, pretending that my guts weren't revolting against me. My mother let the opportunity to make a joking-but-in-a-serious-way chubby-daughter crack pass. She was good like that. I widened my eyes to reinforce that I was listening.

"Your platelets are down. White cells too. Dangerously low. I'm holding chemo," the doctor said.

"How long?" I asked.

"I don't know," he said. "Looking at the numbers, I probably wouldn't advise starting again. Not worth it. It would only weaken her. Lessen the days left."

"Shit," I said, and not for the first time in that office.

"It's okay," my mom said. "I knew this was coming." She looked at me. "What about her? With me having this history? Ovarian cancer? Should she be tested?"

"She should," the doctor said.

"But that's not what this is, is it? Just cancer?" I said. "It came on so hard and so fast, and she's sick, and civilian cancer doesn't do that. Pulling out my stuff wouldn't do anything for me, right?"

"It might"

"So, a lifetime of having poison seed pumped through your insides, that doesn't affect this?" I asked.

My mother looked at me like she had never seen me before and never wanted to. "I'm dying. If all you can do is insult me, you should leave."

"Doc? Nothing?" I asked.

"It's cancer. Isn't that enough?" he said, actually making eye contact.

I stared at them both. Outgunned, I retreated. "Let me know when you're done. I'll help you to the car." I stomped out in one of my more impressive tantrums.

We sat side by side on the couch later that night, eating potato chips. The grease somehow settled her stomach. She ate one at a time, licking each finger completely after. I

shoved them in my face by the handful, pausing
infrequently to wipe my hands on my white ribbed tank top.
If only there was a money prize for complete bodily
disregard. Just another thing I did that made her sad. My
men's undershirts and boxers. Every day. Every night. I
didn't own a bra. I owned a pair of silk underwear, but they
weren't mine.

"You don't have any idea how to be with another
person," she said. "I really don't think you're terrible. You
just have no sense of how to act that isn't mean and awful.
Was that me? Did I do that?"

"You were fine, Mom."

"I don't want you left alone."

"I'm not," I said. " I have chips."

"We're talking days, honey. Days."

"Shut up. You don't know," I yelled at the woman with
cancer. Asshole.

"Neither do you," she said. Not angrily. Not with tears.
Just factual and documentarian.

"I'm not like these other stupid girls. I'm not like you."

"I'm stupid? I haven't heard that since you were fifteen.
I almost miss it."

"Goddamn it, I didn't mean that. You know what I
meant."

"You don't want to wear a skirt and get flowers and go
to dinner. I get that. I don't care. Then you have to find
something else. Whatever works for you and gets you out of

here." She knocked on my chest like a hollow oak door. "You can't curl up in your old men underwear and your extra skin forever."

"I'm just not like you," I said. "All those guys. In and out. All the time. I'm not, I can't do that."

"I don't care if it's with a girl. Or a boy. Or something else. That doesn't matter," she said. Which was cool to hear but didn't make any goddamn difference.

"That's not it. How do you think it felt to see all that? In and out of our house and your bed. And none of them gave a shit about you. Except Carl. But you made sure he didn't stick around."

"Your dad left. That wasn't my fault. That wasn't your fault. It was his fault. And his loss. And no one who came after, including Carl, signed up for the job of being your daddy. You didn't get a good one. I'm sorry. Not everyone does. But you can't take that out on everyone that comes after."

"The ones that come after? At least you make sure you come first," I said. And immediately wished I hadn't. "I'm sorry. I'm an asshole."

"Amanda, there are sides and parts to everyone. The ones you hate and the ones you hate less. You have sides, like it or not. I don't get to know them all. It's okay. So you need to respect that sometimes, you only need to know the mother and not the woman."

"That's not my name. That's a dead name," I said.

"And I'm almost a dead woman," she said. "Go get me a beer. Vit."

After that, you don't say anything. You just drop the crumbs of chips out of your hands and go get a beer. The bottle felt like it weighed roughly fifty pounds when I finally got my hand around it. When I came back to the couch, she was fast asleep. I put down the anvil-weighted beer. She somehow weighed less than the drink when I scooped her up in my arms. The smooth skin of her head connected with the bare skin of my arm, and our flesh dipped and pressed against each other. I pulled her closer to get us both through the narrow bedroom door. She was still fast asleep when I laid her in the hospital bed. Cold even in her sleep, goosebumps rose up on her skin, so I pulled the blankets up to her chin. She still quivered under the layers. I climbed in over the side and pulled myself next to her, trying to fill every concave space in her body with a convexity of my own. It took a few minutes, but I felt her body warm, and she stopped shivering. I, on the other hand, was fevered, and the hair that had now grown to the base of my neck was wet with sweat. Neither of us moved for a long time.

The regular girl wasn't at the deli the next morning. It was a new one. Now, I don't like to disparage the gender or the sex of my birth. Although I gave both up, I don't like to put down those who still inhabit it. QUILTBAG and alphabet soup acknowledgement and respect for preferred pronouns. I personally don't give a shit. And frankly, some bitches are too much. This broad here? Jesus. Far east coast of too much. I stood at the deli counter, staring at my cup and pondering the difficult, sweet, nutty taste in my mouth.

"You ordered soy milk, right?" she asked from behind the counter.

No, honey. Not in this lifetime.

"Regular milk. Red cap. Ice. Two straws," I said, not actually expecting to get it.

"Oh my God, that's right. I'm so sorry. Here. I'll fix it," the girl with the bob haircut said. And before I could roll my eyes at her, the cup was out of my hand. While I waited, I checked out the bagel. As soon as I opened the bag, the smell of onion and garlic salt let me know that things were not well in Bagel Land either. As soon as I looked up, she was shoving a cup across the counter at me.

"So sorry. I'm new. Getting things wrong all day. I'm filling in. She said they needed help in a hurry. She, Tabitha, hired me this morning. I'm Turner," she said as she shoved her hand across the counter. I shook it, at least as well as I could, holding a white paper bag in that hand. She was cute. If I liked…well, anyone, anything, I guess. Bobbed black hair and brown eyes. I'd seen her before. Couldn't place it. "What's the name?" she asked from behind the counter. I blanked. "For the order?"

"Vit. I come in every day," I said, although for the life of me, I didn't know why.

"Oh. My. God. I love that name," she said, blinking on

the downbeats. "Did you make it up yourself? Your mom didn't give you that name, did she? It's so cool. It sounds like—"

Then she stopped and covered her mouth with the back of her plastic-gloved hand. I was curious which rhyme she was considering. Then The Bob went back in for talking. Not talking, exactly, but whispering, as she balanced my new milk on the counter, not quite giving it up for ownership.

"The guy who owns this place, he's at a funeral. Not a regular funeral. Like, a big, important funeral." And then she actually looked over her left and right shoulders to see if anyone was listening. "A super funeral," she said. Eyebrow rise. She waited for a response I didn't give. "Guy turned purple. Not death purple. Like, unicorn poop purple. Isn't that weird?"

I shrugged my shoulders. They were slow to return to their normal place because I was absolutely aching for revenge. My mother was dying and that mutant was at someone else's funeral. She didn't know a sixteenth of it. No one here did.

"I heard Tabitha talking on the phone. Anyway. And I've screwed up every order today. Some guy, like an hour ago, had to give himself an epi-pen shot. Because I accidentally had peanut butter on my finger and I put it on his change. She's totally going to fire me." Then she spilled my second milk all over the counter. Complete with a mom-intake of breath and hands covering her mouth. It was the sound that drew Tabitha out to the counter. Second time I'd heard that sound lately but couldn't remember why. Wasn't from my mom.

Tab stared at both of us. "Hey," she said.

"Hey," I said.

"Sorry," Tabitha said. She had no idea who I was. I watched her swirl the white water across the counter. The Bob had given me skim milk. Closer that time, at least. As they both cleaned the milk, it almost bubbled. Like the molecules were being separated. Or agitated. But probably not. Maybe not. No. Probably not. I kept watching The Bob paint with the milk and didn't notice Tabitha handing out a new cup, until she tapped me on the arm with it. I took a sip. Ice. Whole milk. Two straws. I left without saying thank you.

I sat cross-legged on the floor at work, staring at the door. I refused to use any of my powers. Ever. But if I had such a way to keep customers out that night, I would have considered it. I'd just gotten rid of a pack of stupid teenagers who spent almost two hours surreptitiously tasting the flavored lubricants. I could have cared less. No. False. I actually don't believe that I could have. What I did care about was that I finally remembered where I had seen The Bob before. Here. I had run her out at closing. And there she was again, standing just outside the door. So, of course, I stared at her through the glass. Until I gestured her to come in like a third-grader through a school bus window.

"Oh my God," The Bob said, sliding into the door but stopping just inside on the dinging entrance mat. "It's you. I am so sorry. I've seen you here before, and then again today at the deli, and that was, I was such a disaster."

"It's okay," I said. I realized I was still sitting on the ground. It would have been polite to stand when she came in, but I don't usually do polite. I don't know how to be with people, I've been told. And now it was late, so I just stayed there. I had to make up for the ridiculous come-in beckon. "You looking for something?"

"I'm gay. Totally gay. Like, one hundred percent. No boys. At all. Black and gay. That's me."

"Congratulations," I said. Oh boy. Or oh girl, maybe. "You looking for something?" I repeated.

"I've never, you know, had anything. I just broke up with my girlfriend. We'd been together since college. She left and I finished. She's already dating someone. But, I'm not seeing anyone. It's been a while. So, I was wanting to get something. My first thing. Since you, you know, girls, I thought maybe,"

"I don't like girls," I said. To remind myself.

"Oh. Because I thought, with the hair, that you…"

"I don't like boys either."

"Oh. So, huh," she said.

"Come on," I said, as I pulled myself up from the

ground. I walked back to the toy shelf. She was still standing by the door, so I had to wave her over. For the second time tonight.

"What's the first thing that pulls your eye? First draw is usually the winner."

Of course, she points to the most phallic thing on the shelf.

"Are you kidding me?"

She was horrified. "What? Is that wrong? Did I pick, I picked the wrong one, didn't I? Damn it!"

"It's not wrong. It's just kinda penis-y for a gay girl. Really, really penis-y, actually." And with that, I'd crushed her. Ripped her lesbian membership card up right in front of her face and burned the pieces on a pyre of Gloria Steinem's memoirs.

"What's your name again?" I asked, like I didn't remember. What in the hell was happening?

"Turner," The Bob said.

"See? Turner. That is a really solid lesbian name." It really was.

"Not as cool as yours," she said. It really wasn't. "What's it mean?" Bail time.

"Turner. Absolutely. No way a straight girl has that name. No way."

"Thank you," she said. I pulled the rubber/latex monolith down from the shelf.

"I think you can handle it." I don't remember cashing

her out, but I remember watching her walk out of the store. And thinking again that I was glad X-ray vision wasn't in my clashed-up hybrid mutant DNA, because for the second time that night, I might have stooped to use my power. Because damn. But not that much damn.

The whole way home, I thought about that crazy girl. I hadn't thought about a girl like that for a long time. And it wasn't that I wanted to sleep with her. I just wanted to sit with her. Which made me sound as gross and creepy as I felt. I walked up the steps in the dark, damping down my mind and my physical sounds as best as I could, because I hoped my mom was sleeping. As soon as I opened the door, I heard it. It's not the sound of someone choking. That's quiet, because they can't make any sound. No, this was the sound of ugly fighting air, struggling with going down and then coming back out of a wracked little torso. Then I didn't hear anything except for my own feet running to her body.

As the sun came up the next morning, I first wondered if my mother was dead. I flopped my hand around to find her chest and clarified that it was still working. Next, I wondered if The Bob would be working at the counter. Was she really bad enough for Tabitha to fire her? I mean, she was pretty bad, but it's a deli, not a surgical suite. A spinning, sloppy brain has to be expected during these times, I reasoned. Or I thought I did, but my exhausted nervous system was still computing. There really wasn't any waking up the next morning, because I had never gone to bed. I sat on the floor next to my mother's hospital bed. My shoulder was cramped because I had propped it up all night so I could hold her hand. I squeezed it every time she shuddered or shook in her sleep. I wondered if she was going to make it through the day. And because our brains do monstrous things we can't control, I wondered if the bobbed girl behind the counter would notice I wasn't there. My mother snorted and I got to my feet, leaning over to see what was happening.

"Sorry," she whispered as she made a silly little attempt to try and flip up the sheets. Seems it wasn't a snort. Aside from our brains, our bodies can be some joke-making jerks sometimes, too.

"Nice one," I said.

"Can you get into my drawer? Top one, underwear," she said, pointing in the wrong direction.

"Wait, let me get you cleaned up."

"I don't want underwear. There are papers in the back. Go get them."

Whatever this was, I was not happy to be involved. Near-comatose in a bed, and this woman still had it all over me. I got up and went to fetch the papers. I remember looking in her underwear drawer when I was little. Some of the things I didn't understand. Looking back, ugh, come on, Mom. But I remember looking at all her pretty underwear. The good stuff. The black and red and lacy stuff that she wore on the nights when men came to the door and tried to impress me with flowers that bloomed on command, or once, a stuffed apple that turned into a glass of juice if you shook it. I watched her get dressed and thought she was so beautiful. But I never wanted to look like her. Never tried on any of those slippery, shiny things. Never wanted to slide around with anyone else while I had them on, either. None of those good ones were left in the drawer today. Just variations of big white cotton. And in the back, worn white papers. I grabbed them and brought them back to her bed.

"Good. I haven't seen them for a while. Put them back," she said.

"What?"

"Just put them back. You know where they are. Now you know I want you to read them. Not now. Later. You don't have to think about it. Good enough."

"You hungry?" I asked. She couldn't even get it up to lie to me.

"There's this new girl at the deli," I said, and I had no idea why. I knew I didn't want to. "She botches every order. On a really impressive scale. Yesterday, she was talking about him not being there, and she spilled my milk. But she's really nice about it, so I can't bitch about it. I wish it was Tabitha. I remember once she stole my He-Man to be her Barbie's boyfriend. Broke his leg. I stuck it in her ear."

"Is she cute?" my mom asked.

"Ew. No, she's a vicious, weirdly elongated troll. And why does it always have to be about being cute? How about being decent instead?"

"Is she decent instead?"

"I have no idea."

"Shit, I'm tired," she said, and closed her eyes. I was still sitting on the bed, wondering why the hell I was holding these things in my hand, and she had fallen fast asleep. At a quick flip, I saw they were all in the same handwriting. I flipped to the shortest one and scanned to the name on the bottom. Carl. I wanted to ingest them immediately, without the time it would take for my eyes to scan and my brain to process. And I wanted to bury them forever. Burying won for the night. I barely left that five-foot square space for the next twenty-four hours.

The next morning, my mom wasn't up for talking. I stood guard by her bed. Pacing. Stopping and turning at every sound. Finally, she slapped her hand on the side of the bed to stop my wandering. There was something soothing in the rhythm of manic worrying. She didn't tell me to leave, but with the strength she could muster, she rolled her eyes and tipped her chin to the door.

"You're crazy," I said. She smacked the bed again, flipped me off, and eyeballed the door again.

"Five minutes. Been here all day. You need to eat something," she said.

"Forget it," I said.

"I'm hungry," she said. "Go." I kissed her and ran out the door. It wasn't until I was halfway down the block that I realized I'd just been grifted and fell for it like the world's biggest mark.

I got to the deli just for the slag time between lunch and dinner. As I stepped up to order, I saw Tabitha. Not growling but not mewing either. And Turner.

"Hi."

"Hi," she said. Still bobbed. Still unsettling. "Let me get it for you."

She hummed around in the kitchen, taking things out of refrigerators and cabinets and putting them back in again, but not from where she had taken them.

"Two straws. I remembered," Turner grinned, as she handed me a cup and a bag. I took a sip. She had remembered. Two straws. In two percent milk. With no ice. She was closer. I didn't bother looking in the bagel bag. It wouldn't get eaten anyway. That was really true at that second, and that was hard. This could be my last bagel trip for my mother. It must have shown.

"You okay?" The Bob asked. And it did; her hair really did bob when she leaned her head in and out with genuine concern. I almost forgot what she had asked, the gesture so stunned me. Maybe it was her that was a superhero.

"I am not ideal," I said.

"Hey Tab," she called behind her without looking. "I'm taking off for a bit. Come on," she said to me, as she flipped the counter escape hatch. She took my hand. I let it go. But I still followed her out of the deli.

"You don't need to take care of me. I'm fine," I said.

"Okay."

"And I should get back to her."

"Five minutes," she said. I just kept following.

We walked downtown and eventually to the river front. They had built a lovely running trail along the water. Nice enough for something as miserable as intentional exertion for no creative purpose. It was windy and very un-warm, and I folded my arms across my chest, wearing only a tank top. When one leaves as a sucker, one is likely to be cold doing so.

"I like your hearts," Turner said. I forgot about them for a second. That seemed to happen to me when she talked. "Let me see them," she said, and pulled my elbow out and closer to her face. She didn't ask. "What do they mean?"

Three dark blue hearts in descending size from my shoulder to my elbow. A matching set on both sides. Larger ones ran from both of my hips to my knees and down my back. I wasn't ready yet. At least she got that right.

"Do you want to talk about what's not ideal for you right now? I know you need to get back. But you can just blurt it out really fast. I can listen. Fast. I won't interrupt. And I don't know you, so sometimes it's easier to talk if you don't know."

"My mom's sick," I said.

"Oh my God, really sick? I'm sor—" She literally covered her mouth with both hands like a cartoon. Taking only one hand away, she gave me a flourish/carry-on gesture.

"She's sick, dying-sick. She has cancer. It sucks in every single, evil way." She still had her hands over her mouth and looked like it was choking her not to participate. I took her hands down. "Go ahead."

"I'm sorry. How is your dad? How is he doing with all this?"

"I have absolutely no idea."

"Oh," she said.

A trio of runners came past, bright sleeves and shoes, and perfectly sleek, bouncing ponytails. Odd thing, a threesome of runners. Too many to stack horizontally. Someone has to be the peak or the basin of the pyramid.

"I don't get running," she said. "I tried a few times. I didn't get it."

Seriously. This girl.

"You take care of her by yourself?" she asked.

"Yeah. Except when I leave her alone," I said.

"What about you? Do you have anyone? Outside of her, I mean."

"That's not what I do."

"Oh," she said.

"I'm a half-breed."

"So you have the other half of yourself?"

"No." But that made me think.

"Well, that's okay. I mean, I bet a lot of people are. And it's totally cool. I mean, I'm totally fine. There's nothing wrong with that."

"Yeah."

"So, the hearts, are they tribal? Ethnic?" She leaned in. "Are they a sex thing?"

Who was this girl?

"They mean my mom had a thing for supers. My dad and everyone after." And like I did with this broad, I just kept talking without thinking. "They're magic. I guess." She stared. I plowed ahead. "I got them done by a gypsy super. They're containment spells. Whatever is inside can't get out. Anything I have in me, I can't use. Not that I ever would."

"Ever?" she asked.

"They're not rub-ons."

"Oh. Right. Duh. Course not. Did they hurt?"

"Not getting them. They hurt when they work. Burn."

"That's pretty rad. I guess."

"Not really." Halting tattoos are rad in purpose, nowhere near that in practice.

"I mean, I thought it was a vagina-power thing. Go girls. Something like that," she said.

"I don't have sex, Turner. I don't have 'a sex.' I don't have 'the sex.' It's outside the realm of my consideration."

"Dude, that's just weird," she said. "The sex. A sex. It's such an awesome expression. How can you skip that?"

Wildly libidinous, vicious, weirdly elongated troll. But with cute hair.

"No. Come on, Vit. Superhero is one thing. But you work in a sex shop?"

I stopped her. "So, an alcoholic can't work in a bar? A fat girl shouldn't sell bikinis?"

"No, not at all. It would just gross me out. I'd be sad if I was you. Is that why you do it?"

"This is what I don't do, okay? And this was supposed to be talking about my mom. Who is sick. I can't be here talking about my stupid shit. I need to get back. Now," I said. She grabbed my arm.

"No, really, I want to know. Doesn't mean I want to get all in your parts, or part or whatever you have."

I shrugged her off. Hard. "Stop talking and leave me alone."

"Is your power down there?" And she actually pointed to her crotch. "Maybe it's a forcefield thing."

"Go home, little girl." And I walked away. One more thing to this girl's credit, she didn't try to stop me.

My legs ached hours later as I sat on the floor of the store, my dizzy head leaning against one of the racks. I had walked home and then to work from the river. My mom was actually rallying when I got there. I didn't trust it. She was sitting up in bed. Took a few sips of the soup I had brought home from a different take-out place. After a few hours, she pushed me out the door again. I didn't feel scammed that time, but maybe she was just better than I thought.

I dug into my legs with the knuckles of both hands. Those muscles were not accustomed to such misuse, much as my liver was not accustomed to the whiskey I was dosing it with at the moment. It wasn't my fault I worked on the same block as a liquor store. Probably the government's fault for keeping the sex and booze quarantined to the dirty parts of the city. But I can multi-task like a champion. I clanked my tooth on the glass bottle as I took a swig, being too lazy to turn my head away from the door and actually look at the mouth before I took a drink.

Flailing. My mom was dying. I was lousy at taking care of her. I needed to schedule a collapse but didn't have the time or anyone to catch me when I went down. Went down. What the hell was going on with me? Only person I have is going and I'm thinking about some dingy girl. I didn't want to throw this kid down on the floor and have our anythings touch. But it was just nice to talk to someone. To entertain for a second that some day, someone might be there to help put me back together when I fell apart. I seemed to be doing that more and more lately.

My phone rang. It was buried in my slouchy jeans that were not as slouchy as they once were, so it took some contortion to yank it out of the pocket. I didn't bother to look at the screen.

"Mom!" I yelled into the phone, with much more enunciation than I thought my brain and tongue capable of coordinating at the moment. But they both went into total synchronicity the following second, because in a heartbeat, I was completely sober and totally falling.

"Wait. I'm coming. I'm leaving right now. Listen to me. I'm coming, hang on," I said. I don't remember leaving the store that night or how I got home. I got there and she knew it. I didn't know what to do. I never have. So I just held her. Rocked because that's what my body made me do. Then next thing I have is lying next to my mom in her bed, holding her hand and knowing I'd never get to do that again. My hair was down to the back of my knees the next morning when I finally left her alone in the bed. It dragged across her body when I pulled myself away from her to start my goodbye. I shaved it before I called the funeral home. My body was still rocking back and forth as I ran the razor over my head.

It's remarkable how quickly they can throw a funeral together. To tidy up someone's life like that in the span of a day seems impossible. But it was possible, and when you don't have much money, they get things over in a hurry. I didn't have to rent a casket or anything, but it was definitely a small-scale production. They let me bury her the next day. I asked about it, almost as a joke. Twelve hours later, I was at a graveside. That was what she wanted. Nothing. No viewing. No flowers. She had wanted to donate her organs at one time, but they were pretty much sludge by the time she was done with them.

I was the only one there. She had never really had women friends. I don't know that the entire time that woman raised me that I ever saw another woman in our house. She didn't talk to them on the phone. She didn't really talk about them. She had her boys. And me. So what a surprise that I was the only one that showed up for the funeral. I didn't want a priest or another Jesus-speaker. Not really our thing. I'm not really a feeler, so I didn't make a speech or read a poem. I just sort of stood there looking at the box. The cheap caskets don't have shiny finishes or rounded edges. They're more flat and angular. Pointy edges to really serve as exclamation points, illustrating that no one cared enough to spend that extra two thousand dollars. I hated that box. And I hated my dad. And I hated every man who wasn't standing there to say goodbye. One more than the others. I let the gravediggers do whatever they needed to do. As I walked away, I wondered if I should have tipped them. I don't know.

Back at the apartment, I laid in the hospital bed. There weren't any sheets on it, and I wondered where they had gone. I ran to the bathroom and looked in the hamper. Nothing but her nightgowns and some dirty towels. I took the hamper into the kitchen with me and upended it into a big black garbage bag. And then I needed everything gone.

Right now. I dragged the bag into the bedroom and just
started yanking drawers out and tossing everything into it.
Her old sweatshirts. Jeans from ten years ago. Two drawers
full of old bras and underwear that she hadn't worn since
she actually had boobs and hips to put in them. I saw the
papers tumble into the bag along with the underthings. I
grabbed another drawer and piled more things on top.
Bury everything I can today, I figured. But I couldn't. I
reached into the bag with both hands and scooped out the
letters. One by one, I spread them out on the floor and
squatted on the bag of her clothes while I read them.

*"They were lovely, the days we had. Having you in my life gave
me a peace I hadn't known since my wife left. I hope you can
understand. You want and deserve more than I can give. You should
have a man who can be there with you. All in. Always. But with
Tabitha in my life, I can't do that. She needs more than that. Both our
girls need more than a half-strength dad. And while you never asked,
only a superman can be a father and a lover to two different families.
So I'm choosing to be a father. I wish you every light. Maybe in a
different world, we will meet again. But if we don't, you have my love.
Carl."*

I had never seen that letter, but I had never forgotten
the after. I remembered my mom sitting in a chair, staring
at the wall. She wasn't crying, wasn't making a sound, but
her cheeks were wet. I went to Carl's house that night, after

she had finally given up and gone to bed. I'd never snuck out before that. I stood outside his door, and for the first and only intentional time, I was going to use my powers on him. If I could just talk to him. Make him see how perfect all three of us could be together. If I could just get him back to the house and get my hands on both of them, I could do it. Meld their hearts together. Force them into a family with me as the sweet, creamy center. Not for me, well, not mostly for me, but for her. I wanted his heart for her. But it didn't work. I stood outside and tried to step closer to the house. I felt something keeping me away, so strong it knocked me off my feet. When I picked myself up off the ground, I saw him staring out the window at me. He smiled and then drew the curtains. By the end of the week, I had found the witch and gotten my tattoos. Never again.

The deli was packed when I went in that night. Tabitha was behind the counter, balancing a pile of sandwiches on both hands and up her forearms. Turner stood behind her, holding a single tomato slice and wandering around looking for its home. I started barking from the back of the room like some pumped-up action hero.

"Where is he?" I didn't yell, but more than asked. The crowd didn't part so much as they just looked up from their phones and hoped their order would be ready before I brought any more irritating crazy into their snack time. No response. Well, that wouldn't do. I walked between the crowd up to the counter proper. And punched it like every macho poser I despised. Of course, nothing happened. No shattering or collapsing. But it made noise. A loud noise.

"Where is he?" I said, once more for the flourish, complete with periods between syllables.

Turner stared, still holding her tomato. "Honey, are you okay?"

Tabitha, on the contrary, did not care one whit how I was. "Get the hell out of here. Now," she said. And pointed, in case I needed a visual cue.

"I want to talk to him," I said. Walking closer to the counter, I threw my handful of letters across to the back side. Aerodynamic, they were not, and they had no trajectory toward her, they just floated aimlessly to the floor. "She died and I buried her today and he wasn't there. He said he loved her."

"We were kids, Vit. That was a long time ago," Tabitha said.

"I want to know why he wouldn't even come when she died. He should at least tell me. So go in the back, and get him out here."

Tabitha charged at me from behind the counter. She pushed me. Harder than I thought she would. "Get out." Behind her, the crowd had parted, just a little. Only two teenagers were recording us with their phones.

"Just because he's your dad doesn't mean you have ownership. He owes other people things, and he should be man enough to come out here and see me," I said.

"He's not here," Tabitha said.

"She's right," Turner said. " He's not. He hasn't been here for days. Honest."

"Well, isn't that super. Maybe you should go find him," I said, shoving Tabitha back into the customers behind her. She came at me, grabbing me by the tank top and pulling me to her face.

"Wait, wait, wait," Turner said, stepping between us and prying Tabitha's fingers from my shirt. "I got this." Turner grabbed me around the waist, digging her thumb into my diaphragm. I kept my eyes on Tabitha, but my feet moved outside and onto the sidewalk.

"Vit, I'm sorry about your mom," Turner said. "I wish you would have told me. I could have come to the funeral with you."

"It wasn't a Sadie Hawkins, sweetie. It was a burying."

"Yeah. I know. I've done it before," she said. "Except I put my mom in the ground about a decade after she left us. It was hard. We had to buy two vaults. She was a super. They said that if she came back, or if it was a psuedo-death, that she'd make it out through just one."

"You're a super?" I asked.

"I don't know. I didn't get anything from her. I always wished I had. But, nothing. Like, I can eat gluten and dairy, but those are my only special skills. My dad was just a regular. Based on that, I guess I'm not super. I really don't know all the rules on that stuff."

"How did you know about Carl being a super? No one knows about any of that."

"Well, I mean, I have ESP, a little mind-reading, I guess. That's how I knew about you," she said.

"And that's not a power?" I asked. I didn't like anyone knowing about me.

"Not really. It's because I'm a Libra. That's all," she said. With a serious face.

"That's your move? You knew what was happening, but you still mined into my world about it. Spring your sad shit on me to make me feel like the jerk? Even if I did want to have sex with anyone, and I don't, even if it was face-of-death mandated, I still wouldn't with you."

"I hope not," she said. "And I'm sorry about the other day. I was a colossal jerk—"

"Yes. That is absolutely a fact. Colossal," I said. "I shouldn't even be standing here. That was all kinds of bullshit."

"I'm sorry. I wish there was another way to say it. I've never done that before and I don't know what happened. I didn't mean to get in your stuff. I'm pretty out there with my life and shouldn't expect everyone to do that too. Very uncool of me, and I'm sorry. But I like you and I wanted to know more. But I get it. Not my business. No more questions. I'll mind my own."

"Good," I said. "I don't need anyone in my stuff."

"Agreed," she said. "And as far as the sex thing, it's

cool. Really. Don't worry. That's not why I was snooping around your anthill. You're really not my type."

"What's that mean?"

"I mean I like nice girls," she said with an adorable smile.

"Bully for you. Pity I don't call myself a girl. Or nice."

"You're cranky, whatever you call yourself. And you hate a lot of things. That's just not my jam. Sorry. But, for some reason, I still kind of dig you. Just to talk. And drink beer. Watch movies. Do you like movies? I like bad horror ones. Like, offensively ridiculous bad. But those are even better to watch with someone else. I think I'd like to watch a movie with you. You don't want to? That's cool."

"It's ironic, a heartless bastard like my dad giving me what he did. My stuff. It's not mind control. It's heart control. I could never have made anyone do anything, but I could make them feel things. For people, I guess. Love, mostly. I tried it once on Carl. He fought it. I was a kid, probably wasn't that hard," I said, not really wanting to look and see her reaction.

"Is that why you won't claim anything for you? The whole anti-sex, anti-gender, all from an anti-love thing?" she asked.

"No. The sex and gender thing has nothing to do with my super-stuff. That's really me. But if a heart can be changed with a wave and some finger twinkling, I won't ever trust it."

"You probably like horror movies, then."

"I don't like horror movies."

She just smiled and nodded her head. "Musicals? I kind of pegged you for a musical fan. And you have the worst taste in vibrators. Ever."

"Don't you have to go back to work?" I asked, wiping the tears from my eyes and the snot from my nose with the back of my hand.

"That's filthy," she said. "All kinds of un-hygenic. Use a tissue. And no. I don't. Tabitha fired me this morning, but I agreed to stay through the day. Day looks done to me."

"She fired you?" I asked. "Bitch."

"She's not that bad. You should probably lay off her dad."

"What did we just say."

"What about pizza?" she asked. "Do you have any strong, emotional, jacked-up feelings about pizza? Just the regular kind. Not super pizza."

"I'm okay with that," I said.

"Super duper. We can go to my house. Have some pizza. Not have sex. And talk. Or not. Whatever. I will stay completely on the other side of the world from your stuff. "

"Thank you," I said. I wasn't sure the last time I had said that. Felt like a while.

"You're welcome," she said. "Come on."

I had just lost my mom. And felt really, really shitty. I suspected it would continue to feel so for a rather extended time. But for right now, Turner bobbed beside me and I walked next to her. And that felt okay.

...A Hero Only One
by Paul Smith

"I know who the villain is."

The man behind the counter looks up sharply, glancing around the deli. Satisfied we're the only ones here, he smiles and returns his attention to the food he's preparing.

"Who's that?" he asks. This is a conversation we've had many times over the past few months, and there's a tone of good-humored exasperation in his voice.

"Mister History," I reply. This time his glance is more measured. I've known him for a long time. My entire life, actually, or at least my entire life this time around. I can read the complex mix of confusion and concern in his face as he studies me for a moment.

"Tommy," he begins slowly, "you know History's dead, right? You were there."

"I know History is gone, I don't know that he's dead. You were there too, Carl. He vanished, along with most of Haverland Cemetery, when you pulled apart his time machine. But you've been a superhero long enough to know the rule: no body, no death. Right?"

Carl smirks, apparently relieved by something I've said. He puts the finishing touches on my lunch and passes the

plate across the counter to me. My usual: one All-American
(PB&J), one Olde Fashioned (PB, banana, and honey),
garnished with chips and a pickle spear he knows I won't
eat. I take it and head to our usual table while he takes off
his apron, washes his hands, grabs a couple of cold drinks
— soda for him, milk for me — and comes around the
front to join me. It's Tuesday, our day to catch up over
lunch. "Catching up" usually means me trying to talk him
out of retirement.

"Okay, I'll bite," he says, settling into the seat across
from me. "How do you know Mister History is back?"

The sandwiches are delicious, as always, and I savor
the mouthful I've just taken before trying to answer. Despite
my feelings on his retirement from the hero business, there's
no denying he has a gift when it comes to the delicatessen
arts. True, my usual order isn't particularly challenging. I
basically order off the kids menu. But the menu at Cook's
Deli is expansive, and everything on it is exceptional. Every
week I feel a slight twinge of guilt over trying to convince
him to leave the lunch meats to someone else and get back
in the Game. But this is bigger than that. At least that's
what I always tell myself.

"The bowling ball has disappeared." I let that hang in
the air between us for a second, expecting a suitably
dramatic reaction from him. He stares at me blankly. "You
remember the sphere, that sort of pizza-colored ball that
you pulled out of History's big Time Bomb last time we

fought him? The Actioneer called it a bowling ball? There was a fire at the Barrow-Wake Observatory. Part of the east wing museum came down. Apparently the only item unaccounted for after the clean-up was the bowling ball."

He considers that for a moment. "And you think that means...what? That Mister History is somehow alive and come back for his doohickey?"

"Or one of his minions. I think if History himself were back, he would have done something by now. Something bigger. He never was the most patient world conqueror we faced."

"Ironic," he laughs. "All right, so what would any of this have to do with me?"

"You're his nemesis. Piecemaker dismantled his ridiculous temporal subway stations and turnstiles through time more often than any other hero. And you're the one that 'killed' him the last time. He was never patient, but he did hold a grudge."

The bell over the door jingles as a couple of teenagers come in. Carl looks to see that Aldous has it under control at the counter, and we sit in silence until the customers have placed their orders and taken a table outside on the sidewalk. Even so, Carl speaks quietly.

"I think nemesis is overstating it just a bit, don't you? Besides, there are plenty of other heroes in the city that could look into this. Hell, you could take the lead. You can't be a sidekick forever, Tommy."

There it is. Every time we have this talk, this comes up. Not that he'd remember, of course. The universe won't let anyone remember when they talk about this particular detail of my life with me. I know that. I understand the limits I have to work within, and I don't blame him for bringing it up time and again. Still, it's frustrating. After all these years, after so many lifetimes, to come up against the same wall over and over again and not be able to explain it.

Doesn't stop me from trying.

"What if I'm supposed to be, Carl? What if that's my job? I should be a sidekick. I should be *your* sidekick. You're meant to be the hero, Carl. There's a plan for you, things the universe means for you to do. Maybe I'm just supposed to help you."

He stares blankly at me, his eyes glazed, his face almost frozen. I know from too many years of experience that he's not even hearing me right now. This is a pause in the conversation from his perspective. A hiccup that it won't even occur to him to question.

I wait for a moment until whatever cosmic forces make up these rules decide the forbidden subject has lapsed and my friend comes back to himself.

"You're just as capable as half those guys in the Heralds, I keep telling you," he continues as if I'd never said anything. "They'd be lucky to have you. Or any of the other teams in the College. They all know you. They like you. I think you'd do great things in that environment."

He can obviously read the skepticism on my face.

"Or, you know, you'll always have a place here," he says with a wink. "If you really want to keep being a hero, we fight villains here every day. Teenagers. Suits and ties and business meetings. Health inspectors."

I shake my head in mock sympathy. "I don't know how you can consider any of this retirement. I'll take mad scientists and alien invaders any day."

"I do feel sometimes like I traded one group of evil masterminds for another."

I take the last bite of my sandwich and sit back in my chair. I examine my friend, my former partner, my reason for being. I know that there's something he's meant to accomplish, or else why would I still be here? But in truth, he's never looked better. Out of the outlandish costume, without the dust and debris of constant battles on his shoulders, and the strain of saving the world at the cost of...other things. He looks good.

"But seriously, Tommy. Why don't you come work for me? Be my partner here, instead?"

"Aha, so you *do* want me to be your sidekick again."

He scowls as he reaches to take my empty plate, but he remains seated. "That's not what I said. I said partner. Besides, Tabitha would love to work with you."

"She'd love to be my boss, you mean."

"That too," he chuckles. The ring of another set of customers announces the end of today's lunch. He stands and clears the table, taking my plate and our glasses back behind the counter. I remain seated, staring into the middle distance, letting this and a thousand other conversations like it over the years echo through my head.

Eventually Carl claps his hand on my shoulder, breaking me out of my reverie. I stand up and shake his hand.

"It's good seeing you again, son. I should get back to work. And you've got crime to fight," with another wink.

"You too," I say, pointing at the teenagers out on the sidewalk who seem to have taken up some kind of performance art that involves standing on the table and balancing glasses on their heads while shouting at passersby. He grunts and moves toward the patio door, but I catch his arm. "Just," I pause, wanting to drive home the whole missing bowling ball thing. But suddenly it seems silly. "Just be careful, sir."

"This is the sort of villainy I face every day now. I think I'll be all right." He smiles, knowing that's not what I was talking about.

⚖

In a hundred years, this is the oldest I've ever been.

I mean, I guess that's true of everyone. You're always the oldest you've ever been. But it's not really the same for me as for other people. I'm 25 years old. Which to most everyone else would be, I don't know, early adulthood? But I feel ancient. Every other life I've lived has been a flash. I'm a mayfly, here long enough to do my job, to perform my function and then disappear. Until the next cycle.

But not this time. Not with Carl. I was "born" as a 12-year-old. I spent a year doing minor heroics, purse snatchers and cats in trees, that sort of thing, getting the attention of my soon-to-be partner Piecemaker. He was a bona fide superhero even then. But he was falling from grace. Losing focus. Succumbing to the strain of the public eye. My purpose was to quicken him. That's always my purpose, with all the heroes I bond with. To bring them back to life. Help them find their destiny...whatever that may be. In the past, that's typically taken no more than three or four years. With me as their spunky sidekick, my heroes have always achieved whatever karmic goal the universe had in mind for them relatively quickly, leaving me to disappear back into the ether. Or very occasionally to die a tragic yet inspiring death.

I have now been Crashtest, high-flying "kid" sidekick to Piecemaker, for almost 13 years. Three times longer than I've ever lived before. And it looks like this time I may have failed to inspire my hero to his destiny. Which means...what for me, exactly? I just don't know.

The walk from the deli to my apartment isn't that long, but it's an unseasonably hot summer day. This city doesn't usually have to deal with weather like this. We're more accustomed to fighting the cold than the heat. But every once in a while, the sun remembers we're here. Today it seems to be boiling off the lake, sending a miasma of humidity oozing and bubbling through the arterial streets of New Caliburn's Row District. Within a dozen yards, I'm already soaked with sweat, my too-boyish-for-my-age dirty blond hair matted to my forehead.

The Row, the half-mile stretch just off of the waterfront that used to serve as the print district years ago, before the speakeasies took over during Prohibition, and the tech revolution of the '60s and '70s drove out the last of the large presses and publishers, has seen a bit of gentrification in the past few years. It's been cleaned up, historic structures and facades restored, new businesses — mostly restaurants, diners, and pubs— have moved in. Carl scored himself a nice location for the deli just a block down from the south end of the Verge, the narrow park that runs down the center of Union Street. Weekday afternoons, people leave the shelter of their office buildings to enjoy lunch at one of the hip new eateries that line the Row. And at night, the neighborhood buzzes with the sounds of various clubs and music venues.

The elevator in my building is out of order, because of course it is. No one is about, so I indulge myself and *fly* up the four flights to my modest one bedroom flat. Slowly, and keeping my hand on the handrail, maintaining the illusion just in case any of my neighbors should open a door as I pass. The dry, air-conditioned atmosphere of the room smacks me in the face as I enter, instantly freezing the sweat on my body, and I couldn't be happier. Oddly enough, I have always been a cold-natured person, no matter how many lives I've lived.

My furnishings are simple and sparse. A sofa bed, a recliner saved from an ignominious curbside abandonment, an old television I never actually watch. Pretty bland. I don't spend a lot of time here. The only signs that an actual human lives here are the assortment of bric-a-brac: photos, news clippings, little keepsakes from previous incarnations. I don't ever have any idea how long I've got each time I live. There's no tourist guidebook that comes with my new body and identity. I make do with a powerful instinct, some kind of genetic memory or something that grounds me as...whoever I am each time I manifest. But I don't have a convenient countdown to my final days, so it's not easy to plan ahead for next time. I can't always leave my valuable possessions to my "next of kin" or anything, and I don't get to take it with me any more than anyone else does. But after so many years, I've learned how to go back, to sift through the detritus of earlier identities and collect...just some small remembrances. To satisfy my self-reflective curiosity.

The other thing I've learned how to do is put away a little money now and then. Rainy day kind of stuff. And to pay it forward, as it were. Since I never know who or what I'll be next time around, and I never reincarnate as a relative or associate of my last persona, I can't exactly put anything in a will. I don't leave behind an estate or anything. But there are ways. For obvious reasons, I've never been much of a pack rat. I have my mission, and it satisfies me. But it definitely helps to be able to afford food and shelter when I wake up.

My one true luxury, the only thing I allow myself that might count as an extravagance, are my comic books. I have a box of a few hundred comics I've collected over several lifetimes. Each identity I've inhabited has had slightly different tastes, so there's an assortment of genres; crime comics, and war comics, and a few horror comics. Unsurprisingly, perhaps, the largest chunk of the collection is taken up with superhero comics. Most of them are gaudy, campy, four-color titles from the '50s and '60s. But there are more than a few that are adaptations of characters I myself have played. The closest things I have to old family albums.

I pull the box out of the closet, select a couple titles at random, and plop down in the recliner to try and lose myself in some silly adventures. Unfortunately, what I end up grabbing are two mob books, which don't really meet my "silly" requirement right now, and one *Adventures of Justice* annual. That one features a Piecemaker story, definitely silly and adventurous, even more so than many of the real adventures Carl and I had. But I was trying to forget this life for a little while, not wallow in it even deeper.

I read it anyway.

⚖

Superheroes love their clubs.

As long as there have been heroes, at least enough of them to gather in number, there have been clubs. Groups. Affiliations. Secret societies. Teams. The modern idea of the superhero team, a core group of a few powerful individuals working as a single unit, usually to battle a similar team of super*villains*, is kind of a holdover from the '50s. We were all a little...looser, back then. Nowadays, though organized and identifiable teams still exist, the whole thing is more structured. Blame it on the induction of the first superpowered President of the United States. There's a system now. Fewer unsanctioned, freewheeling Legions of This and Societies of That.

I come in high over the rolling green of Mallory Park and circle the campus once before setting down in the middle of Adamant Square. Welcome to the College of Arms.

The College isn't, strictly speaking, an educational institution. It is that, of course, but first and foremost it's the governing body of the superhero community. Kind of the union headquarters where all of the sanctioned, licensed, approved superheroes come to learn the "business" of being superheroes. Everybody who's anybody in the costumed community registers with the College. Not only does it come with authority and respectability (you get a fancy laminated card to carry in your super wallet), but also the perks and celebrity of it all. Lots of capes and tights enjoy the life of the magazine cover model or nightclub ingénue, and being a College member makes those things seem less frivolous.

But more importantly, the College brings heroes together. It's like a living, breathing classifieds ad for "hero seeks adventure" or "lone wolf needs temporary partner to help fight nemesis, water powers required." If you're a hero looking for some super friends, this is the place to come.

It's also the main base of operations for the Heralds. Which is why I'm here.

The Square is pretty quiet today. There are only a few students walking purposefully from one class to another, and a small group of tourists. Nobody even glances in my direction as I touch down. My yellow costume is too garish to be unobtrusive, but garish costumes are a dime a dozen around here.

The Blazon, the large heraldic lion statue atop the marble column at the Square's center, is enchanted (or possibly it's a robot, I can't recall). It changes position to indicate the current threat level heroes need to be aware of. At the moment, the lion is seated on its haunches, *sejant* I think is the term, which means all's well. If we were on high alert, the beast would be reared up and roaring. Basically, it's the superhero equivalent of DEFCON.

I make my way up the broad steps at the north end of the Square to the entrance of Hall H. I know I'm being scanned and analyzed from a hundred different directions as I cross the threshold, but the only obvious sign of any observation comes from the attractive young woman behind the reception desk. As I cross the lobby towards her, she beams a practiced smile of welcome.

"May I help you?"

"Yes, I'd like to see Helios," I say.

"I'm sorry, sir. Lord Helios is not available at the moment."

"What about Neko? Can I speak with her? It's kind of important."

"I'm very sorry, sir. Lady Nekomata is off-world as well. Many of the Heralds are attending the Acheron Discotheque reopening ceremonies on Mars this week."

Damn. I'd forgotten about the big Martian dance party everyone was so excited over.

A woman in a blue-and-white jumpsuit comes out from a hallway to the left of the reception desk. She has a towel draped around her neck and is carrying a large gym bag. She notices me and smiles.

"Crashtest. It's good to see you again, it's been a while." She extends her hand and I take it. I still feel odd being recognized without my partner. Ex-partner, I guess.

"Alice? I didn't know you were in town. I thought..."

"I'm trying to get back more often. England is...too

small, if you take my meaning? But right now I'm playing Reservist, filling in for the team while everyone's off planet-hopping." The bag she's carrying is massive, and looks far too heavy for someone her size to be holding so nonchalantly. But she's a size-shifter, so there's no telling what that does to her strength. "Sorry the big guns aren't around today. Is there anything I can help you with?"

"I hope so. I've got a lead on a returning villain, and I was hoping someone here could help me work it out."

"Absolutely, of course. Come up to my office. Maggie," she turns to the woman at the desk, "be a dear and let Sutter know I'll have to take a pass on today's meeting, would you?"

"Of course, ma'am," Maggie says.

"I don't want to interrupt anything. I can—"

"Nonsense, it's nothing. Really. Please," she motions for me to follow as she leads me past the front desk and toward a larger hallway opposite the one she just came out of. There's a bank of elevators with elaborate bas relief scenes of epic battles on the doors. The wall across from the elevators is lined with framed pictures of heroes past and present. There's Helios, regal in his primary colors and flowing cape. And his better half, and co-leader of the Heralds, Nekomata. Her picture features her at some UN function, her usual battle armor replaced by drapes of silk and damask. She's shaking hands ceremonially with a dignitary of some sort, who looks perhaps slightly uncomfortable being so close to the statuesque goddess with the head of a Bengal tiger.

We board an elevator, and as the doors close I catch a glimpse of another picture further down the hall. A picture of the '70s hero The Silver Rage and his sidekick Penny. I smile at the memory. I enjoyed being Penny. She annoyed Silver endlessly with her terrible jokes and cockeyed optimism. But ultimately she — I — helped him heal the darkness he struggled with inside and channel his anger. He did some amazing things after that, as I recall.

That was a good life.

The doors open again and deposit us on the fourth floor. A series of winding hallways takes us to the door of Alice's office, which she opens with a thumbprint scan. Inside is a warm, welcoming space filled with plush sofas piled high with pillows of every imaginable color and texture, and floor-to-ceiling bookshelves lined with volumes both stodgy (*A Dissertation on Nebuchadnezzar's Dream*) and whimsical (*The Complete Works of Dr. Seuss*). And, of course, Lewis Carroll.

"Make yourself at home. Can I get you anything? It's cliché, I know, but I'm having tea. You like some?"

"No, thank you. I'm good." As an afterthought, "Isn't it too hot for tea?"

"It's never too hot for tea." She drops her duffle on the floor by the door and begins some complicated mad scientist laboratory cluttering in the little kitchenette. I shift a green fuzzy monster pillow out of the way and sink into the sofa. Suddenly I don't feel quite so vivid in my emergency-sign-yellow tights and cape.

She joins me after a moment, sipping something vaguely minty-smelling from a cup which reads "Drink Me."

"So tell me what's going on. You said you've got a line on a villain coming back?"

"What do you know about Mister History?"

She thinks for a moment. "Was that the guy who used to build Time Bombs? You and Piecemaker stopped him last year some time, I thought."

"Closer to two years, actually. And it was Piecemaker that did it, I was busy with those stupid Split Seconds doppelgängers of his. But yeah."

"I thought he died or disappeared or something."

"He did. But we know that rarely means anything."

She shifts in her seat and sets her tea on the table between us. "Okay, true enough. So what have you got?"

I explain to her about the device Piecemaker destroyed, and the bowling ball that was left behind, and its recent disappearance in the mysterious museum fire. She listens intently until I finish. Then she retrieves her College-issued tablet from her desk and begins tapping out search parameters on the holographic keyboard it projects in front of her.

"What does Carl think about all of this?" she asks,

studying the scroll of data she's pulled up.

"Well, that's the problem. He's kind of retired."

"Kind of?"

I just shrug. She gives me a sympathetic half-smile before returning to her search. "There's...more he's meant to do, Alice. I can't really explain how I know. I just know. And I'm convinced this missing ball is no coincidence. History always seemed like a joke, but he wasn't. He was deadly serious, even with all his goofy B-movie doomsday plots. He disappeared into the time stream more than once, so I'm not really sure why everyone assumes this time he's really dead.

"He's going to come back," I say, trying to sound serious rather than desperate, maybe pulling it off. "He always does. And he'll want revenge on the people who 'killed' him. The fire and the bowling ball are just the first signs."

She sets her tablet aside, its light show interface winking off with a faint *blip*.

"Well, there's nothing in the College database that suggests the 'incognizable artifact,' as they call it, is dangerous, just undefined." Off of my look, "Which I grant you is really just another way of saying dangerous, and should've merited better security than sitting in a display case at some sideshow museum. But from what little I could understand in all the notes, it seems to have been just what you called it: a bowling ball. A plain, polished sphere of black and yellow rock, with some residual temporal distortion field, likely an aftereffect of its use in History's device."

"I'm not sure any of this is actually making me feel any better," I say. The frustration edges my voice more than I'd like.

"Look, Tommy, I believe you, for what it's worth. I completely agree there are more things in heaven and earth, etc. I'll keep looking into this, and I'll let you know if I find anything. I'll have Sagan take a look at the scene."

"Who's Sagan?"

"He's one of the new kids. Another Reservist filling in while Mom and Dad are away." She smiles. "He can see things. Weird things. Maybe he'll be able to spot something everyone else has missed."

"I'd really appreciate that, Alice. Thank you." We both stand up, the meeting apparently over. "Listen, I know you're busy and everything, but I don't suppose you'd consider having a chat with Carl. He's—"

She holds up a hand to cut me off, while her other hand moves to the side of her head. It's an affectation I recognize, putting a finger to an imaginary earpiece. I know she must be receiving a call on her Heralds-issued implant, a stream of information letting her know of some breaking crisis. After a few seconds, she looks back at me.

"Since you're suited up anyway, how'd you like to come on a ride-along?"

⚖

That did *not* go well.

In a very real sense, I've been involved in the superhero business for as long as there's been a superhero business. Longer, technically. But I've always been the sidekick. That's my job. I'm here to guide the real heroes, to be the inspiration or incentive they need to do heroic deeds. I either lighten their load or serve as their comic relief. Or, in a very few cases, I'm the tragedy that pushes them to their ultimate heroic destiny. What I'm not, what I've never been in all my various lives, is a team player. The heroes I fought side-by-side with today didn't need my guidance or inspiration. My instinct is always to play for the cosmic camera, to set my partner up for the metaphorical splash page hero shot. But removed from my natural habitat of sidekick, those instincts just get in the way.

No one was hurt, thank God. It wasn't a major battle, just some minor supervillain and a group of unpowered minions. So textbook that my clubfooted efforts to help Alice and the others clean things up were just embarrassing. Which is fine, I'm not worried about embarrassing myself. Often that's a sidekick's job. But I'm still wearing the gold-and-black costume of Crashtest. I'm still known as the kid partner to Piecemaker, despite not being a kid anymore. What people will remember from today is not how clumsy and awkward I was, but how amateurish Piecemaker's partner was.

So now I hang in the night sky, nearly a mile straight up from the site of today's fiasco. Even from here I can make out the flashing blue lights of the remaining emergency units, still cleaning up the mess we made. I drift upward, hoping that distance will obscure the details; from far enough away, maybe the city lights will blur and wash out the strobing lights of the police.

Gravity is the weakest force in the universe. Did you know that? And yet flight is statistically the least common superpower. Oh, it seems like one of the basics, but that's mostly due to comic books and Saturday morning cartoons. They feed the public perception of heroes and villains, and everyone just naturally assumes all heroes can fly. Sadly, that's not the case. I've done this, been the embodiment of the sidekick stereotype (technically, you could say I am the reason there *is* a sidekick stereotype) over 20 times. This is only the third time I've had the power to fly. And the first two hardly count. Once I had magic boots that let me walk on air, which was pretty cool, but it still meant I was in essence running to get anywhere. And the last time, I could fly by swelling up like a helium balloon. Not really my finest hour, but I made the best of it.

But this time? In this life, I get to soar. Truly, actually soar. Just like in the comic books.

As I slowly rise upward, watching the city that has been

my home more often than any other shrink below me, I feel the feeble grasp of the entire planet trying to pull me back down. I ignore it. I realize I have no idea how high I can go. Or how fast. Or how long I can stay aloft before, I don't know, power fatigue or whatever kicks in. It's strange to think about, but I never really question how my powers work. Every time I wake up in a new life, I always just have an innate sense about things. I know just enough, subconsciously, to play my role. I usually learn things about myself and my abilities as I go, of course. In the line of duty, as the plucky partner of this hero or that heroine, I naturally discover new ways to use whatever gifts the universe has given me each time. But it's never about me. I'm not here to play with my new toys. So that's not ever what I think about.

I've been Tommy Pigeon, aka Crashtest, for a long time. I've had a lot of adventures with Piecemaker. When I first teamed up with him, all I could do was fly and wrap myself up in a force field. So my signature move became the "crashtest special"; I'd fly full-speed (or what I assumed at the time was full-speed) into the bad guys with my shield up and basically hit them like a runaway car. Hence the goofy name. That annoying reporter that used to be obsessed with Carl came up with it after we saved her from Gunrunner and his gang on my first public appearance. It was kind of derogatory, but it stuck, and I just went with it. Yellow-and-black costume designed to look like those crashtest dummies from the TV commercials, and oversized goggles to complete the slightly mannequin-esque look, although they actually protect my eyes from the flash of my shield. I always thought it was poor power design that my force field flashes and glows so brightly when anything hits it, and yet my eyes never seem to adjust for it.

In any of my previous lives, that would have been it. A few years of derring-do and first class sidekickery, my hero achieves whatever destiny the universe meant for him or her, and I'd shuffle off, one way or another, to start fresh somewhere else. As some*one* else. But having so long to flesh out this life, so to speak, I've learned some more tricks than I usually get the opportunity to. For instance, I discovered that I can share my powers with others this time around. That was huge fun, for both of us, when I figured that out. Carl got a kick out of charging into a fight by air. For a few years the world pretty much assumed that Piecemaker could fly on his own, I guess forgetting that he never had in the years before I came along. We didn't encourage that belief...but we didn't really rush to set the record straight either. Then, when I began sharing my shields more and more with innocent bystanders to protect them during big battles, everyone sort of figured it out.

As my mind wanders, I continue to float-not-quite-fly upward, higher and higher. I figure I'm probably three miles up at this point. My shield, normally only visible when bullets and bad guys are bouncing off of it, is glowing very faintly. Again, I don't really know the pseudo-science mechanics of how my force field works. But I know that it protects me from harm, of pretty much any variety. Among other things, it provides a certain amount of protection from environmental extremes. I have to guess that at this altitude, it must be pretty cold, yet I barely notice. Another limit I've never really tested.

From this distance, the city is an amber crescent pressed up against the black hole of Lake Superior. Tiny glints and sparkles play across my shield as some mist or rain, or possibly, less romantically, a swarm of insects cascades around me (not the first time I've smirked at the image of myself as a giant bug zapper). I lay myself out flat, face to the earth, and imagine instead that what lies beneath, the twinkling light of New Caliburn, is actually a giant funhouse-distorted reflection of me, exaggerated out of all proportion by the dark mirror of the great lake.

I hold on to that thought for a few minutes before deciding it's way too self-aggrandizing. Not to mention loaded with complicated metaphors and implications I'm not really smart enough to explore. So I roll over, still willing myself upward oh so slowly, stretched out on an imaginary mattress, my hands behind my head. I look up...and out. And I gaze into a different kind of dark mirror, with smaller glints of light, silver rather than gold. Possibly still a reflection, but not one that makes me feel large and important at all.

⚖

I answer the door on the fourth knock. Tabitha is standing there holding a large plastic bag with the Cook's Deli logo on the side. She's decked out in her usual casual punk attire of jeans, unlaced boots, and stylishly ripped T-Shirt. This time it's for a band I've never heard of, Estonian Polar Bear Seduction. At least I think it's a band.

I'm wearing Mighty Mouse pajamas.

"Morning, T-bird," she says.

"Did...did we have a thing today?" I ask, befuddled. Tabitha is my little sister. Sort of. I've been adopted many times by my partners in past incarnations, but heroes are typically single, lonely, often orphans or outcasts themselves. It's rare that someone I'm sent to help has a family. That's usually one of the roles I end up filling. So I've been legally adopted more than once, had an assortment of guardians and foster parents. But this is the first time I've had a sibling. It's taken some getting used to.

"No, but you had a thing yesterday," she says, moving inside and heading toward the folding card table that serves as my desk slash dining suite. "I thought you might need to talk."

"Thanks, Tab, but..." I begin, then give up. I move to help her clear the research rubble off the table and make room for the perhaps-a-tad-over-the-top feast she proceeds to lay out for us.

"Nice suit, by the way," she mocks, nodding her head to my sleepwear. "Is that the new costume? I like it."

I sigh and take a seat, thanking her for the sandwich she passes to me and staring pointedly at the two sandwiches, soup, salad, chips and pickles on her side. "Umm...are you pregnant?"

She glares at me in mock fury, though there seems to be a hint more steel in her eyes than I remember.

"I'm hungry, shithead. Shut up. I'm going to go raid your fridge for some tasty beverages now. I'll likely be bringing back something specifically to dump over your head for that remark, so if you have a preference...keep it to your damn self." She punches me in the shoulder as she walks by.

I begin unwrapping my breakfast, not surprised to see the egg white wrap with turkey bacon that Tab always makes for me when she's working at the deli, no matter what I actually request. I usually only get to have breakfast with her on mornings after her graveyard shift. She's recently returned to school, much to my surprise. She never really got on with any of her professors before. But she's making another go of it, which eats up the last of her free time. School during the day, work all night at your retired superhero father's restaurant, have breakfast with your less-retired superhero sidekick adopted brother, then back to school. I have no idea where she gets the energy from.

"Hey, there's beer in here," she shouts from the kitchen. "Like, actual beer."

"Help yourself," I reply.

"Are you even old enough to buy beer?" She sets an open bottle in front of me and sits across the table. She has two bottles for herself. "For dumping on you later," she responds to my suspicious look.

"How old do you think I am?" I joke.

"Well, you look like one of the kids from *Sesame Street*, but Dad assures us he didn't actually kidnap you as a baby. You're a big boy, I know. You only look fourteen."

I lift the bottle of beer to my lips with a smirk and swallow a mouthful of the bitter brown poison. I kind of hate alcohol. I only have it in the apartment because, as Tab points out, I still look like a teenager. I bought beer in a panic, suddenly realizing I may not reset this time. I may actually have to do grown-up things. Grown-ups have beer in their refrigerators, right? Though drinking it had actually never occurred to me. Clunking the bottle back down on the table, I say through teeth gritted in mild disgust, "I'll always look fourteen."

"Jerk."

"It's not my fault," I say defensively.

"Oh I'm sure," she sneers. "It's genetics." There's an edge to the word, which I'm pretty sure I only pick up on because of the years the two of us have spent having conversations like this. The arguments. She probably doesn't mean anything by it. Probably isn't even aware she said it. "Or just good clean living. All those superhero battles. It's like the Sidekick Diet, right?"

"Something like that."

We eat in silence for a while, and even though she has three times as much food as I do, she finishes first. Leaning back in her seat, she glances around the apartment. Her eyes fall on the stack of papers and files that have accumulated at the foot of my fold-out sofa bed. I've spent months watching crime reports, studying villains' patterns and habits. Waiting for some sign that Piecemaker was still needed. The morning sun has found a break in the heavy curtains and is shining a golden spotlight directly on the news clipping about the museum fire.

"So," she says casually. "What's up?"

"Nothing," I reply. She looks back at me and raises an eyebrow. "It's nothing, Tab." I start clearing the table, taking particular pleasure in dumping the vile toxic drink down the drain.

"Even if I believed you, which I don't, it would still be a story at least. C'mon, there's nothing there you want to talk about? Not even anything you could embellish for me?"

I know where she's going with this, and I can't help a sad smile. Carl had already been separated from his wife for a year by the time I came into the picture. The divorce was finalized shortly thereafter. His time in the tights had taken its toll on the marriage. Tab's mom got the house in the suburbs, away from the city and its hero academies and spandex politics. She also got Tabitha. Carl got an apartment downtown, and me. Which made for some seriously awkward weekends when Tab would come visit. I was like the son from a second marriage that had to get along with the daughter from the first. Only my "mother" was Carl's superhero adventures, not some hot young secretary or something. A stepmom would've been easy for Tab to hate. But she loved the fact that her dad was a comic book character come to life. And though she resented me as the sidekick that took her daddy away, she also devoured the stories I would tell her. She had her very own comic book being written right there in front of her. But Carl refused to bring any of his costumed life home with him. He didn't want his daughter to be hurt by any of the craziness he dealt with, and so didn't like talking about it with her. In public, he was, for a few years at least, a golden boy of the superhero set. But in his private life he tried to be...normal. And so Tab's insatiable desire for thrilling tales of Piecemaker battling the Primate Pope and his Monk-Ee's, or helping the Heralds fend off the Xi'ard Armada from Dimension Pi, ended up coming from me. And thus was an uneasy truce, and eventually bond, formed.

"I was at the College doing some research, and Alice invited me along on a call. It was nothing. A local skirmish that didn't need me involved. Too many cooks in the kitchen, I guess."

She doesn't look very satisfied with that answer. Growing up, I used to try and sneak in the occasional story taken from my previous lives. I had hoped that the relationship with my "sister" would somehow be different enough that the universe would let me share even small bits of my past with her. But it never worked. At the first mention of any detail the Powers That Be deemed off limits, Tabitha's eyes would glaze over and she'd tune out until I returned to the approved narrative. This is far from the first time I've wished I could talk about some of my finer moments with her.

"Did I ever tell you about the time your dad saved the world?" She had started to push back her chair and get up, but she sits back down and gives me an odd look. "This was a few years after I became his partner, and we were sort of experimenting with being out on our own, away from the teams and the leagues and all that. I'd convinced your dad he needed to find his own rogue's gallery, y'know? I thought he needed a nemesis. So we followed a lead we'd gotten off some squirrelly little villain pawn broker and headed south. Way south. Supposedly there was a new evildoer who'd discovered a buried UFO in Antarctica, and he was just days away from getting it working again, complete with all its alien weaponry. Taking apart weapons and gadgets and doomsday machines has always kind of been your dad's thing, so this seemed right up his alley."

Tabitha is leaning back in her seat now, listening

intently.

"I'm not really sure what we were expecting," I continue. "Some base of giant robots digging massive holes in the ice shelf, maybe? What we found was a small camp of two-bit thugs huddled in tents around the mouth of a tiny little cave in the side of a glacier. They were barely alive, starved and freezing. We did them a favor by beating them senseless and tying them up. At least they'd be going to a nice, warm prison somewhere with hot food when this was all said and done. When we made our way down into the ice cave, we didn't find some new villain trying to make his mark with a recycled flying saucer. We found Mister History, wannabe time lord and first class schmendrick. And he did indeed have a buried flying saucer, but he wasn't trying to dig it out from under the South Pole. He had turned it into another of his crazy time machines and was using it to send the core of the planet back in time. Basically, I guess, he was trying to reset Earth to the way it was billions of years ago. You know? When it was still coalescing from the cosmic rubble. Essentially he would have wiped us all out, just for...well, I have no idea what for. We never knew what in the world he thought his crazy plans would accomplish. Maybe he'd rather be ruler of a molten world than a D-list villain on a planet he could actually live on.

"In any case, crashed alien spacecraft or wacky MacGuyvered time machine, Piecemaker could've dealt with the thing easily enough. He could've used his power to pull it into its component parts and used them to make a cage to lock History in, or whatever. Plug pulled, world saved. Unfortunately, History wasn't alone. He'd found himself a tribe of...well, cavemen. Cliché, club-wielding cavemen. Hundreds of them. They were like extras from a Buster Keaton movie. But they were fast, and strong, and somehow knew that we were the enemy. And like I said, clubs. Not guns Piecemaker could pull apart. Not complex devices, things with moving parts. No seams for his power to get ahold of. Just solid wooden sticks that they proceeded to pummel us with.

"It's funny now, thinking the world almost ended because Piecemaker and Crashtest got pig-piled by a bunch of leopard-skin-wearing Neanderthals. But...we were cocky. And those little buggers hit hard. My force fields weren't as strong then. And your dad wasn't expecting a street brawl with Stone Age unibrow minions. And while we were fighting, Mister History's machine was continuing to burrow down into the center of the Earth, while he stood on top of it cackling like a lunatic."

I pause for a long minute. Some of this is hard to remember. Either because it's painful, or because sometimes my memories from different lives start to bleed together. I can't be sure which.

"So what did you guys do?" she asks. It's like we're kids again. I let myself imagine for a moment what it would be like if the last ten years hadn't happened. If neither one of us had grown up.

"Well, your dad fought his way through the horde and made it to the ship. I did my best to shield us both as he began fighting with History, and I kept the cavemen occupied. But the machine was doing things to us. There were these waves of alien energy washing off of it, playing havoc with our powers. My shields kept getting stronger and weaker, blinking on and off. Carl's power, too. One minute he'd feel more powerful than he ever had, and the next it would fade to nothing. He could never get a lock on the ship long enough to do much more than pull a few panels off before another wave of energy hit him and his powers went wonky again. And there were just so many cavemen. We were outnumbered, and off-balance, and out of time.

"And then...the cave collapsed. The ice of the glacier and the rock of the mountain just crumbled and came down on all of us, crushing the machine, the cavemen and their sticks, and, we thought, Mister History. Oh, and us, of course. But whatever weird energy it was that thing was putting out boosted my powers just at the right moment, and I was able to get a shield up around the two of us strong enough to protect us. But...only us. And as the ship was destroyed, the boost quickly faded, so Carl and I made our way up out of the cave as fast as I could fly us.

"As it was all happening, I assumed the fight and the

machine and all of it had just caused a massive cave-in. But I found out later it was your dad. He'd gotten the same power boost I had at the end, and as the machine started to phase out of time or whatever, and he lost his grip on it, his ability to rip it apart and shut it down, he made a decision. With his power amped up to the nth degree, he reached out to the mountain around us and pulled *it* apart. He chose to pull a glacier thousands of years old into its component pieces, chunks of ice the size of train cars and boulders the size of houses just...came apart. And then came down. And Mister History's crazy machine broke. And the world didn't end. Or reset. Or whatever."

We both sit then, quietly reflecting on the tale I've just told.

"So," I say, a little embarrassed.

"Why..." she begins, "why haven't I ever heard that story before?"

"Carl...your dad doesn't like to talk about it. He doesn't consider it one of our finest moments."

"But why? You guys, like, saved the world. Literally."

"Your *dad* saved the world," I correct. "And it was ugly. He's not proud of the way he did it. Doesn't want people to know what happened. Doesn't..." I look at her again, sheepishly. "Doesn't want you to know."

"So...why did you tell me?"

I cross to the windows, consider opening the curtains but instead reach up and pull them tighter closed, shutting out the knife's edge of light that had been cutting into the room. I stand there, hand gripping the dusty fabric, staring as if I were seeing out another window, watching the city street below me as it is in my mind.

"In 1943, I was partnered with that German superhero, Soldat, the guy that fought alongside the Allies." I know she can't hear any of this right now, I don't have to turn around and see the vacant look in her eyes to know this subject is taboo with my cosmic bosses. But I'm talking for myself this time.

"He was a good man, but also very violent. It was a violent time, of course. We always try to clean it up when we talk about it, to make it more colorful, less gruesome. But it *was* gruesome. Soldat was a warrior, and we were fighting against monsters. And I did what I could to bring some light to him, to all of them. But he had his own mission, and it meant getting bloody. And there was collateral damage.

"For almost a century now, even when we costumes aren't fighting such indisputable evil as we were back then, there's always been collateral damage. People caught in the crossfire. Needless death and destruction. It's gradually just become part of the game. We all just accept it. But I think your dad...I think he got tired of accepting it."

"Wait, 1943? What the hell are you talking about?" she asks.

I turn around like there's been a gunshot. She spoke.

She reacted. *In context.* She asked a question in response to what I was saying. As if...

There's a whisper, a rustle of air. The space between me and Tab is filling with faint, feathery white light, like electric mist. It's only for a fraction of a second, almost too brief to even be sure I saw it, and then there's a figure standing in my living room. Floating, actually, about a foot off the floor. He's small, and slight, even smaller than me. He seems to be naked except for a cloak and hood. His skin is jet black. Blacker than black, almost a hole in the air in front of me. And that hole is filled with stars.

I instantly wrap a shield around myself and another around Tabitha. She's standing now, near the kitchen, but I notice that she doesn't seem afraid. She hasn't moved away but actually stepped around the table, come closer into the room. She's looking directly at the intruder, and her hands are clenched in fists at her side.

"You're Crashtest," the figure says, and his voice is surprisingly normal. After years of playing the hero game, I naturally expect someone this outlandish, who makes so dramatic an entrance, to have a booming, intimidating voice. But he just sounds like a guy. "I apologize for disturbing you, but there's a situation I believe you may wish to attend to."

Suddenly, there comes the sound of an explosion in the distance. The apartment trembles, dust falls from the ceiling.

"Oh dear," the soft-spoken man says. "I suggest you hurry. This could be--" He flickers and then blinks out of existence. The air loses the faint static charge I hadn't even been aware it had before, and Tabitha and I are alone again. At the sound of another explosion of some kind outside, I throw open the curtains and look out east across my little corner of the city. In the distance, there's a column of black smoke rising.

"Is that the waterfront?" Tabitha asks, joining me at the window. Then the apartment shudders again, and windows in the building across the street shatter. "*Earthquake!*" Tab yells.

Without a word, I lift her in my arms and carry us both through the glass of my window, shields sparking as we burst out into the air above Dyer Street. I fly quickly to the open area a block away, where the Row meets at Five Points, and set Tabitha down in the plaza. "Stay here, stay clear of the buildings." I drop the shield I put around her and lift up and east, streaking toward the smoke and rising sounds of destruction.

And yes, I'm still wearing my Mighty Mouse pajamas.

ᛉᛉ

The smoke seems to be coming from Railway Park, about eight blocks to the northeast. I arc in high over the condos and office buildings that border the park and swing in across the top of the mall. There, in the large cobblestone courtyard, I see a burning crater about the size of a swimming pool. I circle once, looking for bad guys, but the only signs of life are the Saturday morning crowds fleeing the lawns and park benches, many of them heading inside the mall.

The Roundhouse Mall is built in the old railway maintenance building, a massive three-story semicircle which used to service the trains that dominated shipping and commerce in New Caliburn in the early twentieth century. Now it's a sleek brick-and-glass shopping center and tourist attraction. The center of the circle formed by the Roundhouse is the Coal Car Diner, a converted train car that serves breakfast and lunch from the rotating turntable, old tracks radiating outward from it like spokes on a giant wheel. The smoking crater is right at the edge of that turntable, debris and detritus being carried along its perimeter like a smudge as the platform continues its slow rotation. Early morning diners are hurrying to exit the area and seek what they obviously assume is the safety of the mall.

I approach the crater, and through the haze, I see a figure lying motionless, partially buried. The rubble is superheated, glowing hot in some places, but my shields protect me as I rush to pull the person out. And then I freeze.

It's a man, large and muscular, wearing the remains of

a silver-and-white costume, cape tattered and tangled around his body. Even covered in blood and soot, I still recognize the chiseled angles of his face, the stark white hair, the frostbitten grey of his eyes as he struggles to look at me.

Enceladus.

My former partner. The hero I was "assigned to" before Carl. Almost twenty years ago, and a world away.

"E?" I say, horrified.

"Don't—" he chokes off. He's barely conscious, not really seeing me, though of course he wouldn't recognize me anyway. "Don't let her...have—"

For the first time, I notice he's holding something, clutching it close to his chest. As I kneel beside him, he tries in vain to shift, to hand me the object. I gently take his hand and pull his arm aside to see what he's holding.

Well, I'll be damned. The bowling ball.

I'd allow myself a moment of...I'm not sure what exactly. Amazement? Shock? Perhaps just a bit of, "I *knew* it?" But then the world explodes. Enceladus and I are both hurled into the air as the ground beneath us erupts in fumes and fire. I cast a shield around Enceladus as he falls back to the ground almost thirty feet away. I, however, stay aloft and keep my eyes on what was a crater but now is more of a gaping wound, an open chimney belching ash and molten rock. There's no doubt in my mind that the not-as-dead-as-everyone-thought Mister History is about to rise up out of that maelstrom, nestled in the cockpit of some new ridiculous robot spider from the future, or maybe this time he'll be riding a T. rex. He's come back for the ball, the artifact, whatever it actually is, to use as the power source for his next temporal apocalypse.

Where's Carl? Where's Piecemaker?

But the only movement I see in the crater isn't a giant robot, or a dinosaur. No laughing maniac with antigravity boots and a staff shaped like the arms of a clock. Down low, scrabbling up out of the hole, a small, feminine figure. She climbs to the edge of the rubble and surveys her surroundings. She appears to be carved out of stone, rough-hewn, sharp. There are cracks and fissures in her skin that glow, revealing a molten inner core. And then I see her face.

The woman is Io, self-proclaimed Living Flame of Jupiter. She was the archnemesis of Enceladus, the Spear of Saturn. Even back then, when I was the sidekick caught up in the middle of their war, I thought it was all kind of silly. They were both very melodramatic and over-the-top, very faux-Shakespearean about everything. Also, Io never created actual volcanoes in the middle of the city like she seems to have done now. She used to be just a young woman, rather mousy actually, with simple fire-based powers to offset E's ice-based ones. And she had a really goofy costume...not nice, like the pajamas I'm presently wearing.

Then she killed me, and things got a little more serious.

I don't hold a grudge. That's the way it had to be. It kicked Enceladus into gear, got him to step up and accept the responsibility that a crazy hero/villain rivalry brings with it. Last I'd heard, Io had been gone for a decade, and E was living it up as the resident champion of the great white north somewhere.

But now they're here, and Enceladus is unconscious, maybe dying, and the living statue that used to be a goofy villainess is stomping toward my city. Literally stomping, her every step echoes and booms like a cannon shot. I look around quickly, judging where E's body is, where all the civilians are. Whether there are any other heroes nearby. No luck. So I ramp up my shields and turn back to engage. She's not going for the city, or the people, or even her nemesis, prone and vulnerable. She's made her way to the bowling ball, which flew from E's grasp when we were both blown up. As she takes it in her hand and lifts it, they both...swell. She and the ball grow, their relative sizes doubling in a matter of seconds. The bowling ball loses its glossy black and yellow marble look and begins to boil, becoming a sphere of sulphurous oranges and greens, now almost as big as a motorcycle. Io herself shrieks, or perhaps it's the sound of the tectonic plates that now form her skin shifting as she balloons to nearly 12 feet tall, the seams and cracks covering her body oozing molten lava.

Simultaneous with all of these really alarming transformations, the earth around us lifts and shakes. Even in the air, I can feel vibrations as the quake ripples outward from Io and the cobblestone courtyard buckles. Some of the huge plate glass windows fronting the mall shatter, and over the sound of the destruction, I begin to hear screams.

I plow full force into Io's midsection, giving her the most powerful crashtest special I've ever executed. There's a blinding flash as my shield takes the impact, but even with its protection, I feel like I just flew into the side of a mountain. Io is caught off-guard, and the ball is knocked from her hands as my momentum carries us both into the Coal Car Diner. We tangle in the twisted metal of the train car, and as my vision clears, I begin to hover up and back, trying to free myself and get some distance. I don't have super strength or anything, I just fly really fast and hit things. It won't do me any good to trade punches with Io right now.

She has a different idea, however. Still blinking away stars from my shieldflash, I feel a stony fist close around my ankle, and I'm swung like a sledgehammer into the ground. Another blinding flash, and I find myself staring up at the blue morning sky, buried in a foot-deep, me-shaped hole. I spend just a second wondering how cartoonish this must look. I just survived what has to have been one of the hardest hits I've ever taken, dazed but relatively unhurt. I feel like the Coyote after some typically disastrous scheme to catch the Roadrunner has left him to plunge over the edge of a cliff. All I'm missing is a little sign to hold up that reads, "ouch."

Then Io pulls herself clear of the diner wreckage and steps square on my face as she heads back out to retrieve the ball. I come back to my senses and stop worrying about looking professional.

As I pry myself out of the ground, I notice that, while Io and the ball both still look transformed from their brief contact with each other, both have shrunk back down to the sizes they were before. But with each thunderous stride she takes toward the artifact, the tremors get worse. We're on the still-spinning turntable platform now, and the ball has come to rest near its edge. Due to our rotation, it is currently situated directly in front of the mall's main entrances. What windows remain are rattling, bricks crumbling loose. I see the faces of people who thought they'd be safe inside. I feel the impact of every footfall. I remember what happened when Io touched that thing for only a second. And I'm still trying to climb up out of my pothole. I'll never get to her before she can reach the ball. And when she does, that mall is gone. In blind desperation, I throw a shield around the bowling ball, trying to keep her from being able to grab it. Knowing it won't work.

But it does. Somehow, I manage to wrap a shield around the object just as Io reaches for it. I've never been able to shield inanimate objects before. I can only share my powers with living things. But Io's hand brushes up against a glittering golden force field mere inches before touching the pulsing sphere. I...I'm stunned.

And Io is pissed, because as she fumbles and pounds on the shield, she lets out an otherworldly roar, and the earth around us splits. The entire turntable platform tilts and grinds to a halt, the heavy gears beneath screeching. The face of the mall structure begins to collapse, and the Roundhouse sign on top of the clock tower in its center shears lose and begins to fall. Even the hotel attached to the south end of the mall semicircle, the only building within 200 yards more than a few stories high, begins to shift.

Everything around me stutters into slow motion as I watch tons of glass, steel, and concrete collapse on top of the people huddled inside. Innocent bystanders, about to be crushed by the random arrogance of two supers fighting about who even knows what?

"*NO!*" I scream out in horror. With the same desperation and fury I felt when I reached out to protect the ball, I cast every last bit of my shield powers around every single face I can see under that cascade of debris. Time ramps back up to speed as the sound of destruction pummels me. Through the choking cloud of dust and the smoke of the growing fires, it's impossible to see if I succeeded in shielding anyone. The mall is gone, just a sagging lump of girders and stone. But I can feel them. Hundreds of them. I can feel the weight and pressure against my power as it holds open little pockets of what I hope is safety for all of those people. I have no way of knowing if I was in time, or if my powers will hold for long, being spread so thin over so many different individuals. But Io is still raging, the ground still shaking, and I have to get her away from here.

What little shield I still have left for myself is weakened and reduced enough that I easily slip out of the hole I've been stuck in. I remember from my time as Enceladus' sidekick that both his and Io's powers were rooted to the Earth somehow. They both needed to maintain contact with the ground for their powers to function. I take a couple of shaky steps forward and then launch myself at the villain. I close my eyes against the flash as I slam into her, but this time I don't just ram her into something hard. This time, I wrap my arms around her and turn up, carrying us both skyward. As I suspected, the second her feet leave the ground, the tremors stop.

Unfortunately, here I am, trading blows with the superstrong villain made of hot rock. In its diluted state, my shield takes much of the brunt of the powerful blows Io now rains down on my head and shoulders. But not all of it. I can feel every impact, each punch twisting my head around, filling my eyes with stars not just from my shield's light show. And she burns, like hugging a red-hot stove. I look into her face and see none of the campy, cartoon villain I remember from my past life. I see none of the humanity, as warped and twisted as it may have been even then. All I see is fire and rage and primal instinct.

And then one more horrifying realization hits me. I can't fly her away from here like I'd planned to. I can't take her out to the middle of the Great Lake and drop her in, miles from the city. I can't even take her to the College of Arms, to let the real heroes and heavy hitters deal with her. I can't get more than a few hundred yards from here or the shields I've put up around those people will fade. I have to stay close to maintain them or all those people will die. Have I already gone too far? Am I too high above them?

I stop climbing, and in my distraction, the problem is solved, sort of, as Io lands a blow so powerful it hurls me back down to the ground. My fall, or rather my landing, knocks the breath out of me. I struggle to rise to my feet, looking around for my opponent. I think she came down somewhere over—

And I'm punched in the face again. I manage to catch myself with my flight before I'm thrown too far back. I even manage to keep my feet, which considering it felt like I was just hit by a bus, I'm understandably proud of. But no time for that. I have to get her back off the ground, at least enough to keep her from shaking this place apart any further. I manage to suck in some air at last and square my shoulders to face her. As she storms forward, I can just make out the *pop pop pop* of gunfire and see Io stagger to a halt about twenty feet from me. More gunfire, and I see tiny little flashes, little Christmas light sparks of color across her body. She reflexively raises her arm to shield her face, and two perfectly symmetrical divots appear in the palm of her hand, chips of stone flying away.

I spare a glance over my shoulder and see The Actioneer, standing majestically atop the remains of the diner, twin .45's blazing. The cavalry is, it seems, finally here. Unfortunately, The Actioneer's bullets are digital. Being a video game character come to life, his weapons are all just special effects. They're the opposite of my powers, only really useful against inanimate objects, with very little lasting effect on real people. In this case, they sting and distract, but Io quickly recovers and she stomps her foot, sending a tidal wave of stone and dirt rolling to bury her attacker. The Actioneer dives forward over it, nimbly rolling to his feet several feet away, maintaining his hail of computer-generated gunfire.

I turn back to Io, now basically ignoring the bullets as she continues toward me. Or more probably toward the ball, which is somewhere behind me. I clench my fists and brace for impact, but Io's approach is cut dramatically short on account of having a train engine hammered down on top of her. Alice, grown to her impressive full size, steps back from the train car, catching her breath. Even as big as she is, that was a strain, wielding something that heavy with that much force. She looks at me for a second, tilting her head. "Crashtest?" she says, surprised. I can hear sirens in the distance.

"That," I begin, trying not to collapse to my knees.

"I'm not really sure that will stop her." I motion to what had been a lovingly restored turn of the century locomotive, now flattened and crumpled on top of the petite but terrifying woman I've been fighting. And as if on cue, there comes another rumble from deep in the ground. Then another, even stronger one which finally gives me an excuse to fall down for a minute, and causes Alice to stagger back a few steps. The remains of the train engine begin to glow.

"Who is that?" Alice asks, shrinking down just slightly to lower her center of gravity and keep her balance. Molten metal begins to slough away, and Io pushes a hand through, clawing her way to freedom.

"I have to keep her off the ground," I say frantically. "There are people in there, in the mall. I can't shield them for long, you guys have to get them out. Please." Another shudder and what remains of the clock tower tumbles down. "*Hurry!*" I'm practically in tears.

A heartbeat as she considers me. Then she turns, grows to full size once more, and heads toward the destruction of the mall. The Actioneer is already in motion, climbing back atop the diner car. With only a glance, he assesses the situation, takes aim, and fires a single shot. There's a metal snapping sound, louder than the gunshot itself, and a steel cable stretched between the crumbling clock tower and the fallen mall sign frays and gives way. The sign sags, swings to the side, and smashes into a large slab of concrete from the collapsed roof. The concrete shifts slightly, then slides forward across the steep pile of rubble beneath it, like a surfboard down the face of a towering wave. And just like that, there's a large opening into the interior of the mall, into which The Actioneer immediately disappears.

And then it's my turn, because Io has just stepped clear of her melting prison. Her eyes sweep the area, passing over me as if she doesn't even notice me, and lock on the ball, still shielded, only a dozen or so paces away. There's so little recognizable human emotion in her expression, it's unreal. She takes one step forward, and then I'm at her again, wrapping my arms around her from behind to limit the amount of face-punching she'll be able to do this time, carrying us both upwards. Just like last time, once she's clear of the ground, her powers fade. Also like last time, once she's airborne, she goes mental, flailing and thrashing and making a gravelly, gurgling sound that I guess is what passes for screaming in her mutated throat.

It's so strange that even with everything that's happening, I can't help but feel...pity, maybe? I remember her as crazy, and obviously a bad guy, but human at least. She was an attractive young woman in horrible spandex, and she did insane things. But she was just part of the game at that time. I don't even hold my death against her. Enceladus had this elaborate history set up for himself, for all of us, actually. In his mind, we were all the spiritual incarnations of the moons of the solar system, made flesh to continue our eons-long battle. He claimed to be the icy moon of Saturn, while Io was, you guessed it, the living soul of the moon of Jupiter. Me? I was young Amalthea, one of Io's sister moons, but I was a renegade, fighting for the forces of Saturn. I really didn't know how much of any of it they took seriously. But I played along. And when the time came, I sacrificed myself. I used my powers of intangibility to get inside Io's pyramid and faced her alone, distracting her long enough for Enceladus to destroy the mirrors she was using to bring Jupiter to Earth. It was all very arch and overwrought. But my death made it real. I think it shocked *both* of them into reality.

Now, however, the woman that was Io seems to have no footing in reality whatsoever. She is giant, and monstrous, and there's nothing about her actions that seem like a game anymore. This all feels beyond me. This is a job for Helios. He should be here to deal with this, not off christening a Martian dance club. I chance a look back down to see how the others are doing. Alice is using her size and strength to move the largest pieces of rubble. I see that Errant has shown up as well and is using his power of random teleportation to 'port away chunks of rock and debris. I can only hope none of that stuff reappears anywhere it will cause even more problems. But in the short term, at least he's clearing a path for rescue personnel. And Crowdsource is there, dozens of him, a one-man chain gang passing debris down the line, helping paramedics lift survivors out and carry them to safety.

"I apologize for startling you earlier," a voice says from directly behind me, startling me. I spin to see the hooded figure from my apartment hovering a few feet away from us. The creature in my arms becomes even more frantic, kicking back at me, trying to reach behind to grab me. Thankfully, what little shield I have keeps her from getting a grip. "I failed to introduce myself. My name is Sagan. Not actually my name, rather, the sobriquet my fellows have assigned me. I was researching the artifact stolen from the observatory, at Alice's request and on your advice."

Io manages to twist in my grasp just enough to drive her left elbow like a jackhammer into the top of my skull. It hurts, like you might imagine it would. I taste blood and feel us losing altitude. I begin spinning us in the air, cartwheeling, rolling, twisting and banking, doing anything I can think of to distract her. Sagan, meanwhile, remains locked in perfect position with us, matching every erratic turn.

"Help?" I struggle to say it through clenched teeth. I'm not even sure he can hear me, but he replies.

"I'm dreadfully sorry, but I am only a projection. I possess no physical properties that would benefit this scenario. And as I discovered earlier when I was abruptly interrupted while speaking with you, your foe seems able to harm me despite my insubstantial state."

"Yeah, she does that," I almost laugh, remembering

her burning touch even as I was ghosting around her the last time we met.

Back on the ground, Alice has gotten all tiny in order to squeeze though smaller gaps and find people buried. No sign of The Actioneer, so I assume he's still inside as well. Everyone else seems focused on treating the people pulled from the site. Which means I can pull back the shields on those people, thank God. The shield around me brightens as I reabsorb some of the power I'd been sharing. Io's kicks and punches have less effect now, though I'm still in bad shape.

"The artifact in question," Sagan continues. "The item colloquially referred to as the bowling ball. I've had an opportunity to analyze it. As improbable as it may seem, it appears to be a satellite of Jupiter. The fifth orbital body of the Jovian lunar system, more precisely. How it came to be here in its present state is a mystery. But there is a very heavy stasis force at work, obviously. And a strong chronal resonance field surrounds it as well."

"*English!*" I shout.

"It's a moon from the future. At a guess."

That would explain why Mister History was so hung up on using it as a power source. He must've been tapping into the time energy or whatever it has after being sent through time. Or maybe he's the one that brought it back in time. Who knows? Also, those claims that Enceladus and Io were actually the spirits of living moons might seem less comic booky than they used to.

"Why does she want it so badly? Can we let her have it? Maybe she'll stop fighting if we give it to her."

"Oh, I rather suspect she would," he says in an irritatingly calm voice. "I surmise that she and the object are connected. Both share similar energy signatures, patterns and spectra that suggest they are each pieces of a whole, both alive and dead in equal measure. It is likely your opponent's existence in human form is cause and/or effect of that moon being held in its current stasis. Her desire appears to be to return to her natural state."

"So you're saying...?" I ask angrily.

"Allowing her to bond with the sphere will have one of two possible outcomes. Either it will boost her power levels to an incalculable degree, or it will break the stasis binding the sphere and the moon itself will manifest physically here in New Caliburn."

"Can't you fly it away from here?" I ask, pleading. Though I already know the answer.

"As I explained, I am intangible and thus unable to physically transport the sphere. If I may though, sir, I have another suggestion. Why not have Errant teleport the object away? Since the creature's only desire seems to be its acquisition, sending it away would remove her need for local destruction."

"Yeah, but Errant can't decide where it goes," I say. "We can't just ship it off somewhere random and let other people deal with it. We need to—" I'm cut off as Io twists enough to get a knee into my ribs. It pulls her free of my grip, and she begins to fall, reaching out in single-minded need for the ball a hundred feet below us. I panic and rush to catch her. By the time I've got my hands on her again, we're both moving so fast the arc of my flight carries us through a concession stand at the edge of the park, reducing it to splinters. We skip off the ground once, like a stone across a pond, before I can correct our trajectory and take us back up. Sagan keeps perfect pace with me the entire time.

"If it's of any consolation, Alice reports that all of the survivors have been cleared of the damaged structure. Perhaps you could take the villain to her and enlist her aid in subduing it." His voice is not quite robotic, just casual and distant.

"I have a better idea," I say. Glancing quickly to confirm what Sagan said, I see Alice and The Actioneer now at a distance from the mall destruction. Alice is waving me down. I pull back the last of the shields I'd cast out before, reabsorb all the spare power I'd been sharing, and ramp my shield up to full. I take us higher, several hundred feet at least. Untangling myself from Io's flailing limbs for just a second, I reposition us with her beneath me. With my hands on her shoulders and my knees in her back, I drill us full speed straight down into the ground. We hit with the force of a bomb. At full shield, I survive. Barely. So does she.

I hover up out of the fresh new crater I've created and look around quickly, searching. Io pushes herself up on her elbows. Already the ground around her is rumbling and turning to magma. By the time she is fully upright and looking around for me, I'm floating ten feet above her head. In my hands, I hold the bowling ball.

"Hey, looking for this?" She opens the smoking furnace that serves as her mouth now and roars like an erupting volcano. "Come and get it." And I rocket straight up into the sky. She reacts with primal rage. Her need to pursue, to hunt, to have the artifact, drives her to leap after me. What little human consciousness she still possesses must surely be surprised to find itself flying, lifting into the air and following me even as I soar. I look down to see if my gambit has paid off and permit myself a grim smile when I see that it has. By sharing my flight power with her and taunting her to chase me, I've gotten her to take herself off the chessboard. No more earthquakes.

Now to see if the rest of my so-called plan will work.

We continue to climb, arrowing straight up as fast as I can fly. Of course, as I've said, I don't really know how fast I can fly. Io's pursuit is clumsy, less experienced than mine, but her drive to obtain the ball clearly compensates. She matches my speed, laser-focused on me. So I reach up and see just how much I, we, have in us.

Part one of my plan was to get her to chase me. Part

two, I hope, is to freeze her. My shield protects me from the cold, as I've said. But I'm not currently sharing that power with her. Of course, she's basically a walking inferno, so this part of the plan is probably a bust. I keep increasing speed, hoping the higher and faster we go, the colder it will get. I don't really know much about aeronautics, so I'm functioning on a "things-I-learned-in-movies" level of science right now. If she doesn't freeze...maybe she'll pass out from lack of oxygen?

Neither thing seems to be happening. My shield is glowing fairly steadily now, reacting to the omnipresent threat all around me, the cold and thin air and who knows what else I'm flying through. Io is leaving a contrail behind her as she rockets after me. We're well above the clouds now. I still don't feel like I've reached top speed. I don't even know how to describe what it feels like. I just push myself in a direction and I go that direction. There's no sense of fatigue or anything to tell me I'm pushing too hard. So...I keep pushing.

Without warning, Sagan appears flying beside and a little above me. He's just moving with me, keeping exact pace, though he's not inclined like a flying superhero, not stretched out with his hands in front of him. He's just sort of hanging there, facing me, flying backwards with no effort whatsoever. He would look like an illusion or hologram if not for the cloak and hood, which flutter in the breeze as if he were physically here, though moving at a much less terrifying pace.

"If I understand your intention, you will need to adjust your angle of ascent," he says, as casual as ever. His voice is somehow perfectly audible, even now.

"Will this kill her?" I shout as loudly as I can to be heard over the roar, but to my ears no sound comes out. Still, he shakes his head as if he has no trouble understanding me.

"It is impossible to be certain what the limits of her physiology are at this stage. But due to my interpretation of her true nature, I suggest death is unlikely."

Comforting, I suppose. I mouth the words, "Will this kill me?" But I don't even try to raise my voice, and Sagan offers no clear response. The black starscape of his skin is becoming difficult to distinguish against the quickly darkening sky above us.

"Your ascent is too steep. Follow me." He turns and begins speeding ahead of me, gently leveling so we are moving more parallel to the ground. The ground that is now far, far below us. How high are we? Twenty miles? Forty? I have no way of knowing. Even through my shield, I can tell it's freezing, but after a while, I begin to imagine it's actually getting warmer. Isn't this what happens when you get hypothermia? When you freeze to death, don't you start to feel warm? Right at the end?

I look back behind me to make sure Io is still following. She is. The look of determined hate in her eyes is undiminished. So I push on. Sagan seems to be weaving a very particular path, climbing then leveling off, then climbing again. And the temperature keeps fluctuating. My shield continues to glow, just faintly all around me, like a halo. And now I can feel the pressure, or maybe the lack of pressure. I can feel that my shield is now holding in rather than pushing out. It's strange and new, and not *not* terrifying.

Finally, far ahead of us, I can make out a...change, in the air. A crispness, maybe. Sagan falls back to my side.

"This, I believe, is what you were looking for. Continue on this trajectory for a few more miles and it should work. I will return to Mars and inform Helios of the situation. Good luck." And with that, he blinks out of existence.

I don't know if Sagan actually knows what I'm trying to do or not, but I decide to go with it. We're here now, and this seems like the smarter version of what I thought I was doing when I took off. So...

I try to cut back on Io's portion of my flight powers just a bit. I've never really paid attention to this, to the more complicated math of my ability to share. I've always just shared or not; I've never tried to assign a percentage of my powers. But I make an effort now to pull back some of what I'm giving her and apply it back to myself. Can't really tell if it's working, but I pour on even more speed now, deliberately trying to pull ahead of Io, to increase my lead. The atmosphere up here is weird. The faster I go, the less sound I seem to hear. Once I feel I'm far enough ahead, I pause. Turning to face the oncoming missile that is Io, my heart skips a beat as I see the proverbial thin blue line. I can actually *see* the edge of the atmosphere. It's...it's so fragile. I am bobbing I have no idea how high above Earth, and behind me, around me is the deepest blackness I have ever known. I have the ridiculous notion that I can reach my hand up and pierce the edge of space like a bubble and let out all the air below me.

Speaking of below me, Io is approaching quickly. Against my better judgment, I now try to reverse that mathematical sharing division I did moments ago. I try to give her more than me, try to up her power. As I do so, she picks up speed. She is a burning red streak. A comet in reverse. Behind her I notice the swirling white clouds of a storm, and I make out a bit of land, a coastline. Oh my God, is that Africa? I can't tell. I have no idea where I am.

She's almost on me now. I hold the ball, the moon, out in front of me. I brandish it for her to see. It boils and sparks in my shielded hands, color shifting from yellow and green to orange, copper, fiery red. Io is like a charging bull. The miniaturized moon is my matador's cape. And the cold vacuum of space is the sword I've concealed behind it.

At the last possible second, I pull back every ounce of my flight power from her, flooding myself with it, using my restored power to pivot and dodge to the side. Her momentum, hundreds of miles an hour, carries her past me like a bullet. Without my borrowed flight to save herself, Io bursts through that imaginary bubble and cartwheels grotesquely into what I hope and pray will be a safe orbit.

I watch for as long as I can, making sure she's still moving. She continues to grasp and reach out, even as she drifts away, and I try to convince myself I did the right thing. Then, at last, the adrenaline of the last hour drains from me like the stopper has been pulled out of the bottom of a bathtub. I'm shaking, I'm sore, I'm freezing, and that power fatigue I mentioned not feeling before? Here it comes. If flight were a muscle, I'm now having the world's biggest charley horse. I consider doubling over in pain and weeping, but instead I just sag. The constant faint halo of my shield, the gold-colored glass I've been viewing the world through for so long, winks and fades. I have a brief thought of, "Oh, that can't be good." And then I'm falling. I always assumed that shooting stars, meteors burning up in the atmosphere, would glow red. But the last thing I see as I burn up in the atmosphere is silver.

♎

The deli is more crowded than it usually is on a Tuesday. The sidewalk tables are full, and there's actually a line at the counter inside. Standing room only. The lunch crowds are getting better every day. That's good. It's a good deli. I bite back a little tear as I look over and see, despite

356   The Deli Counter of Justice

the crowd, my table at the back is empty, a little RESERVED sign set on it.

There are still several people in line in front of me waiting to order when Carl looks up from his prep and sees me. There's a moment of sheer panic as we make eye contact. A moment more frightening than hanging a hundred miles above the Earth. What do we do now? What do we say? Is he angry? Should he be angry? Maybe he knows. Maybe someone from the College, Alice or one of the others, has already spoken to him. Everything else around me drops away as I wait to see what he does.

He smiles.

And then he goes back to serving the guests in front of me. When I get up to the counter, Aldous tries to take my order, but I motion that I'd rather speak with Carl, so he takes the woman in line behind me. Carl finishes the croque-monsieur for a large man in an ill-fitting suit and then I'm standing there, and we're face to face, and we don't say anything. I haven't spoken to him in a week, probably the longest we've gone without contact in the entire time we've known each other. Though I wasn't in costume, I'm sure he knows it was me in the fight at the park. True, I've been a little busy since then, but I should have come sooner. I should have let him know I was all right. He should probably be upset with me.

"Hey," he says.

"Hey."

We hold each other's eyes for a few more seconds, and then he smiles again, one of his big, goofy, genuine smiles, the kind I used to live for when I was his kid sidekick. He hands a plate across to me. All-American and an Olde Fashioned. My usual.

"I told you so." That's all he says. And that's all I needed to hear. I take my food, grab a drink, and settle into my seat to enjoy the noisy, messy chaos of lunch rush at Cook's Deli.

About an hour later, the rush has begun to die down. There are only a handful of customers still inside, most everyone having had to paddle through the afternoon humidity back to their jobs. From my table, I have a view out one of the large windows on the north side, facing the side street coming off the Row. There's a little boutique, and a tobacco shop, and a real estate agency with apartments up above. About a block and a half west down that street, I know there's a library with a little playground on the side. This area has really cleaned up. The edges of New Caliburn have kind of been burned and frayed over the years, but this side at least has stitched itself back together, maybe better than it was even in its prime. And yet just a few days ago, just back over my shoulder a few blocks, someone tried to pull at the loose threads again, threatened to unravel what the people of this city have worked so hard to rebuild. I guess that's life in the superhero capital of the world. But it feels damn good to know that I did something to protect this little oasis here. Destruction and collateral damage have always been part of the deal with superheroes and supervillains. We need to be better than that. We really need to look out for the people that always get smacked upside the head by our stupid little feuds.

And then I'm smacked upside the head. Tabitha falls into the seat across from me. She has a coffee and a newspaper and a scowl. "Hey, T-bird," she growls.

"Hey, Tab," I say, rubbing my head as if it actually hurt. She glares at me and sips her coffee. I look everywhere but at her. I glance over at the counter, hoping Carl might offer some help, but he's not looking this way. He is smiling, but it doesn't seem reassuring. I fidget with my empty glass, wondering if I could get up for a refill and just keep walking out the back door. Finally, I say, "Look, I know—"

"Three days," she interrupts. "Three. Fucking. Days. You fly off to stop an earthquake and disappear for three days. Tell me you were being held captive by the Rock Trolls of Sewergate or something. Explain to me how you've spent three days battling your way out of Undertown and you only just got back. That's the only excuse I'm going to accept for you not letting me know you were all right, jackass."

"I'm sorry, I know. I...I'm sorry. I wanted to come back here straight away and let you guys know what was going on, but..." I trail off. She unrolls the paper and drops it dramatically face-up on the table in front of me.

"But you were busy," she finishes for me. After my brief trip to space, I fell. Hard. Witness reports after the fact claimed to have seen a glowing silver UFO crashing down in the woods of upstate New York. That would've been me. When I came to, I was in the bottom of yet another crater, fortunately out in the middle of nowhere. I was nearly naked, weak, my powers temporarily tapped out. It was quite the adventure finding a way to call the Heralds' Hotline from the little town nearby. When Alice and the College recovery team got to me, I faced a couple of days of "debriefing" and testing. Seems in the process of pushing myself so hard, I managed to "level up," in the words of The Actioneer. My flight capabilities have advanced, according to some science doohickey thing Technocrat scanned me with. My ability to share my powers seems more controlled, like a tool I've learned more precise applications for. And my shields are stronger, and apparently silver now instead of gold. That's what saved me. My new and improved shield kicked into survival mode as I was tumbling out of the sky, even though I was unconscious. Which is a neat trick that I hope sticks around.

During my downtime, Helios returned from Mars and managed to locate Io, who was in fact still in orbit. Though I'm told it was a decaying orbit. Another day or so and she would have reentered the atmosphere; Sagan predicts she'd have come down in the Ukraine somewhere. As it is, she's presently in Heralds custody pending determination of her security requirements. The bowling ball, which I somehow managed to keep hold of most of the way back down to the ground, was recovered less than a mile from me and is sitting in Sagan's lab right now. Or it's in an unmarked crate in a huge warehouse full of unmarked crates. I'm not really sure.

Oh, and Enceladus is alive and recovering. I haven't gotten to speak with him yet, but I'm told he should be up and on his feet in a couple of weeks.

Of course, none of that is on the front page of the newspaper. The headline reads, "NEW HERO AIDS HERALDS IN RAILWAY RUCKUS." There's a picture of Helios introducing the new guy to a crowd of reporters, while Alice and The Actioneer stand behind us clapping.

"Aegis, huh?" Tabitha smirks, indicating the caption beneath my photo. "Better than Crashtest. And at least you got a decent costume out of it. Silver looks good on you. I'll miss the cape, though."

"It's a work in progress," I say, smiling. "The College has an entire program dedicated to fashion and superhero accoutrements. This is what they came up with on short notice. I may tweak it. A little bit."

"I was kind of fond of the Mighty Mouse pajamas, personally." She takes another sip of her coffee and winks at me.

"Listen, Tab, I really am sorry about how all of that went down. I didn't know I'd be gone like...well, like I was. I'm sorry."

She crosses her arms and tries to look more put out than I suspect she actually feels.

"My purse was still in your apartment," she finally says, looking out the window with a mock pout.

"Oh crap, I didn't think about that. I'm sorry..."

She cuts me off. "It's alright. You'll just need a new lock, is all." She smiles slyly, still looking out the window. I smile too.

"Hey," she says after a while. "Before you flew off after that weird guy in the hood, you started to tell me something about being somebody else's sidekick. Before my dad. What the hell?"

I stare at her for a long time. I thought perhaps I'd imagined her reaction in my apartment earlier. I'm not really sure what to do now. I fix her with my eyes, studying her reaction. "Soldat, you mean." I watch for the familiar glaze to pass over her eyes, the light of comprehension to go out, as it were. Nothing. She continues watching me, raising an eyebrow in surprise.

"Yeah, that was it. I've heard of that guy. What was that about?"

I've felt...different, since my fall back to Earth. I mean, aside from the changes to my powers. I'm not sure how, but I can just tell that I'm human now. Truly human. It's like my entire life, every life I've lived, has been ticking in slow motion, and suddenly the movie around me has started playing at normal speed. And I know, somehow, that I'm finally just living. Just this once. Just one last time.

While I was recovering at the College, during all the tests and talks, I never got a sense that my new status quo had changed anyone's perceptions of me. No one seemed to suddenly realize that I had ever been anyone else. And at least once, I'd tried explaining my history with Io and Enceladus, and been met with the usual vacant stares I was accustomed to. But Tabitha seems to be hearing me. Even right before the fight, she seemed to have heard what I was saying about my past.

There are butterflies in my stomach as I lean in toward her. In a testing tone, I say, "I've been a sidekick before." I'm studying her, terrified by being able to say these words out loud and still hold her gaze.

"Yeah, okay," she says, amused. "This sounds like a story."

Leaning back in my chair, I can feel every cell in my body as I take a deep breath. I smile widely. "It is a story. Several stories, actually."

And she listens.

Epilogue

Another late night.

Wiping down tables, straightening chairs, throwing out old bread. Maybe the average 52-year-old wouldn't enjoy doing these things until the wee hours of most mornings, but Carl Cook hasn't been average for a very long time. The routine of it all is refreshing; he'd always liked working with his hands, and this sure as hell beats punching out The Pulverizer.

Not that it's boring. In between your soups and your sandwiches, you also have superpowered brawls just down the Row, Ursatron stomping past your front door, even the occasional break-in by your old, forgotten foe.

(He hopes there'll only be one of the latter; for a number of reasons, sure, but replacing that lock had been a son of a bitch.)

Then there are his hires from The College. Just today, he'd started a new one, a kid named Jim. Jim looked normal enough. He'd wandered off on a field trip, had the misfortune of getting trapped in a lab with some birds, took a hit of radiation or whatever they use these days, and now grows feathers on command. Jim the Feather Kid. Hell of a thing.

He'd be lying to himself if he said he didn't miss it
sometimes, the whole hero thing. Fighting crime, palling
around with other folks stupid enough to put on capes,
going on official-like missions when the big guns were out
of town (or off-planet)…what could he say? It was fun.
Gave you a sense of community, like you were all in it
together to save the damn—

He stops himself mid-thought, shakes it away. These
are the things he tells himself when he gets cold feet, starts
thinking he's made a mistake, considers taking Tommy up
on all those offers to get back in the ring. Push all that away,
he tells himself. Push away all the self-aggrandizing bullshit,
what do you have?

Did he save lives? He knows he did, and he wouldn't
give back a single one of them. Whatever damage his
personal life suffered, whatever price his family had to pay
for his costumed adventuring, it was all worth it if he saved
even one life. But he has his own life, too, and so do his kids.
There are younger heroes out there now, ones who don't
have to worry about arthritis and back pain when they lift
off into the sky.

New heroes like Tommy. Carl doesn't make a lot of
time for TV, but he watches ENN every morning
(afternoon) when he gets out of bed, always on the lookout
for a familiar face. Carl gets a kick out of it whenever Aegis
pops up, silver flashing across the screen. It makes him
proud to know that his sidekick, his "stepson" — however

you want to put it — is moving on. Tommy was so hung up on Carl's retirement for so long that Carl wasn't sure he'd ever recover. He's finally becoming his own hero, his own man. That's all a father wants, right?

Well, no. Not all. Because Carl doesn't have just one child to think about, a mistake he sometimes made when Piecemaker and Crashtest were still going. His relationship with Tabitha in those years was...strained, he thinks is the right word. Always loving, mostly amicable, but strained. Fighting in the trenches alongside Crashtest, he too often figured Tabitha's mother would be there for her, to handle the side of things he couldn't.

Just because he could tear apart terrifying, razor-sharp death machines didn't mean he could deal with his own daughter, right? Not very heroic of him. That was his biggest regret, the one thing that made him wish he'd never thrown that cape around his shoulders. He'd missed out on so much of his daughter's life, there were times he thought he didn't know her at all.

One thing he does know is that she's smarter than she lets on. Sure, she wears that tough exterior, makes sure everyone knows she's got more witty put-downs in her arsenal than they've ever thought of. But there's more there, a lot more. When she gets this old, she won't be slicing pepperoni like her old man. Carl doesn't know what Tabitha's future holds, but it's gotta be great.

As Carl double-checks the ovens, as he turns off the

light in the kitchen and switches off the ones in the dining room, he takes another look back at the deli, the one with his name on the door. He knows Tommy will be there soon, at his usual table, regaling him with his feats of derring-do. He knows he'll see Tabitha tomorrow night, working side-by-side with her.

And he thinks,

Yeah. This was worth it.

Acknowledgments   367

Acknowledgments

This was a joke.

Not this, the final book you hold in your hands — at least I hope it isn't — but the mere idea of *The Deli Counter of Justice* was originally a Twitter punchline. I'd been airing some of my writerly complaints when Paul and Eric jumped in and started arguing over who'd get to murder me first. This is how my conversations with Paul and Eric usually go.

Eric said *he* wanted the satisfaction of my blood on his hands. Paul: "There's a LIST of people who want that particular satisfaction. Take a number." Eric: "I hate the Deli Counter of Justice." I then quickly latched onto the title, said it should be a creator-owned comic book about a "retired, aging superhero [who] opens a deli. Hilarity/ poignancy ensues."

I was still joking. Eric was not. His response, terrifying in its immediacy (as Eric's responses usually are), was simply, "Want to write some anthology short fiction?" By the end of the day, it was beginning to dawn on us that this was actually going to happen.

That was March 7, 2013. As I write this, it is September 22, 2014. The past year-and-a-half has been a wonderful journey, traveling from the kernel of an idea shared by the three of us to a full-blown anthology featuring a number of contributors. The names of these authors and poets are elsewhere in the book, but here I'd like to thank them again: Kitty Chandler, Thomas Dorton, Rahne Ehtar, Alyssa Herron, Amorak Huey, and C. Gayle Seaman. Without you, we'd be a few guys with a funny idea; together, we've created a whole world, one I'm not done exploring.

For kicking the book off in grand fashion, I must thank Mere Smith. Mere is an extremely gifted writer, not only for her brilliant collection *Cowface And Other Hilarious Stories About Death*, but her television work as well. At the risk of making every other person involved in this project feel incredibly old, *Angel* was one of the shows I grew up on. If you had told my 15-year-old self 1) that I would actually write a book, and 2) that the writer of such genius *Angel* episodes as "Orpheus" and "Birthday" would write the introduction to said book, I would have called you a crazy person. Thanks, Mere, for making me less likely to hurl knee-jerk insults at people (except for Sipple).

Thanks also go out to Blair J. Campbell and Karen Wellenkamp (you may know her as QuoterGal) for making our book look so damn good. Blair graced us with the brilliant image of a superhero standing at a deli counter, shopping basket in hand; if ever there was a perfect visual shorthand for the book's mission statement, taking the heroic and making it mundane (and vice versa), that's it. Karen designed all the fonts used on our front and back covers, deciding where every word should go and what they should look like. Thanks, guys, you make us pretty.

On a personal level, I'd like to thank my parents, who have always encouraged me. A lot of people never get that kind of encouragement; I recognize my great fortune in receiving it from the day I was born. For reading my story early and offering their feedback, I have to thank Joseph Lewis, who is almost always my first reader; Wesley "Wezzo" Mead, who I can count on to offer a positive word when I feel like nobody could possibly have one to give; Kenn Edwards, the funniest man I know and one of the more thoughtful; and our very own Rahne Ehtar, who really should consider a second career as an editor.

Last but not least, Paul and Eric: thank you. This has been the most rewarding creative collaboration of my life. Two years ago, I read Eric's great YA fantasy novel *Broken Magic* and knew he was someone I wanted to be friends with. He always made the at-times farfetched possibility of this book's existence seem like a sure thing. He was this project's rock.

I've known Paul for nearly a decade now, bonding over a shared love of Joss Whedon. We've been hosting the podcast *Gobbledygeek* together for four years, and he's the real deal. He didn't just come up with the inventive power sets for his characters; he also helped Eric create the ground rules for Tabitha's Pixels and gave Carl Cook his defining ability to disassemble. You know the one I came up with? The guy who gives people static shock.

In the words of a punk song you both probably hate: *I love you more than all the others…and I salute you, my brothers!*

☖

Arlo J. Wiley

Akron, Ohio

September 2014

Contributors

Campbell, Blair J.

Blair J. Campbell is an illustrator from South Jersey. He spends his day designing everything from geek shirts to tattoos to novel covers. If you need something drawn, doodled, or designed, he's probably had some experience in it.

⚖

Chandler, Kitty

Kitty Chandler has been writing for over 20 years and has published several short stories for various anthologies, as well as blogging at great length on certain television shows. She resides in Asheville, NC, where she is Queen Under the Blue Ridge Mountains and Mistress of her Battlecat Army.

⚖

Dorton, Thomas

Thomas Dorton is a writer from Delaware. When he's not writing, he's making noise rock under the name Fierce Deity. He has written study guides and music reviews, and has an ebook called Have I Become Sassy Enough to Ascend.

ᛪᛪ

Ehtar, Rahne

Rahne works hard to give the impression of working hard, when in fact she spends most of her time reading and making up stories. Sometimes she tells them to other people, this is the first time one has been in print. Frequently mistaken for a boy, and is partial to oversized sweaters.

ᛪᛪ

Herron, Alyssa

Alyssa Herron is a writer and actor living just on the Pittsburgh side of New York. Her film scripts have been finalists for both the Steeltown Film Factory and the Sundance Institute. Her short plays have been staged by various regional companies and awarded by the Pittsburgh New Works festival. As an actor, she has appeared in both theatre productions and independent films. She has her own blue hearts tattoo for a very good reason.

ᛟᛟ

Huey, Amorak

Amorak Huey is a longtime reporter and editor who left the newspaper business in 2008 to teach writing at Grand Valley State University in Michigan. His chapbook The Insomniac Circus is forthcoming in 2014 from Hyacinth Girl Press, and his poems have appeared in The Best American Poetry 2012, Poet's Market 2014, The Southern Review, Poet Lore, Rattle, Menacing Hedge, The Collagist, and many other print and online journals. Follow him on Twitter: @amorak.

ᛟᛟ

Seaman, C. Gayle

Gayle has always lived in a fantasy world populated by superheroes and magical, mystical beings - some even real. In the past few years, characters from Joss Whedon's creations have been added. This has led to her being the organizer of Can't Stop The Serenity Vancouver fundraiser for nine years, part of the global event to raise money for Equality Now.

⚖

Sipple, Eric

Eric Sipple is a lifelong fan of books, computers, and Moleskine notebooks. He writes, builds software, then writes some more. His debut novel, Broken Magic, is available on Amazon. His inspiring rants about art and geekery can be found on his website, saalomuyo.com.

⚖

Smith, Paul

Paul Smith is the co-host of the more-or-less weekly, critically acclaimed pop culture podcast Gobbledygeek... because that seemed like the thing to do at the time. Raised on a diet of epic fantasy and superheroes, he currently makes a "living" training dragons. Also, he's old, and rarely wears pants. Follow him on Twitter: @Haunt1013.

⚖

Wellenkamp, Karen J.

Karen J. Wellenkamp (QuoterGal) has been a graphic artist for over 35 years. Though she has worked at numerous jobs over the years (actress, wardrobe mistress, bookseller) she always returns to graphic design as her one true love. She is an obsessive geek about a number of things, including but not limited to: reading & books, typography, Golden Age Hollywood movies, the graphic & fine arts, social justice, the works of Joss Whedon, the BBC, third wave coffee, perfume, antiques (especially Victoriana) and too much more. She is a fan of this book & its creators.

ひひ

Wiley, Arlo J.

Arlo J. Wiley co-hosts the pop culture podcast Gobbledygeek and has written for online publications Screen Invasion, The Ann Arbor Review of Books, and Blogcritics Magazine, among others. He currently lives in upstate Maine with his wife Nicole and their daughter McKinley. One of those sentences is not true.

Made in the USA
Lexington, KY
21 December 2014